SADDLEBAG DISPATCHES MAGAZINE PRESENTS

WEST OF DODGE

WHERE THE LEGENDS OF THE WEST BEGIN

Saddlebag Dispatches, LCC
A Subsidiary of Oghma Communications
Bentonville, Arkansas
www.saddlebagdispatches.com

West of Dodge: Where the Legends of the West Begin
Description: First Edition | Bentonville: Saddlebag Dispatches, 2023
Identifiers: ISBN: 978-1-63373-854-6 (trade paperback)| ISBN: 978-1-63373-855-3 (eBook)
FICTION/Westerns | FICTION/Action & Adventure |
FICTION/Thrillers/Historical

Trade Paperback edition July, 2023

Cover & Interior Design by Casey W. Cowan
Editing by Dennis Doty & Amy Cowan

SADDLEBAG DISPATCHES MAGAZINE PRESENTS

WEST OF DODGE

WHERE THE LEGENDS OF THE WEST BEGIN

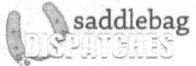

saddlebag
DISPATCHES

For Bob and Velda.
Gone but never forgotten.

The Empty Saddle by Frederic Remington

TABLE OF CONTENTS

How I Met Wild Bill Hickok by Tom Teti 7

Cephas by Stephen P. Cook 19

Dancing With Snap Turtles by Mark Arvid White 33

Three Little Crosses by Rickey Pittman 45

Paint the Town Red by Benjamin H. Bailey 53

One Eye or Two? by JD Arnold 71

Clowns for Bandits by Brock Poulsen 79

The Great Burro Revolt by P.A. O'Neil 95

The Mystery of the One by Ralph Greco Jr. 99

Piano Player by James A. Tweedie 111

On the Rio Grande by Will Ames 121

The Hanging Day by Grant Eagar 139

Shoot, Shovel, and Shut Up by David Birdsall 149

Vigilance Committee by Benjamin Thomas 165

One and Fifteen More by Ken Snyder 181

Comanche Woman by John O'Donovan 193

Waltz to the Wind by Dusty Richards 207

The Fighting Editor by Mark Mellon 209

Playing the Loot by Keith "Doc" Raymond 215

My Vow To Keep by Velda Brotherton 229

American Buffalo by George Catlin

LIST OF ILLUSTRATIONS

The Empty Saddle by Frederic Remington vi

American Buffalo by George Catlin xi

Emigrants Crossing the Plains by Albert Bierstadt xiii

Attack on the Herd by Charles Schreyvogel 2

The Messenger by Charles Schreyvogel 18

Trailing Texas Cattle by Frederic Remington 44

Smoke of a .45 by Charles M. Russell 70

Singing Cowboy by Thomas Eakins 110

In Without Knocking by Charles M. Russell 120

Riding the Range by William Dunton 138

The Flight: A Sagebrush Pioneer by Frederic Remington 148

Indian Woman on a Horse by Frederic Remington 192

Sentinel of the Plains by William Dunton 206

One of Geronimo's Braves by William F. Farny 214

The Scout by Frederic Remington 245

Emigrants Crossing the Plains by Albert Bierstadt

PREFACE

WELCOME, MY FRIENDS, to *West of Dodge: Where the Legends of the West Begin,* the inaugural anthology of *Saddlebag Dispatches* Magazine. In 2014, the late Dusty Richards, a legend among Western writers, and Casey W. Cowan, the visionary CEO of what is now Oghma Communications, joined forces to champion a cause close to their hearts—to "make Westerns sexy again." As Dusty once said, "Westerns are at the heart of the American story. Brave men and women from all walks of life challenging the wild frontier for a chance to find and be more than they were. What could possibly be more inspiring and relevant to us in today's world?"

Our mission for *Saddlebag Dispatches* was thus made clear from early on: to resuscitate the Western genre, to breathe new life into its timeless tales, and reignite the flames of passion it once stirred.

With unwavering determination, we set out on a remarkable journey. From humble beginnings, our magazine has flourished beyond our wildest dreams. We have been honored with prestigious awards and established ourselves as a steadfast platform for Western literature, unearthing hidden treasures and introducing readers to both emerging talents and celebrated authors who have dedicated their craft to the genre we hold dear.

In the pages of *Saddlebag Dispatches*, you have encountered riveting short stories that transport you to dusty trails, gun-slinging showdowns, and the resolute hearts of those who dared to tame the frontier. We have immersed you in the rich tapestry of Western history, weaving together stories of triumph, struggle, and the indomitable human spirit. We have celebrated the rugged beauty of the West, capturing its essence through breathtaking art, photography, poetry, and prose that invite you to journey alongside us.

But now we yearn for more.

This anthology marks a significant milestone in our quest to expand the horizons of Western storytelling. Within these pages, you will encounter a diverse array of voices and narratives from an equally-diverse group of writers—newcomers as well as seasoned veterans—each capturing the essence of the genre in their own unique way. From thrilling adventures that stir your soul to introspective tales that unravel the complexities of the human condition, these stories will transport you through time and space, allowing you to witness the untamed West through a kaleidoscope of perspectives. These stories capture the essence of the American frontier, with its rugged landscapes, fearless pioneers, and moral dilemmas that shaped the Wild West. From the dusty streets of towns like Dodge City to the vast expanses of the Llano, this collection offers a glimpse into the lives of cowboys, outlaws, lawmen, and ordinary folks who faced extraordinary circumstances.

As the wild frontier once beckoned the brave and the bold, we invite you to venture forth and explore the untamed pages that lie ahead. Within them, you will discover the indelible spirit of the American West, a spirit that continues to inspire and resonate with us even in our modern world. These stories remind us of the enduring power of resilience, courage, and the pursuit of something greater than ourselves.

One of our contributing authors delves into the bond between a grizzled lawman and an impressionable youngster. Through their unlikely friendship, we witness the marshal's unwavering dedication to protect and guide the next generation.

Another tale unfolds, highlighting the enduring bond and sacrifice that exists between a rider and his horse. Prepare to be moved as this story explores the profound connection that can develop between man and animal.

A bride and groom's quest for happiness is challenged by unforeseen circumstances, reminding us that life can be both unpredictable and fleeting.

THE PUNNY EXPRESS

by George "Clay" Mitchell & Victoria Marble

A man seems cursed forever to ride the Llano seeking revenge. Will he find solace or succumb to the relentless pursuit of vengeance?

The bonds forged on the frontier are celebrated when a couple of trailhands hit town. Through thick and thin, they exemplify the loyalty, trust, and brotherhood that sustains them in the face of danger.

The familiar names of Wyatt Earp, Prairie Dog Dave Morrow, and Texas Jack Vermillion make an appearance in JD Arnold's "One Eye or Two?" These legendary figures remind us of the heroes who emerged from the West.

A traveling theatrical group blends the art of storytelling with acts of heroism. When faced with danger, these performers unite to protect the innocent, underscoring the notion that courage can be found in unexpected places.

Childhood innocence and the desire to prove oneself take center stage when four little boys conspire to declare their maturity. It was a time when childhood was short-lived.

A piano player introduces us to a seemingly unassuming character with hidden depths. Behind the keys of a saloon piano lies a story of resilience, secrets, and the power of love.

We extend our deepest gratitude to the talented authors who have graced these pages with their words, painting vivid landscapes and breathing life into characters both heroic and flawed. Your passion and dedication have helped us forge new trails, ensuring that the Western genre thrives for generations to come.

We also musn't forget the tireless and hardworking members of our staff that made this publication a reality—Anthony Wood, Chris Enss, Amy Cowan, Staci Troilo, Casey Cowan, George "Clay" Mitchell, Victoria Marble, and Rachel Patterson, our late friends and partners Bob Giel and Velda Brotherton, and, last but certainly not least, our dear departed Ranch Boss, the man that started it all, Dusty Richards. Thank you all for your time, your work, and, perhaps most of all, your faith in what we're doing.

Within the pages of this anthology, you will encounter an array of unforgettable characters, each navigating their own unique challenges and moral choices. Through their stories, we explore themes of friendship, redemption, revenge, love, and the enduring human spirit. So, saddle up, grab your hat, and embark with us on a journey *West of Dodge.*

—**Dennis Doty**
Publisher, *Saddlebag Dispatches*
Corbin, Kentucky
June 24, 2023

SADDLEBAG DISPATCHES MAGAZINE PRESENTS

WEST OF DODGE

WHERE THE LEGENDS OF THE WEST BEGIN

Attack on the Herd by Charles Schreyvogel

HOW I MET WILD BILL HICKOK
TOM TETI

H.F. BURKETT
SPECIAL TO THE *ABILENE STAR REFLECTOR*

IT IS THE one-year anniversary of my retirement from this newspaper, but since that warm June day, I have been pestered unmercifully by readers and colleagues alike to come forth with this story, which most everyone knows I have lived through, but no one has heard me tell. I reported on land deals, state boundaries, races for congress, scandals in the Governor's mansion, the residue of Reconstruction, Native American issues, the effects of the Great War, the Depression, unrests, regular and irregular, and most of the simple joys of our small and ornery community, but I was never exhorted by my various and numb-headed editors to deal in reminiscences from my own life. The new and current editor of the *Star*, however, is young yet, and hasn't had time to develop his full potential numb-headedness, and so does not demonstrate the usual fear that one of his writers will attempt to be interesting. So, before he gets any older and less humble, with your permission, reader, I'll get personal.

There was a chilly early spring wind where I stood at the edge of the graveyard when I spotted a tall figure on a horse that was too small for him. A big hat and a big mustache were standouts, even from a couple hundred yards away. He was coming from the west, and the Abilene cemetery is on the western outskirts, as you all are aware. The arrival was slow, mostly because the horse was burdened too much, approaching on a slight uphill incline. I stood and watched, with a modest bouquet of flowers in each hand, just prairie clover and coneflowers.

Hickok got closer on his own pace, which we were all going to find out was his only pace. I don't know if he was deliberate in his youth, but by the time he got to Abilene, he was downright funereal. Drink and bad sleep had put him that way, more than likely. There's photographs of him as a slender, handsome figure. The man who rode toward me that day was bloated and jowly with circles under his eyes. One thing he could do was stare, and he stared at me the whole time he approached, never wavered. I stared back. At fifty paces, he pulled up on his mount.

"Mornin', son."

"Mornin'."

"Paying respects?"

"Yessir," I said.

He nodded and, for the first time, moved his eyes off me and surveyed the street into town.

"Abilene," he said, almost to himself. Then he looked back at me like he didn't know how much to tell me. "I'm your new marshal, son—"

"Mister Hickok, I know."

Hickok was used to people reacting to him in one of two ways—

fear or awe. The absence of either one of those in me seemed to take him aback.

"Huh," he muttered. "Saloon this way?" he said, pointing in front of him.

"Yessir," I replied.

With a nod to me and a quick look at my flowers, he spurred his horse forward.

So, meeting the man was no more than that. But it doesn't tell the story, even a little. The source of it came before. The "why" is always more important than the "how," and this is why I met the man known as Wild Bill.

He didn't ask who the flowers were for, so, right off the bat, I wasn't impressed with him. My mom told me I was too sensitive.

"After all"—her favorite way to start a sentence—"he's a lawman, and they aren't usually sentimental." Maybe not, but the good ones notice everything, they don't miss a trick, and they like to get explanations. One bunch of flowers was for my father. He'd gotten sick a couple years before that and never recovered. Mom liked me to place the flowers on Saturday so that when we visited after services on Sunday we could see them as we walked toward the cemetery.

"It looks more lovely when we get closer and closer," she'd say.

The other bunch I always placed on the grave of the previous marshal, Tom Smith, the best lawman anybody here ever knew.

Thomas J. Smith arrived spring of 1870. Abilene's mayor and business council were desperate. Our town was called Cowboy Town, and it was a wild and wooly mess, with cowhands rambling through all year and getting rambunctious every day. We were preyed upon by the ugly, the dangerous, the careless, and the corrupt. Dad made and repaired saddles and holsters and such and settled here because there were so many horsemen coming through all the time and punchers coming off cattle drives and plenty of leather hides. After he died, Mom took in laundry, sewed, and gave lessons in the church, numbers and letters and reading.

The day I first saw Marshal Smith I said to myself, "Oh no, he's too small!" Men around town were either skeptical or downright defeated. "Better dig another grave," one said. "Ain't got nary a prayer," said another. But he saw me and another boy watching him, and he smiled and tipped his hat. I wasn't confident, but he was, and that made me curious.

Marshal Tom Smith came to town with the moniker "Bear River." He was Tom "Bear River" Smith. Two old codgers who sat in front of the barber shop all day told me why.

"He was marshal in Bear River over in Wyoming," said one.

"Big problem where townspeople hanged a murderer, and the army came in—"

"Shootout—" interrupted his companion.

"But he stopped it. Told them vigilantes where to get off."

"But the people didn't take to him. He was too bossy—"

"Same thing in Coloraydo where he went next. With Kit Carson."

"Oh, get your pants on straight, Jake, it wasn't Kit Carson hisself. He's dead. It was Kit Carson, Coloraydo, the town."

"Anyway, he always wants to be the boss, and he takes away your guns. He's handy with his fists, is told."

"Heh, we'll see about Abilene."

I went away despondent—too short and no guns. My friends, Joey and Caleb, and myself were looking for somebody who could stand up to the big, the bad, and the stupid. It appeared too much like Marshal Tom Smith's smile would either follow him out of town or into an early grave.

Before his first week was up, Marshal Smith nailed notices all over the main street. The notices said there would be no more carrying of firearms in the center of town and visitors must leave their guns at the Marshal's office. A protest developed within the hour in the form of a rowdy palaver outside the saloon, which was named the Even Chance. One of the largest and most combative drunks in town, "Big Hank" Hawkins, yelled about it until he had an audience, then pulled the paper off the saloon wall, dropped it into the dirt, and discharged three shots into the marshal's name. Much laughter ensued from other midday drinkers who had less of a reputation than "Big Hank" Hawkins by virtue of being not as tall... or as fat.

Well, others commenced to firing at other notices, on hitching posts and beams supporting the shade roofs on the street. Laughter increased. Women got the children off the wood walk, merchants locked up, and old folks peeked from behind curtains, all with a familiar "here we go again" look on their faces and in the language of their movements. Then suddenly, from out of nowhere, Marshal Smith was standing in the street behind Hank Hawkins.

"There's an ordinance against guns in Abilene, that means firing them, too. I'll take your weapon, sir."

It had to be the first time anybody ever called "Big Hank" sir. He turned around.

"Talkin' to me, Shorty?"

Now, if you've never squared off against somebody or never gone in for fighting much, you might not understand what was distinctive in that formation or why nobody who was watching gave the new lawman a chance. The marshal was no more than five feet seven or so, and Hawkins was past six feet, plus he was more than a foot higher from being on the wood walk, and the marshal was on the dirt of the street.

"Marshal Smith. I'll take the gun."

"You'll take the gun." Hawkins was smiling and had his hands on his hips, as he had holstered his firearm. "Well, you think you're going to take it," he sneered, and he leaned down and put his face in the marshal's face, "I think it's a pretty funny idea, don't you, boys?" The others laughed. Then Hank turned mean. "You pipsqueak," he said and reached to grab the marshal's shirt by the neck.

The first time you saw Tom Smith's hands, it was hard to fathom. They were like lightning, like the swiftest panther paws you ever beheld. He grabbed Hawkins by the left wrist, pulled him down closer, and jabbed him in the nose with his own left. There's jabs, and then there's jabs. This one broke Hawkins's nose, spouting blood all over his shirt, the Marshal's face, and into the dry dust of Main. Hawkins swung down at the marshal, but Smith ducked under it and launched a right hand to the solar plexus—more coming about how I know that was the target—then he pulled "Big Hank" Hawkins face down into the street. One of the others, a fellow known only as Wyoming Frank, jumped off the walk into a comical fighting stance and was met with a right to the chin that put him down and out. The birds were chirping for him. Tom Smith straightened up and addressed the two tough guys still standing.

"If you gents wouldn't mind escorting your friend"—he pointed to Hank—"to the jail, whereupon he will spend the night and will be banned from Abilene hereafter. There, you can leave your guns in my charge. He'll catch his breath, by and by. And if one of you citizens would inform this fellow"—he pointed to the knocked-out Wyoming Frank—"when he comes to that I'm taking his gun, and I would be obliged if he would find a hammer and nails and nail up the posters they rudely pulled down." Then he said, "Thank you," to no one in particular. I moved forward and picked up the marshal's hat, aiming to hand it to him.

"Thank you, young sir. Drop it by the office later, would you?" It became a signature move of his—he finished off an arrest without his hat, leaving it to one of the loyal townsfolk to drop it off later. I heard my mom's voice calling me. She was worried. I saw her at the end of the street, blonde curls and frowns waiting on me. All the mothers worried when there was trouble. I signaled I was coming, then turned to watch the dark-red, wavy head of the marshal progress to the jail.

Shoot, he called me "sir." It was a day for a lot of firsts in Abilene.

Incidents like that one were to become spectator sport in our fair town. Residents and merchants were, at once, pleased for the calm they were living in yet looking forward to the next disturbance, for our faith in the new marshal grew whole and secure. He was outnumbered, more often than not, and faced the threat of six-shooters as well but came out on top using only his two bare hands. And gratitude toward Tom "Bear River" Smith took on various forms, many of them edible.

I had delivered his hat to the office, but he was busy with his first inmates, so I slipped away.

"Did you thank him?" asked Mom.

"I didn't have a chance. He was busy with those guys."

"Agh!" she said, exasperated. Her eyes rolled toward heaven. "This boy. You don't want to be rude." Mom made it a two-syllable word. Roo-*ood*.

So, she got to making a bread with some storage apples and oil of clove. It was still warm as I walked it to the Marshal's Office, the next day, wrapped in a light green cotton napkin with a thank you note on top. My mother had beautiful handwriting. But just as I got there, I encountered a difficulty in the form of a boy a couple years older than me by the name of Ben Sykes.

"What you got there, Burkett? Some goodies from your ma? Widow got her eyes on the new man in town."

I saw red, and truth be told, I was ready to cry at the same time. My pa wasn't gone that long. The loss was not far away. But I chose the color red over the tears. I hard-dropped the loaf on the jail steps and charged that boy, calling him everything but his real name, and none of them suitable for public repeat.

Ben was older and bigger and tough, at least as reported by him. I got to him fast, and he let my shoulder catch him in the midsection, but he pasted me with a hard fist from above. I think my forehead began to swell the instant it hit me. We went down, and I whaled two shots on his face that may not have caused much damage, but he stopped smiling. He got on top of me and tried to pin my arms under his knees. A crowd gathered and started rooting for who-knows-who in the general din. I was a wiry little whelp, and I bucked him off.

"You're a lying bum, Sykes!"

"Who you callin' what, you Hump, little Hump bastard!"

"Take it back!" I kept swinging.

"Go cry to mommy, Hump! And get a good name, Hump!" And I kept getting hit, but I didn't stop swinging. Then the noise went hush, and I felt my shirt pull up on my neck. Ben's shirt scrunched up on his neck, too. Next we knew, both of us were being held two inches off the ground like a couple of cats. I couldn't see the hand on the back of my neck, but the one behind Ben's was big as his head.

"We having a disagreement, here?" It was Marshal Smith, and, as usual, he was smiling. "You go on home," he said to Ben.

He took me into the office, picking up the bread on the way. "Be more respectful of your mother's labor," he said, sort of shaking the loaf at me. Inside, his desk was crowded with expressions of thanks—cookies, muffins, pie, even a baking dish with something that smelled more dinner-like. It was later made factual that he shared his food with his prisoners. He placed the bread at the edge of the desktop.

"Your mother is very kind. You live at the end of the street. Your dad had the saddlery, right?" I answered yes. He poured some water onto a red bandana and dabbed the bruises on my face, which I was to learn later were fairly numerous. "Your mom won't like to see you like this, so we'll try to keep you looking calm. I watched your scuffle there with that boy, Ben, is it? You did okay." He stopped and looked at me, more serious. "Would you like to learn how to be more scientific? As a fighter, I mean, 'cause you're all over the place, swinging wild. All your power goes up in the air. You want to concentrate toward the opponent." I said I'd like to learn. After all, the whole of Abilene had seen how good the marshal was with his fists.

"All right. I'm going to lesson you this first time. Then you have to tell your mom and get permission before we have another." I said okay.

We went out back where no one could see us. He removed his shirt, and so did I.

"What's your name?" he asked.

I mumbled, as I was accustomed. "Hump Burkett."

"Hump?" he said, and he turned my shoulders and looked at my back. "I don't see a hump." Then he laughed real big. "Come on, what's your mother call you?"

"Humphrey," I said, quietly. "That's my name. It's dumb. People call me Hump."

"Well, that can't always be easy. But, from now on, people are going to call you Humphrey. Or if they call you Hump, they're going to smile when they do." His big hand pushed my shoulder.

"Now, you want to get your hands in front of you and be ready on your feet. People think a fight's won with the fists, but it's not. It's with the feet."

"How'd you learn to fight," I asked. Probably how I came to be a newspaperman, I always had to know how, why, when, where.

"I was a professional boxer, years ago."

"Professional? Where was that?"

"New York City, where I was born—mean, tough place."

"New York?" The other side of the map. That explained his funny accent. "How'd you get here?"

"Long story," he said. "Now start with the left, moving from right to left."

And so it went. Marshal Tom "Bear River" Smith pranced to his left and taught me to counter. He jabbed and taught me to block, then threw his right and taught me to duck. Punches were to score, he said, and to imagine you were fighting a dummy.

"Remember the body, don't see the head. Look at the eyes but see the body. Here," he tapped the center of his torso. "Because the stomach's big and blubbery, we aim for it. It's too general. This here is the solar plexus. You know what it does?"

"No."

"It's a like an egg and just as delicate 'cause there's more nerves centered right here than anywhere else in the human body. Aim your body shot there, and you'll bring a man to his knees."

I went home on cloud nine.

Mom admonished me for fighting—Mom's then always thought their sons started everything. She was darning some hose when I approached the subject of being taught to box. She halted, immediately. Usually nothing could make her stay a needle. She could handle any conversation while she sewed, except that one.

"I don't want you learning to punish people because you know how to hit them better than they know how to hit you. I don't approve of fighting, you know that. Look in the mirror. You'll see what it does by those red marks on your face."

"But this is…. It's like a sport, a game like target practice."

"I don't approve of shooting, either, and you know that, too."

"Aw, Mom, it's the mar—" There was knock on the door.

"Now who can that be," said Mom as she got up from her table. She opened the door, and we both almost fell over. Marshal Tom Smith was standing there. He removed his hat.

"Hello, Mrs. Burkett, sorry to disturb you this afternoon. I wanted to apologize for not keeping the boys from fighting with each other. It shouldn't happen." He was real serious.

"Oh," started Mom, changing to her "sweet" voice, "boys do get into it, sometimes. No one should be surprised, though we aren't pleased."

Now, the marshal put on his charming face. "Well, I don't know if your boy has yet mentioned to you that I would like to teach him some of the finer points involved in pugilistics or boxing, as you prefer, but I will not if you decline to give permission." And he was off to the races, polishing the proposed lessons with every positive repercussion possible. Mom gave in. The marshal said to me, "See you tomorrow, after lunch." His dark, brown hat went back on his head. "Oh, and thank you for the delicious bread!" I knew he didn't have time to taste it, but it didn't matter. We all felt good.

When I arrived out at the back of the jailhouse the next day, there was Ben Sykes, looking at me kind of expectantly. The thought to thrash him for his insult and general boorishness had been on my mind as a potential result to weeks of training with Marshal Smith. I hadn't figured to have to dig in so soon, but, I thought, here goes. However, Ben walked up to me with the marshal watching.

"I'm sorry I said that about your ma," he said. It seemed like he meant it, too.

"O—Okay."

"Only remedy to a wrong word is a sincere apology," said the marshal. "Mr. Sykes now knows that a real man leaves a man's mother out of a spat. And an apology accepted is the banner of honor." Of course, when he said it, it sounded like it was spelled *"honnah."* "Shake hands."

We shook.

Ben and I trained with Marshal Smith and became sparing partners. We wrapped our hands in bandanas so as to not hurt each other too much, though it happened, at times. We reveled in it.

Hardest for us was to control our wild punches and concentrate on developing the ones Tom Smith said were our best. He told Ben that he should save his left hook for a concluder.

"You have height and strong arms. Nobody will stop that one even if they try to block it."

And for me?

"You have big shoulders for your size and sturdy legs. Don't avoid getting in close. Get your head pointed toward the chin, then spring the right uppercut. Just follow through and watch him drop."

We had a friendly, peaceful summer, the marshal with me and Ben, the other kids, me and Mom, all of Abilene. The town's collective satisfaction cantered into fall. We boys of Abilene had to confess to an excitement in being voyeurs to the fights our marshal won. We peeked under saloon doors to watch or found a safe corner to peer around if he was pulling rowdy drunks off their horses. It happened less and less as Abilene became famous for its peace officer.

I asked my mother if we could invite him for dinner. I wasn't really cognizant of the signals that would send for a young widow. She gave a measured answer.

"Maybe sometime down the road."

"Like when down the road?" I was four square for the marshal.

"Down the road is down the road, Humphrey."

A silence ensued, strange for us. I've always believed we were both thinking about my dad.

"Now, here." She took the brown paper her yarn had been wrapped in and tore it into sheets, then handed me a pencil she made me sharpen with my knife every day, it seemed like. "Do some sentences before you tidy up the backyard."

In late October of that same year, a farmer named John Shea was murdered by two Godless no-goods whom I have never stopped hating for the last sixty years, even though I never met them and whose names I will not stoop to spell. Mr. Shea left behind a wife and three little ones. The marshal for the neighboring district had an arrest warrant for the two men, was going out to their farm shack hideout to deliver it, and he asked Marshal Smith for his help.

I saw him riding out. He grinned at me. I grinned back, then I noticed he was taking his gun. That was a first.

"Where you off to, Marshal?" I asked.

He kept on at a trot. "Situation," he said.

That was it. *Situation.*

Some hours later, a rider came up the road at a gallop, and behind about a quarter mile, a buckboard was approaching. I allowed a bad thought, a feeling that cut to the bone. The town started to pay attention, and by the time that buckboard hit Main, the rumor was waxing toward reality that Marshal Smith was lying in it and was dead. I wanted to see him. I'd seen death before, dammit. I wanted to see him! But Mayor Henry and others gathered round the wagon and kept everybody away. They were white as sheets. There were alarming cries and frightened questions. Abilene was wounded. I don't know who held me back, but somebody did. I carried on something terrible, not with tears, but with fury. And if you don't see a body, you don't have to believe the person is really gone.

Tom "Bear River" Smith was buried in a sack that was placed into a coffin. When he and the other marshal got to the hideout, a gun fight started. Marshal Smith was fatally wounded. The other guy ran for help, he said. With Marshal Smith unconscious, one of the murderers took an axe and nearly severed his head from his body, which is why nobody was allowed to see it. I know Tom Smith, in all likelihood, tried to settle things without using his gun and got shot for it.

It was hard on my mother to have to deal with me when she was pretty mournful herself. She worried that I didn't cry, at least not that she saw. One can shed no tears and make no sound, but the weeping goes on inside.

A week after Hickok came to town, I was passing the saloon on the other side of the street when a voice called out, loud and indelicate.

"Boy!"

I stopped. It seemed to come from the saloon.

"You, Boy!"

Hickok leaned through the swinging doors, swayed two steps forward, and came to a halt with his hands on his holster.

"You Burkett?" He called out.

"Yessir."

"Humphrey Burkett?"

"That's right" I called back.

"In the jailhouse, on my desk.… There's a letter with your name on it."

My name?" Mail, especially for a young lad, was a rarity in the West back then.

"Addressed to Marshal Smith, but he wrote your name on the front. I found it in my drawer."

I just stared at him and, of course, he stared back.

"You can go git it, right on top.… Humphrey… huh." He turned and leaned back into the Even Chance.

I walked back home without looking in front of me at all. My eyes were on my letter. *FOR HUMPHREY BURKETT* was written on the front in block capitals. It was from the Public Library in New York City. Inside was a small page that had been copied from a book.

Dear Marshal Smith,
    Below you will find the answer to your query per our research.

Regards,
Edward Pettit, Reference Librarian

Humphrey, origin and meaning: a boy's name, origins in Germany and brought to England by the Normans. Translates to mean—Peaceful Warrior.

The tears had finally come to my eyes by the time my mom opened the door. She hugged me, and we cried together for a while. *Peaceful Warrior.* That was Tom Smith, too. That would do.

And that's how I met Wild Bill Hickok.

—Tom Teti has been a professional in American Theater for four decades, serving in productions mostly in the Philadelphia area but all over the east coast and Los Angeles as well, as an actor, director, playwright, and teacher. He has also done television, movies, and recorded short stories as a vocal artist. He began writing fiction about twenty-five years ago, and his work has appeared in various literary magazines and journals. He is a founding member of People's Light and Theater Co. and a long-standing participant in the Rittenhouse Writers Group.

The Messenger by Charles Schreyvogel

CEPHAS

STEPHEN P. COOK

I KNEW—WE *all* knew—you ought to put down sand and not straw because straw will catch fire, and so it did. R.S. Jones, the Boss Man, insisted that spreading sand on the floor of the stock car would take too long and cost too much, so us hired men forked straw off a wagon into the stock car. Sand cushions a horse's hooves and legs, and straw will too, but a bare floor would have been better than what was there because one spark from the locomotive was all she needed to set off the straw, and then the stock car went up with all our horses inside. The fire burned fast and hot since the speed of the train fed it, and the nervous, snorting, shuffling of hooves became outright panic as the horses threw themselves against the slats holding them in.

We got the train stopped, slid open the loading doors, and the horses flew out of there, scattering in all directions. A few horses collected into a herd of six or so, turning north, the direction we had been heading. My gelding, Cephas, was one of them. We unhooked the stock car from the locomotive and from the passenger coach to let it burn to ashes and cinders, but that would take considerable time. God knows why Jones had ordered the stock car be hooked up behind the locomotive, what with all the sparks flying from the smokestack. So, with no siding available, we were stuck. It would be a while before we could put the train back together, which would give me time to look for Cephas, who had taken off like a rifle shot. I couldn't tell how burned up or not he was, but I was thinking he could be hurt bad and that I should go see. I had walked maybe fifteen feet when Jones spoke.

"Leave 'em go, kid."

I was just eighteen and full of rebellion, so I kept going.

"You heard me!"

I turned and held out my hands palms up. "We got at least a couple hours."

"We'll get new mounts in Newcastle."

"I don't want a new horse!"

"This is an order!"

"Yeah, well I quit! You're nothin' but a straw boss anyway!"

I snorted and laughed and showed Jones my back, and as they say, that was my first mistake because a bullet dug a furrow alongside my head. I fell forward, deaf from the gunshot, not feeling pain, just wetness on the side of my face. The Boss Man walked to where I was laid out and stood to my right. I could make out his boots and, in particular, the John B. Mull spurs Jones always wore, silver ones with the many-pointed two-inch rowels.

"Always did like them spurs," I said, or maybe I just thought I said it.

"Okay smartass. Brave boy. You want to go, is that it? Fine. Crawl on outa here. You stand up, and I shoot again."

I looked away from the Boss Man's boots and calculated my situation. So, there I was, once again in a fix of my own making. I needed money and had signed on to work with Jones, a regulator hired by somebody in Cheyenne, never knew who exactly, to play havoc with small ranchers in an area going from Casper to Douglas to Lusk on up to Newcastle. We would cut barbed wire, pull out fence posts, confiscate horses and cattle, put them in stock cars in Newcastle, and roll on out of there to Cheyenne right after we cut telegraph wires and spliced 'em back together with leather strings to hide the breach in the lines. Any sheep we found we would scatter along with the sheepherders. This sort of business ran against how I had been raised, but I had agreed to the man's terms, loaded Cephas onto that stock car in Casper, and hoped for the best as we headed for Douglas and on to Lusk. About ten miles north of Lusk, the stock car went up.

I shook my head to clear my mind and said quietly to myself, "Either he missed me, or that was one hell of a shot. If he kills me, I'm going straight to hell, but I'm not gonna crawl."

So be it. Devil be damned.

I took a deep breath, got to my feet, and waited for the second shot, which was into the grass by my right foot.

"You got sand, boy!" Jones yelled. "We'll speak again!"

I went on, walking north and in the general direction of Newcastle, keeping the Central Wyoming Railroad tracks off to my right, which would help me head more or less straight, getting me to where my family's ranch was located a bit beyond Newcastle, almost in Osage. Going north was risky as my mother had banished me from the ranch, calling me a bully. One look at me would tell her I hadn't changed much or at all, and hard-hearted Leonora Merinda would most likely turn me away. My father James Jasper Sampson ran the ranch operations, but she ruled over the house. Putting myself in this position over a horse would have been surprising to the boys I usually run with in Casper, but I had quickly become tired of Jones and knew my mother was right about the cruelty in me because I saw it in him.

He was a cold man, someone we called "Rough Stock" since we didn't know what "R.S." stood for and weren't about to ask.

What I had heard was that, in town, Rough Stock Jones was a killer of stray dogs but then graduated to shooting one sitting outside a saloon waiting for its owner. Also, it was said he might even be part of the Stranglers, regulators hired by big ranchers to hang rustlers, folks who might really be thieves or could just be nesters taking grass for their stock. Didn't matter. At one homestead, they found an old man and a half-breed boy. The old man they hanged right off. The boy they allowed to play a fiddle for them all night, but come morning, the Stranglers left the boy to choke and kick away his life, the corpse of the old man hanging from a nearby cottonwood branch like a plumb bob, perfectly still. Who knew if the stories were true?

My mother and father were small ranchers who deplored the high-handed ways of the Wyoming Stock Growers Association and their hired killers, men like Tom Horn. Feelings ran especially high in Buffalo and Johnson County, but even in Newcastle, and twenty-some years after the fact, hard feelings still existed over the hanging of Tom Waggoner, who had been taken away from his family by men pretending to be law officers and then lynched for the crimes of minding his own business and being a successful horse trader. Talk in the saloons had been that surely there was no honest way for him to have accumulated almost a thousand horses, but maybe Waggoner was simply a close trader. The point was that success could only be enjoyed by a certain class of men.

I acquired Cephas for one dollar about six months prior in the late spring from Cecil, one of the rough boys I worked with in the Salt Creek oil fields, and this horse was similarly bad-mannered, sometimes refusing to move or worse, declining to stop when running all out. I had been a top hand since twelve and tried everything I knew, but at last I considered shooting him since you really couldn't use him for ranch work. Still, I had an inspiration one afternoon as the scenery flew by. We were at a flat-out run, so I tied my rope hard and fast to the saddle horn, made a loop, roped a middle-sized fir tree, and bailed out. The horse hit the end of my rope, the fir tree bent so as to touch the ground, and then that horse flew backwards, knocking himself out. I sat next to his head, and when his eyes flickered open, he saw me, and he saw the light. From then on, his manners were impeccable, so that when I reined him in, he stopped and stood like, well, a rock. If you know the Good Book, you will remember that Cephas is what Jesus called Peter, meaning "Rock." That name fit that horse, and now, I might have killed him, the thought of which hit me with a prickling jolt, roiling my gut with a queasy regret, and in those days, I never felt sorry for anything I did, no matter how wrong I was.

Being exiled to Casper meant nothing to me. I broke horses for a time but began making real money working on oil rigs out in the Salt Creek fields, where some ranchers had got lucky and never needed to run another cow because of what was under the grass. One old boy I came to know had so much money, he would order expensive China, throw a big dinner party, and when it was over, wrap dishes and all in the tablecloth, and toss the whole mess out the window. Then he'd order more China. So, during the day, I was a wildcat, and at night, I was a tomcat, a regular in Casper's downtown bars and bordellos on Center Street. Tough as whang leather, I loved to scrap, not stopping until three or four men pulled me away. I loved Old Crow whiskey, but it fed the bully in me. One Sunday afternoon, a greenhorn was riding a high-wheeler up and down Center Street, showing off, really pleased with himself, doing all this in horse country, so I rode him down, roped him, took a dally, and went off in the other direction. I didn't hurt him much, and the other cowboys and roughnecks got a big kick out of it. I didn't pay for another drink that day.

A coyote yipped in a draw to my left, and two more joined in, their racket funneled toward me by the ravine. The hair on my arms raised up even though the coyotes were no threat, and anyway, I had left my firearms on the train. I stopped, did a full turn very slowly to see if I had missed anything, and walked on in a zig zag pattern as I didn't want to back track. I located two horses, both burned and in bad shape. They were down in a dry stream bed, both standing but trembling, shivering, and sweating, water rolling to their bellies and dripping off into pools on the ground. The sick feeling returned with even more force looking at them, knowing I had been a party to their pain, and I fell back on what I had been taught growing up, trying to pray that Cephas wouldn't be as bad as these two. But the words fell away as that sickness rolled into a knot in my stomach and traveled to my face, which burned with a flush I now understand was shame, another feeling not familiar to me in those days. I kicked the ground, knowing I had to gather myself. Figuring the rest of the little herd I had seen must be close, I whistled and called for Cephas until I heard some low nickering, and there he was, crumpled in brush and sage, right at the edge of a cut bank, all played out.

Now, pulling him up off the ground was a puzzle. We had saddled the horses before we loaded them, and Cephas was still carrying my saddle with a coiled rope next to the horn, so we were in business. I tied the rope tight around the base of the tail, which is the best place on a horse when you got to get it upright, and started to pull, the muscles in my arms, legs, and back straining, then cramping. My groin began to pop, but Cephas was moving and sliding. Good thing it was just a matter of inches. I didn't stop until his back legs were dangling over the edge of the bank of the stream bed, which was about four feet high. I grabbed his mane with both hands and pulled with all the strength I had left, Cephas falling over the bank and him stretching out his front legs for purchase, and when his front hooves touched the dirt, he had no choice but to try and stand. I jumped to his hindquarters, put my hands under his tail, and jerked his ass end up, so then he was all the way standing, albeit none too steady. I wasn't much better since I was breathing hard, and the right side of my head pounded. I leaned the good side of my head against Cephas's withers to catch my wind and to get steady enough to stand on my own. I ran my hands all over him, looking for cuts and burns and fractures but finding only a shallow cut on his right front fetlock. He didn't appear lame, only tuckered out. I checked his hooves, all while he talked to me as horses do. I looked into those great big eyes, me thinking one more time how I had sold him out by loading him in that stock car.

The saddle had slipped some, so I loosened the cinch and moved the saddle back to where it belonged, but Cephas had lost his bridle and was slick headed. I pondered the situation and decided an Indian bridle would be just the ticket. I cut four sections of rope, two for reins, one for a bosal, and one for a head piece, knotted everything together, and off we went. I didn't ride him for quite a while, not until I knew he was going to be all right.

I led Cephas east, in the direction of the road between Lusk and Newcastle, which had been part of the old stagecoach trail from Cheyenne to Deadwood. We walked until the Wyoming Central tracks were in sight, the road beyond the railroad line a mile or so more, but we froze as I heard an engine clacking down the line, pretty sure it was the regulator train. Being seen didn't seem likely since dusk was coming on, and smoke from what was left of the stock car was drifting past the coach windows. The regulators were probably all drunk by now anyway, but damned if I didn't hear the popping of gunfire. I went to the ground, not because a pistol had the range to get me, but because I was pretty sure one of those boys had a Sharps Big Fifty, the rifle favored by buffalo hunters. Imagine what it could do to a man.

In the early morning of the third day after leaving Casper, me and Cephas snuck into the barn on my parents' ranch. We were played out and hurting and real glad to rest in a safe place. I give Cephas some grain and had two handfuls myself. I pulled the saddle from Cephas, slipped off the bridle, wrapped myself in a couple of my dad's saddle blankets, and fell dead asleep in some straw. I awoke to a thrashing and tried to blink my eyes open, and when my vision cleared, I realized Cephas was stretched out in the straw close by and with his back to me, conked out but legs swimming in the straw, hell bent for leather.

I woke up a second time when Dad came through a side door, whistling and humming to himself, and when I stood up, he hollered and jumped back.

"Lord Jesus!" Dad made a little dance, his knees high and his arms loose and flapping.

"Hello, Pops."

"Damn it all, Ed. You scared me. If I had a gun, I might've shot you."

I looked at my dad like I missed him while being gone, and I had.

Dad started to relax. "Dang, you look pretty rough. What happened to you? Let me see."

Dad made like he was going to touch the side of my face, so I pulled away.

"Well, your head will heal in time. Why don't you wash it good, and I got some iodine 'round here, too. How about some breakfast?"

"All I been thinking about is biscuits and gravy, you know with bits of sausage. That would be great."

"I think I can serve that up, but son, what are you doin' here?"

I changed the subject. "I suppose Mother is up there in the kitchen."

"Well, where else would she be?"

"I don't suppose she's softened her thinking on my being here."

"See, there's the difference between you and her. She never supposes. You will have to go after I feed you. One look at you and that horse will tell her all she needs to know about what you been up to."

"Can I borrow a bridle?"

"Of course." Cephas had jumped up, and James Jasper walked to the horse, running his hands over him, speaking softly, too low for me to hear. Cephas raised a hind leg for my dad to check his hoof. "This horse is a beauty. My lord, but a blood bay color is fetching. I bet he can go some distance, too."

Dad dropped the hoof and straightened. "Let me take a guess. This horse is a mite crazy, but you fixed that."

I smiled and shrugged.

"So, why in the world are you hooked up with Jones? "

Of course, Dad knew the score. I wasn't hiding a thing.

"Not anymore."

"Well, I can see that. Let me take a chance and guess that this horse here was in that stock car that got all burned up. This horse took off when they opened the doors, and you left to go find him. Which I completely understand, but Jones took offense and winged you as you walked off. Or maybe ran off like an antelope. You always were fast."

"Nah. I walked away as he fussed and carried on."

Dad shook his head. "I'm glad he didn't back shoot you. That would just be his play. Well, he and his crew are in Newcastle. Bold as brass, they are. That Jones is a bad man, and he's stupid, too. If you're gonna steal livestock, you need to be sneaky, but no, it's like the circus come to town. So now, everybody'll be watching their stock real close. I suspect they'll go into the Black Hills. Not much fencing up there."

"Sounds reasonable."

"I'm sorry you got in with those boys, but I'm glad you walked away. Maybe you only did it for your horse, but you were still going in the right direction. Feelings are strong about the Association. Folks don't appreciate its arrogance. It seems no lesson was learned in 1892 or any time since then."

With that, Dad nodded and turned on his heel. "Be right back."

But he stopped and looked back at me. "I wonder what Owens will do?"

"He's still sheriff?"

"Judge gave him his job back, at least for the next six months."

John Owens was a legend in Northeast Wyoming, a shootist of unnatural speed and accuracy. He was marshal in Newcastle for a lot of years. Even that day in 1912, which put him in his early seventies, nobody would challenge him. He had beaten Wild Bill Hickok in a shooting exhibition at Cheyenne many years before, but locally the story that locked in his reputation happened in his own drinking and gambling establishment called the Castle. A one-eyed drifter was hunkered down at the end of the bar, drunk, mean, and insulting everyone within earshot. I suppose he was mad about being half-blind and ragged, but he shouldn't have talked that way to Owens, who told him, "You shut up now, or you won't have nary an eye."

The drifter made a motion as if to reach under his coat, and that was it. Owens put a bullet through his one good eye and into the wall behind him. My dad was friends with Owens. How that came about Dad would never say, but I called the Sheriff "Uncle Johnny." I didn't know what he would think of my connection to Jones, however, because Owens was ever the gentleman who favored a long frock coat like preachers wore while Jones was a hard-bottom man who had lived a mean life.

Dad smiled. "Owens is good friends with Jo Lefors, who definitely worked for the Association, but that's as close as he got. Knowing Owens as I do, I think he will protect the property of the people he took an oath to defend. If I was Jones, I would clear out and go east into the Black Hills."

"He won't. Jones is made of pure contempt. To him, small ranchers are just a higher form of anklers."

Dad laughed, and in a few minutes, he returned, in his left hand a plate heaped with biscuits and so much gravy it spilled off the edge and onto the ground. The other hand held a flour sack, which I nodded at.

"More biscuits, a ham, and coffee. How's that?"

"Fine as frog hair." I took a deep breath. "So, how is she? Mad?"

"Nope. She just walked into our bedroom. Closed the door."

"I would prefer being cussed out."

James Jasper Sampson Cook held out his right hand, which I shook, man to man. He said, "Ed, you go on and eat up. Come back home at Christmas. I know you will do the right thing."

In less than an hour, Cephas and I had left the family ranch behind and were approaching the four corners, the intersection of four roads, one the way I had come, one heading south to Lusk, one going east to Custer and the Black Hills, one heading west to Newcastle. The meaning of being at a crossroads did not escape me, and as Cephas headed south, I thought of returning in December, the prodigal ready to be a good son. I felt a sort of glow, and then I thought how good a beer would taste. I was dry and thought of how far away Lusk was and figured I could sneak into Newcastle. I could drink in the Castle. The Jones regulators wouldn't dare come in there.

So that October morning, my good intentions now up on a shelf, I turned toward town and was shortly on Main Street. I rode past where Teddy Roosevelt got down from his train and delivered a speech in 1903, which was a big deal for such a young town. In the Castle, Bam Osteen was wiping down the bar, and I was glad to see him and to jawbone. We were rounders together, and Leonora Merinda said Bam was a bad influence on me. I told her I didn't know which of us two influenced the other more, a remark that was the last straw for my mother, and off I went to Casper. Bam got his name from how hard he could punch, and like me, he loved to brawl. Normally, he had sharp, blue eyes, but after a fight, that blue turned black and didn't change back for quite a while.

Once, we jumped a train leaving Newcastle to get off in Lusk, where we didn't have such awful reputations, and as the train closed in on town, he challenged me to see who could throw the other off the top of the boxcar we were riding on. Bam won that contest, but then he jumped from the train, and we walked the rest of the way to Lusk together. In the Castle, Bam and I made up for lost time, talked a lot about girls we both knew, and then Bam really got himself going as the beer kicked in, making big talk until morning was close to midday. He started in on my banged-up head and said how he would have knocked Jones on his ass.

"Well, here's your chance" said a drover at the big window looking out on the street. "He's out front unhitching a horse."

I flew out of the Castle bowlegged from drink and went right at Jones, knocking him into the dirt of Main Street. All around us, the boys from the rustler train jumped back to give room to me and Jones, who was up on his feet likity-split, a Colt Peacemaker in his left hand and pointed at my head.

"What is it with you and this goddamn horse?" Jones shook his head and cocked the .45, extending his left hand, the barrel inches from my forehead.

"You wouldn't understand."

"Oh, I guess not. You got some special relationship, that it?" Jones laughed, and the regulators joined in but seemed uneasy, looking left and right and touching their side arms.

"Jones!"

Heads jerked toward the voice, and I smiled. "Uncle Johnny," I said under my breath.

"Get away from the boy. Now!"

"We got something to settle, him and me."

"He's a boy. Let him be. We all do stupid things when we're young. I'm taking him with me, and you and your mob can git on your train and go back to Cheyenne and the Association."

I turned to look at Owens, and my heart nearly stopped when I saw my mother behind him. In an instant I understood how she figured I would go into town instead of riding straight away, and of course, she was right about that and how trouble would find me. Owens gazed at me and gave a slight sideways movement with his head. I gathered the reins to guide Cephas away, and Jones grabbed the back of my collar. Uncle Johnny stood calmly, both hands empty.

"Let go of the boy."

Jones dropped his right hand from my shirt collar and stepped back.

"Don't never come near him again," Owens said. "Consider me the blood of the lamb covering him and this big mistake he made by joining your crew." The old lawman gazed steadily at Jones until the rustler dropped his head. He seemed to be thinking.

"You know I'll kill you. I'll drop you before you can even raise that gun. Go back to Cheyenne. All of you!"

And just like that, I was free of Jones.

I stared at Leonora Merinda, who returned my gaze with a message in her eyes that I have always thought said, "I didn't raise you to act like this." Uncle Johnny held out the crook of his arm to my mother, who took it, and the two of them strolled away perfectly at ease.

I dropped my head and closed my eyes, knowing that coming to town was yet another boneheaded mistake in a long line of them. And it finally got into my hard head that my mother wasn't mean but only expected the best of me. I had been too set on being my own man.

"One more for the road?" Bam asked.

I shook my head. "Time to go." But before riding away, I threw my arms around Cephas's neck and drew him to me until my nostrils filled with the smell of salt and sage and smoke. "Time to start over," I whispered.

• • • • •

NEXT TIME I rode the train, the date was December 22, and for this trip I bought a ticket. I put Cephas up with my friend, the rancher who threw expensive dishes out the window rather than wash them. I held in my hands a thumb-worn telegram from my mother, inviting me to the Cook Ranch for Christmas, a message I had read again and again, like the letters might have magically re-arranged themselves into words telling me to stay away.

But no, the invitation was clear. Like Cephas, I had been given a second chance, and I wasn't going to throw it away.

For my grandfather, Edgar Miller Cook

—*Stephen Cook is Emeritus Faculty in English at Sacramento State University. He writes because he loves it and because he occasionally gets recognition through being published and winning awards. He lives in the Black Hills of South Dakota.*

DANCING WITH SNAP TURTLES

MARK ARVID WHITE

"I NOW PRONOUNCE you m— m—aww, tar feathers…." I said, closing my Bible with a snap. "Congratulations. You're now hitched!"

The crowd of ranchers, farmers, Sunday-best folk, a few Indians, and two shopkeepers burst into handclapping and whoops. Anyone that lived within twenty miles of this rickety old church had crowded inside for the wedding that everyone had been waiting for. The buckskin-clad bride and groom stood and stared at each other with sheepish smiles.

"Well, go on, Ory," said Grandma Minny with a toothless grin. "Give 'er a kiss!"

"Okay, Grandmother," said Ory with a grin of his own as he took his bride in his arms. "But you're next!" With that he pulled his new wife, Yura, close, giving her quite the lengthy kiss as folks laughed and lined up to offer their blessings.

A dusty cowpuncher shouted, "That's long enough, Ory. You need to get yer fiddle roused. I was promised a dance with that bride o' yers."

"There's a time and a place for dancin'," I said, shouting above the rising din. "Ecclesiastes 3:4. Amen. But not in m... my church. Everyone, shoo!" I started guiding people out the door, using a bit more physical persuasion with the unready.

I shielded my eyes from the somewhat less than blistering, but still near-blinding, sun as I stepped outside of the church. As usual, there was a bit of nodding at gents and ladies and shaking of hands, but most of the wedding guests had made their way a hundred feet distant, to a newly built raised floor where a few tables were spread with roasted corn, beans, and fire-baked biscuits, with plenty of floor left for dancin'. Truth be told, as many folks had come to hear Ory play as see him get married.

Even now, Ory had taken his fiddle from a saddlebag and was busy tuning it, drawing the long bow across the strings. A few children and a couple of adults were standing nearby watching. Ory looked up and grinned.

"Be careful of that fiddler, kids," I said, walking closer. "I've heard he's descended from the pirate Jean Lafite, and his m... mama was an alligator."

"No," said Ory with a laugh. "Maybe a possum, though."

I didn't believe the alligator part, but I knew very well that many of the stories about Ory were true. Orin Fayus came to the Indian Territories from the bayous of Louisiana. Whoever his parents were, he was tough as a tree root, sometimes gambler, sometimes trail blazer, and the best fiddle player west of the Mississip'.

A small boy chewed on a blade of grass and took a step forward. "My pa says that you played a song, and a snap turtle came out and started dancin'."

Ory feigned surprise, putting his hand to his mouth. He played a few notes on his fiddle and bowed low. "Do you think you could out-dance a snap turtle?" The boy grinned and shook his head. The people around him laughed.

At the other end of the floor, three Indian gals, maybe Osage or Wichita, were filling water cups. They had served as Yura's bridesmaids, though they were not of her tribe. They waited now for her to be free, to take her into the long grass for something of a pre-nuptial bride ritual, whether something from their past or from Yura's own, I couldn't say.

I watched her now, moving gracefully among the tables, dishing up slices of pies. For two years I had known her as Yura Three-Dice, a pretty, firestick of a girl with a past full of questions. I had heard her mother was French from up north, while her father was Choctaw or Chickasaw, maybe. She was on her own while still just a girl and somehow came under the sway of one Grufius Smith, a traveling huckster who had overstayed his welcome in one town too many, ultimately being torn apart by an angry mob. Yura had fought hard to get away during the ruckus, ultimately aided in a timely fashion by one Orin J. Fayus. Ory left her in my care until she came of age, and then he came a-courtin'.

Folks were finishing up their vittles, and Ory stood at one corner of the floor, buckskin from boots to neck, with a red scarf given as a wedding gift, flashing a loving smile at his young bride. She beamed up at him, green and yellow bead necklace, her gift from him, worn proudly, her raven hair glinting in the sunlight. The Indian gals hovered near, giggling amongst themselves. Ory waved for old Joe Jenkins to come up on the floor, and he handed him his fiddle and bow. Offering his hand to Yura, he pulled her into the steps of a steady waltz, and they gazed into each other's eyes as they danced.

It was then I noticed the dusty cowboy who had spoken up after the wedding. He was watching the new couple intently. I moseyed closer.

"Afternoon, stranger," I offered with a tip of my hat, sizin' him up as I spoke. He wore a tall hat, a dark red shirt, chaps, and what seemed to be a pair of goatskin boots. I held my hand out to him. "Haven't seen you 'round these parts. I'm Jacob M... Mueller, pastor of that old church back there."

"Reverend," he nodded, barely looking away from the newly wedded and giving my hand a brief shake.

"Are... you a friend of Ory's?" I asked, becoming a bit more curious.

"No," he said, still watching the dancers. "Friend of the bride."

"Oh...." was all I could manage, now feeling quite suspicious. "How long will you be stayin'?"

"Just long enough for my dance," he said, hopping up onto the raised floor just as the waltz ended. He walked over to the couple, tipping his hat.

"Afternoon, Yura," said the cowboy. "Yer lookin' mighty fine these days."

"If that's so," said Yura with a sharp glance, "then it's for my husband and no one else."

"Not here for a quarrel, Yura Three-Dice," said the cowboy with a grin and tilt of his head.

"I'm Yura Fayus now," came the reply. She scowled at him.

"Harris Tess," said Ory, taking his fiddle back from Joe Jenkins. "I hear that my wife promised a dance to you."

"She did, Ory Fayus," said the cowboy, glancing at Ory before staring again at Yura. She looked away and did not meet his gaze, hanging on the arm of her husband.

"Then I'll allow it," said Ory, "but only conditionally, since it's my wife and my wedding day you're dancing to. You can dance to a dance of my choosing."

"Agreed," said the cowboy.

At that, Ory stomped three times on the floor and his fiddle came to life with a few short notes, and then he turned to the crowd. "Step up with your partners, folks! It's time for Bite that Wagon Wheel! Don't be shy! We're doubling the mix, so we need seven more couples."

As others began to come onto the floor and pair up for the dance, Harris Tess moved next to Yura, but his smile had vanished. He glared at Ory, then held out his hands for the traditional dance. He spoke in low tones to Yura, who put her hands to his but did not look at him.

Ory stomped once more, and his fiddle began to sing a rousing tune. The song evoked the image of an old wagon with one squeaky wheel that would pause-stop and then start again. Each time it would stop, Ory would shout out a command, partners would change, spin around, and then dance with their new partners in an Allemande Left and a Promenade. Every squeak of the wheel made Ory's fiddle squeal, and then the song would play again. At every turn around the dance floor, partners would change again, and each time that Harris Tess would get to dance with Yura, he would quickly say words to her, and she would not look at him and say nothing, and then the partners would change, and she would be swept away. The cowboy's face was now set to anger and frustration. Two full turns before the end of the dance, he threw off the hands of his present partner, stormed across the floor, unhitched his horse from a nearby post, and galloped away. Many people watched him go. Some paid no mind. The song came to an end, and people cheered Ory's playing. I walked closer to Ory before his next song began.

"You m... might have just made an enemy, Ory," I said.

"He's been hounding Yura for some time now, Reverend. She's my wife now, and it ends."

I nodded and moved over to sit at a table, having a bite of cherry pie. Song after song played the afternoon away. People danced and sang and laughed as Ory played. Yura was smiling again, and she danced and stayed close to Ory. Soon the Indian gals came to Yura and spoke to her, and she nodded. It was time for their ritual.

Ory saw them and knew what was up. He drew up to his full height and shouted out, "This song I writ for my woman!" He stomped three times on the floor, and his fiddle came to life with sounds that evoked the wind in the trees, the sunlight spreading on the meadow, the baying of seeking hounds, and the hunt for the wild hare. In between these moments were four repeating notes full of life and joy that could only be for Yura. She laughed as she heard the song and danced across the floor to give Ory a quick kiss on the cheek before hopping from the dance floor to the ground. Soon she was dancing past people and horses and wagons, smiling and twirling around. Hand in hand with her Indian sisters she skipped and danced away into the tall grass and beyond.

"You said I'd get the next kiss, Ory Fayus!"

Everyone looked up to see Grandma Minny in her powder blue dress scurrying across the dance floor to the fast-fiddlin' Louisianan. Ory saw her coming and grinned, whisking her up with one arm, even as he plucked his fiddle strings to a steady beat for the dancers.

"Swing your partner!" He whirling around with Grandma Minny.

"Oh, slow down you catfish!" said Grandma Minny, trying to catch her breath. Ory stopped his own dance, still plucking on the fiddle strings for the others. "Minny," said Ory, "everyone knows that had I not fallen for my Yura, I'd have set my sights on you." At that, he leaned close and gave her a kiss.

"You're a liar and a polecat, Ory Fayus!" said Grandma Minny, pushing him away. "But I do love ya." With that, she scurried back from the dance floor to the laughter and cheers of the gathered crowd.

Ory led the dancers for one more turn and then brought the song to an end. "I need some refreshin' folks. I'll be back soon." He turned and walked across the floor to sit down at my table to quench his thirst.

"Careful son," I said with a wink. "One wife is a blessing. Two wives require divine intervention."

"Aww, Minny don't mean nothin', Reverend." Ory grinned and stretched his legs out, one boot over the other. "She's a good gal."

"I do know it," I said with a laugh, noticing a shadow move across my sunlight. I turned to look as a tall lad of fifteen or so made his way gingerly across the dance floor and stopped near our table, hat held in both his hands.

"Mister Fayus?"

Ory looked up at the lad, tilting his head somewhat. "Yessir? Ah, I know you. You're Jamus Torey's son, Bud, right? Pull up a chair and join us!"

"Are... are you sure?"

"It's our pleasure, Bud," I said, "What can we do for you?"

"Reverend, sir," said Bud with a nod, sitting down at an offered chair. "I was just wonderin', well, where Mister Fayus got his fiddle." He looked at Ory with a bit of reverence. "I've heard," I said with a wink at Ory, "that our M... Mister Fayus won that fiddle in a card game with Jim Bridger, Jason Hargon, and Uncle Dick Wootton." I glanced over to see Bud Torey's eyes widening.

"You were on the Hargon trail?" said Bud Torey to Ory.

"Woah, woah" said Ory, holding up his hands. "I was on the trail with the Hargon wagon train, but I never played cards with those other estimable gentlemen. And my fiddle, well, that was handed down to me by my own papa."

"Jean Lafitte?" asked Bud.

Ory laughed and rose to his feet. "Believe nothing, Bud, that the good Reverend tells you, excepting it be about the Lord or the prophets." He picked up his bow and fiddle and sounded a note, then turned and shouted to the crowd, "More music in just a moment, folks."

As Ory was showing his fiddle to Bud, I began to notice a commotion from the far end of the floor. One of the young Indian women had approached and was in tears. Ory saw her and ran across the floor to her side. I could not make out what he said to her, but with her reply he leapt from the floor still holding his fiddle, jumped on his piebald mare, and galloped away to the west.

"What is all that about?" asked Bud, watching the fading horse and rider.

"Nothing good," I replied. "Round us up some horses, Bud. I'm going to gather a few men."

In a matter of minutes, five of us were mounted and riding after Ory. None of us knew where this special ceremony was to take place, so we all kept a lookout as we followed the Louisianan best we could.

It was Zeke Brown spotted things first. At the top of a small hill sat a copse of some twenty trees. Off to one side a single tree grew gnarled and bent by weather and years. Near that tree we began to see a couple of horses and two human figures. As we drew closer, I could make out the other two Indian gals. They were sitting on their haunches, hands raised to the heavens, chanting words I did not know. Now and then their voices rose to a higher, mournful pitch.

We pulled to a stop on the hill. One of the two horses standing there was Ory's mare. The two Indian gals continued their chanting, ignoring all of us. Ory's fiddle and bow lay nearby, but Ory was nowhere to be seen. We dismounted and started toward the Indians, but something else pulled us away. Against the larger, twisting tree was the partially slumped body of Harris Tess. Ory's knife was imbedded in his chest. The cowboy's right hand was extended to his side and open, a pistol fallen to the ground nearby. His hat was resting up-side down in his lap, while his head leaned over in an awkward po-sition, revealing open, sightless eyes. Tess's goatskin boots had been removed and tossed to the side.

"Here's Ory...." said Zeke, almost beneath his breath. I looked up to see Ory behind the tree, rising up from some sort of depression in the ground. In his arms was the limp body of Yura, her face and much of every part of her body that could be seen was quite swollen. Ory lowered himself to one knee and lay the body of his bride gently to the ground next to his fiddle and bow. His face was ashen.

"Ory...." I said, rushing to his side. "Is she—"

"Dead," said Ory. He sat upon the ground, pulling her head into his lap.

"I'm so sorry," I said. "She's with Jesus now. I know she believed."

A couple of the others had stepped behind the tree, and young Bud's voice suddenly sounded, "There's a mess of snakes in this pit!" I could see him on the edge of the hole that Ory had climbed from.

"That's gruesome," said Jedediah Campbell, who had moved for-ward for a closer look. I spoke a few more words, trying to comfort Ory, but he just sat quietly brushing the hair from his young bride's face. The Indian gals continued their chanting as Ory picked up his fiddle and bow. Zeke had moved closer, holding his hat in his hands. He motioned for me to come talk to him.

"What should we do with that one?" said Zeke, motioning with his chin towards the dead body of Harris Tess.

"Maybe you could ride back and find Sherriff Warner. He'll have to decide if this calls for the law."

"I reckon it does," said Zeke.

He started moving to his horse but pulled up quickly as the sharp squeal of Ory's fiddle sounded. We all looked to see Ory sitting with his dead bride upon his lap, his eyes closed, and his fiddle and bow in hand. He played to the Indians' chanting, the four beautiful notes of Yura's song repeating, only to be broken by a sharp, squealing cry of the strings. Every time the four notes sounded, they ended in the shriek of death. Then the song changed. The four notes altered to a different four, like the first but lower on the strings, from joy and the sweetness of life, to sorrow, emptiness, longing. The two Indians ceased their chanting and looked on with pain in their faces. All of us gathered there at that moment could only watch and listen, our hearts rending with Ory's song.

And then he stopped. All that could be heard was the rustling of a soft breeze in the trees.

Ory stood up, laying Yura's body gently on the earth. He walked to his horse and placed fiddle and bow in a saddle bag. He returned with a blanket, carefully wrapping Yura's body, then lifted it into his arms and placed it on the horse. No one said a word as this was done, all of us fearful to break the silence. At last, Ory gained his saddle, and I had to say something but could only manage, "Where will you go?"

"I don't know," he said, steadying his horse. "God or the Devil took Yura from me. I just want her back."

Orin J. Fayus spurred his horse from the hill on which his wife had died, galloping hard into the west. I knew that, if he could, he would do anything to have Yura alive again. All my Bible learnin', all my faith convinced me that such a thing would never happen. But I'd also heard him play. If Ory ever set his fiddle to the task of moving Heaven or Hell to bring his wife back from the dead, I would watch and wait and wonder.

—*Mark Arvid White lives and writes in Alaska, perhaps one of the last Western frontiers. He has had his stories, poems, and other writings appear in such publications as* The First Line, Infinity Wanderers, Permafrost, Wild Violet, *and* Modern Haiku. *He is past regional coordinator in Alaska for the Haiku Society of America.*

Trailing Texas Cattle by Frederic Remington

THREE LITTLE CROSSES
RICKEY PITTMAN

MICAH AND RAMON rode southwest, leaving Jacksboro and the Yankees far behind them. It was late October, and the air was crisp—good hunting weather—and the herd of buffalo stretched out across the horizon.

"Not as many as there used to be," Ramon said. He pulled the mule's rope. "Come on, mule." He raised himself up in his stirrups, turned, and scanned the horizon behind them.

"What's wrong, Ramon?" Micah asked.

"Where's there buffalo this time of year, especially when it's a big herd like this, there's likely to be Comanche."

"Let's go to that clump of cottonwood, build a fire, and stake down this mule," Micah said. "We'll kill us a couple of buffalo, skin them out, take the hide and meat home. We'll be back home in no time."

"Or the Comanche could kill and skin us, and they'd be back home in no time."

"You're a bundle of optimism, Ramon."

They shot two cows, skinned, and butchered them. Ramon put the buffalo tongues and a bit of the hump on spits to roast for their supper. As Micah folded up the hides, he looked up from his bloody work and saw a man on a horse a hundred yards away. Micah nodded to Ramon. "We got company."

Ramon stood, cupped his hand over his eyes, and eyed the man. "White man. Has a coonskin cap on. Riding a mesteño."

The man raised his arm, waved, and rode slowly toward them.

"Do you think he's all right?" Micah asked. "Could be a trapper or hunter, but one does not see trappers alone anymore. Sane ones at least."

"He'd have a pack horse or mule if he were a hunter. He means no harm, or he wouldn't show himself so obviously. And if he does mean harm, we'll kill him."

As he neared, Micah got a better look. The horse was as feral looking as his owner. What Ramon thought was coonskin was actually a skunk cap. He wore a long-fringed buckskin shirt and pants and had two rifles—a two-band Enfield slung on his back and a long flintlock in his hand. A tomahawk, a Colt revolver, and butcher knife were stuck in his belt, and another knife protruded from the top of his boots. His hair was long and disheveled, his skin weathered and wrinkled, and his blue eyes piercing and wild.

When he reached them, he reined in his horse and nodded. "You boys know the Comanche are right near, don't you?"

Ramon said, "We figured they might be following the herds. You seen any?"

"Not in a spell, but I've seen sign. They're around somewhere. Probably camped on that creek a mile east of here. You can bet they've seen you."

"Well, if they've seen us, they've seen you too. You're welcome to eat with us. Get down and rest your horse."

"Much obliged." He slipped off his horse in a fluid motion, the rawhide soles of his spurred boots touching the ground without a sound. The man slipped his haversack and powder horn from his shoulder and tossed them to the ground. "Name's Jeff Turner." Taking off his cap, he ran his hand through his long, matted hair. His face was tanned from too many days in the sun and wind, and the wrinkles suggested to Micah that he had a few years behind them. His eyes were blue and restless, shifting from Micah to Ramon to the horizon, to the fire, to their horses and back again.

Ramon stood. "I'm Ramon. This is Micah Evans."

"Pleased to make your acquaintance." He led his horse to a cottonwood tree, hooked the end of a rawhide lariat to its halter, and looped the end around the trunk of the tree. His horse snorted, pawed the ground once, and started grazing. Micah thought the horse's eyes resembled the man's—wild, feral, and moving constantly as if on the lookout. The horse turned, and that was when Micah saw them—a string of a half-dozen scalps hanging from the saddle.

"You a scalp hunter?" Micah asked.

"Of a sort. Only Comanche. Kiowa too." He looked at Ramon. "Don't scalp Mexicans, nor am I like some I've seen who'll scalp any Indian they run into. Don't sell the scalps I take neither." He sat down. He looked at them again as if measuring them. To Ramon he said, "By the way you wear your pistols up high, I'd say you were a Ranger. You said your name was Micah? By those gray britches you got on, I'd say you're just back from that war some idjits started that ain't done a thing but make things harder on people."

"You're right on both accounts," Micah said. "About those scalps. If you don't sell them, why do you take them?"

"That's a fair question, but it's a hard question. And the answer is even harder, and it's hard on a man to remember such things."

For a second, Micah was afraid they had hooked up with a madman, but Turner continued.

"Why do I take scalps? Revenge. Pure, unadulterated revenge. As long as I have a breath, I'm going to feel it. As long as I'm alive, I'm going to hunt them down and kill them and lift their hair. I'm nearing a hundred scalps. I guess I need to count them again when I return to my house on the Chicolete in Lavaca County."

He picked up a cottonwood stick and jabbed it into one of the tongues. "Should be ready to eat directly, not that I've much of an appetite anymore. Like I was saying, I live for one reason now, and that's hunting down Comanche and their no-good Kiowa friends. I done it enough that they know about me, and they try to avoid me. Likely, they think I'm touched or I'm some devil come up from hell to hunt them down. They ain't far wrong on that.

"So, I'm always on the go now, even winter. I roam their land and hunt them till I run out of powder, then I take their scalps back to the... the house."

"They killed your family, didn't they?" Ramon said.

"They did. For a fact. And worse than that." He reached into his haversack and retrieved a twist of tobacco and a clay pipe. He pinched off some of the tobacco and stuffed it into the pipe bowl, then he lifted a small stick from the fire and lit it. He blew white smoke upwards toward the blue sky. "I'm from Kentucky. We were having a hard time there, so when we heard of the cheap, rich farmland in Texas, we thought we'd make a go of it. It was hard as everything on my wife to leave her folks, but she did because she loved my sorry self. So, me and her and my three little boys came here and settled near a stream that runs into the Guadalupe River. Fine, rich land. Full of wild game and clean water and a beauty that doesn't belong on this dark earth. I told her we'd found our paradise. She said there weren't no paradise on earth that didn't have its snakes. It took a while, but she began to love our new place too. Our daughters grew like weeds. I kept adding land, started having dreams a man on this dark earth shouldn't have—of my three boys growing up and marrying, giving us grandchildren, of me and my wife growing old and dying in peace, leaving my children and grandchildren a rich legacy. But she was right about the snakes." He made the hand sign for snake two times.

Ramon lifted the tongues from the fire, set them on a plate, and began slicing the meat. He set one helping on another plate and handed it to Turner. "A man needs those kinds of dreams."

"No," Turner said. "He don't need them at all. They don't do nothing but disappoint and break a man's heart. It was about this time of year. We'd harvested our corn, planted our winter vegetables, and I went hunting buffalo. When I got back, I found my wife on the cabin floor, dead and scalped. Not a stitch of clothing on her. Her arm was wrapped around the body of my youngest. I found my other boys behind the house in the same condition. I felt this feeling swell up inside me, eating at my heart and head until I thought they would both burst. I just sat down and cried. 'Bout that time, the Indians came back for some reason, and before they knew I was there I shot one through the heart with my rifle, drew my butcher knife, and rushed them. I hacked several of them to pieces. A couple of the others shot me, and that slowed me down a bit or I would have gotten them too. The combination of wounds and grief rendered me senseless, but I must have scared them, or they would have come back for my scalp and their dead friends.

"A neighbor happened to pass by the house, and he knew things were too quiet. He came in the house and found my dead family and me grasping a dead Comanche's throat with one hand and my knife with the other.

"My neighbor didn't think I'd make it neither, but he took me to his house and did his best to nurse me back to health. My strength finally returned, but I wasn't exactly right in the head. Don't reckon I'll ever be. Can't even lie down at night without seeing the bloody corpses of my wife and boys.

"My neighbor dug their graves and buried them in the grove of elm trees near our home. When I recovered, I made three little crosses, sat and talked to them a while, and told them how sorry I was I had brought them to this suffering. Told them I wouldn't rest till I had got my revenge and made things right. But things are never going to be right. I know that, but I ain't going to stop hunting Comanche neither. I started twenty years ago. I'm near sixty now, and I know sooner or later I'll run into bad luck, or they'll kill me, but I still ain't going to stop. It's the only comfort I have had for many years now. I hunted them along every bit of water from here to the Rio Grande. They've been moving north more lately, so I reckon I'll follow them up the Corridor, even into the Llano Estacado if I have to."

"You got a lot of hate in you. I'm not sure that's good for a man to have that much," Micah said.

Turner gazed at Micah, then it seemed as if those steel-blue eyes looked through him, at something none of them could see. "I'm sure it ain't good. But you ain't lived as long as I have. You'll likely find you can hate them just as much as I do, though I hope you don't never have cause to."

"You always go about by yourself?" Ramon asked.

"I do. Though once I found some boys in a bad way. I reckon you've heard of Bigfoot Wallace."

Ramon nodded. "I knew him. Fine, tough Ranger."

"Well, I joined up with him and his bunch after they had lost some horses to the Comanche. They were on foot ten miles away from wood and water. When we finally caught up to the savages, they were in camp. I guess they thought those Texans would just let them take the horses and be glad that they didn't scalp them." He tapped his pipe with his palm and emptied it. "They thought wrong. Those boys were plenty riled up. They walked until they reached Zumwalt settlement where they bought some half-broke horses from a Mexican. That's where I found them. Of course, I weren't about to miss a chance to get me a scalp, so I went with them. Good thing I went with them, as they weren't much at tracking a cold trail.

"We found the Comanche camped in some post oak timber. I led the way cause my horse Pepper Pod was the only one that would follow orders directly. You should have seen those Texans on those ornery horses. I couldn't tell if they were cussin' the Comanche or the horses more. Anyhow, we killed six Comanche, and I took every man's scalp. There were a couple that got away, but after the Texans left to return home, I followed them and got them too."

Micah and Ramon ate and listened to Jeff Turner as he told them story after story of how he had sought and found revenge. As far as Micah could tell, Turner's hate was the only anchor pin that held him to this earth. While Turner talked, Micah scrubbed out their tin plates with sand and put them in his saddlebag. A couple of coyotes carried on in the distance, but for some reason their howls sounded sadder to Micah tonight.

After talking a long time, Turner said. "I can't talk no more about it. You boys get some sleep. I'll keep watch."

That night Micah dreamed of Erin and of their twins, Skye and Benjamin. The dream shifted, and Micah saw himself kneeling by three little crosses. He jerked awake before dawn with a dull pain in his gut.

Jeff Turner and his horse were gone. His tracks pointed northwest, toward the Llano Estacado—the Staked plains. A sea of grass and thorns and thirst and extremes where a man can easily lose all sense of direction. A wild, hostile expanse as limitless as Jeff Turner's own hate.

—Rickey Pittman, the Bard of the South, is a storyteller, author, songwriter, and folksinger. This Dallas native was the Grand Prize Winner of the 1998 Ernest Hemingway Short Story Competition. Pittman presents his historical songs and stories presentations at schools, libraries, museums, and Celtic festivals throughout the South.

PAINT ᴛʜᴇ TOWN RED

B.H. BAILEY

DESPITE POPULAR BELIEF, the saloon was not always the first spot cowboys hit up on their way into Dodge City. With just recently being paid what was coming to them for the many long miles on the trail, Chick Wilson and Dusty Simms reined up at the Beatty and Kelley Restaurant.

Being on the trail for the last couple months, both cowhands were ready to see the town and paint it red. Dodge was the perfect place for cowboys to blow through their hard-earned money.

Dismounting and tying the reins to the hitching post, Dusty stretched out the kinks that had shown up throughout his back.

"I am sure glad to be able to get some real food for a change." Dusty said to Chick just as much as to himself.

"C'mon now, Cookie's grub wasn't that bad until we pulled that stunt on him," Chick said, a grin on his face.

"That old coot always seemed to get rocks in the beans. I feel lucky that I have any teeth left after eating what he cooked."

Truth be told, the rocks showed up in the food right after Chick had convinced Cookie that Indians were attacking in the middle of the night. Coming from a background of Indian fighting, Cookie had jumped up in his long johns, still half asleep, and grabbed his shotgun. The part that Dusty forgot to take care of beforehand was pulling the shells out of the shotgun. Remembering too late, he yelled to the rest of the crew to hit their bellies as Cookie let the buckshot fly from both barrels into the night.

"Thanks to you, we almost all got killed." Chick said.

"I don't know how he survived all those years fighting Indians when he jumps out of his skin like that and is shooting at shadows."

"Well, it was good for a laugh," Chick said throwing his cigarette to the ground as he stepped up on the board walk. With their spurs jingling, the duo walked into the restaurant.

The place was packed, and the newly arrived cowboys were lucky to grab the last table. Sitting down, they both removed their hats. There was a board on the wall that listed the specials. One of the options was oysters, something which Chick or Dusty never had before.

"What is an oyster?" Dusty asked and had to say oyster slow to sound it out.

"I ain't ever seen one, but it is something folks from back east eat. Sure is a fancy place," Chick replied looking over the room. Dusty nodded, and his gaze fell upon a site that caught him by surprise.

"Chick, what the hell is that?"

Chick followed his gaze to the side wall and was also caught by surprise. They had just been up the trail from Texas and had been among cattle and other beasts, but they did not expect to find something like that in the restaurant.

"I think it is a baby buffalo," Chick said starring at the hairy beast by the wall.

"It might be a bear cub," Dusty added.

Before Chick could say anything else, the beast started moving toward them. Dusty grabbed his pistol and took aim.

"Welcome, gentlemen, I will take your order here in just one minute." A female voice called from the back of the room. "And please do not shoot the owner's cat."

Dusty and Chick looked back at the waitress who had come through doors from the back that led to the kitchen. She was carrying three plates of food and took them to a table of other hungry cowboys.

"That thing is a cat?" Chick asked in amazement. Dusty stayed standing with his gun at the ready.

The waitress came over to their table. Her brown hair was pulled up tight on her head, and her cheeks were slightly flushed from the running back and forth from the kitchen to the dining area.

"Yes, that monster is Miater Beatty's Nancy cat. Weighs about eighteen pounds."

"Lord almighty!" Chick said.

"Just some friendly advice, firearms are not allowed in town. The marshal would not take too kindly to seeing you wearing them."

"Thank you, ma'am, we must have missed the sign riding into town. Our bellies have been growling something fierce and can become a might distractin'."

Still looking at the cat, Dusty holstered his pistol and sat down.

"You come off the trail from Texas?" she asked looking from one cowboy to the other.

"Yes, ma'am, just got in actually. This is our first stop," Dusty said.

"Well, welcome to Dodge... and to the Beatty and Kelley. My name's Hannah."

Dusty seemed at a loss for words for a few seconds as his eyes got lost in Hannah's.

Clearing his throat that had all of a sudden gone dry, Dusty said, "It is very nice to meet you, Hannah. People call me Dusty. This here is my pard, Chick."

"It is very nice to meet you boys. What can I get you?" she asked. "We have a fresh delivery of oysters."

"I think, as appetizing as that sounds, I will just stick to some bacon, eggs, biscuits and gravy," Chick said, feeling his mouth water at just the thought off all that food. "Oh, and some coffee."

Hannah did not write anything down and turned to look at Dusty.

"Oh, I will have the same," he said, stumbling over his words.

"Okay, two cups of coffee, eggs, bacon, biscuits and gravy coming up." She turned and went back into the kitchen.

Dusty watched her go, and even after the back door shut behind her, he still stared at it.

"You get lost there, partner?"

Dusty didn't seem to hear his friend. Chick eventually snapped his fingers in front of Dusty's nose.

"What?" he asked a little testy.

"We might have had to find a different place to eat if you shot that cat," Chick said with a humorous grin.

"I might still shoot it. I still ain't exactly sure that is a cat."

•   •   •   •   •

AFTER ABOUT FIFTEEN minutes, Hannah brought them their food. Nothing had tasted this good to them in all their lives. The gravy had been cooked with bacon grease and was thick and delicious. The cowhands ate their fill, and Hannah kept their coffee cups full.

With the food gone and sitting back from the table, Chick rolled a smoke. Holding the cigarette in his mouth, he searched his breast pockets on his shirt for a match. Not finding one, he looked at Dusty who just struck a match for himself and lit his own cigarette. Chick leaned over and Dusty lit his as well.

Hannah came over to their table. "Is there anything else I can get you boys?"

"No, ma'am, I think that hit the spot and then some. The food was mighty good," Chick said.

"I will make sure to tell the cook. We are open all the time, so come on back if you get hungry." She laid their bill on the table. She held her gaze on Dusty for a few seconds and then walked back to the kitchen.

"Oh, Chick, I think I am in love," he said, again watching Hannah go back to the kitchen.

"Well, lover boy, then you won't mind picking up the check," Chick said getting up from the table and walking outside.

Dusty sat there at the table dumbstruck a moment. "That son of a gun just got a free meal out of me," he said out loud hitting the table with the palm of his hand.

•   •   •   •   •

LEAVING THE RESTAURANT, Dusty and Chick took their horses down to the livery. After haggling a price to take care of their horses, they both made their way down Front Street.

"Next thing I want to do is find a bath house," Chick said.

Besides the occasional swim across rivers with the herd, they had not seen a bath since San Antonio.

"Let's get a bottle first. All I want to do is drink and soak," Dusty said.

They made their way farther down the street and turned a corner to run right into a man coming from the opposite direction. Chick kindly apologized, and they walked on.

"Hold on one second, gentlemen." The man turned to face the two cowboys. He was a tall man with steel-laced eyes. There was a badge pinned to his coat.

"I am sure you might have missed the sign, but there is a city ordinance against firearms."

Dusty, feeling a little edgy with the coolness coming from this lawman, started to talk, but Chick nudged him to be quiet.

"We just found out about it in the restaurant and have not had a chance to shuck our hardware," Chick said.

"I understand, but we do have the law for a reason. It is for everyone's safety. If you boys will follow me, we can get them checked in at my office," the lawman said pointing toward the Marshal's office.

Chick and Dusty were no gunfighters, as many cowboys were not real handy with a gun. Their pistols were more of a tool rather than just a weapon of death. They had their guns if they needed them while out on the trail or back in Texas on the range, but no fancy shooting came from these cowboys.

* * * * *

AFTER GETTING THEIR guns checked in with the lawman, they were both able to finally get to the bath house. Sitting in their tubs, they rolled cigarettes and passed a bottle of whiskey back and forth.

"I sure feel naked without my shootin' iron," Dusty said looking up at the ceiling, his cigarette dangling out of his mouth.

Chick had closed his eyes and was starting to doze. Hearing his friend's random comment stirred him back awake.

"You probably feel that way because you are naked." Chick shook his head and reached for the bottle. Dusty handed it over and sunk back down into his tub.

Chick took a swig of the whiskey and set the bottle back between the two tubs. Both men sat for a moment in their own thoughts.

"That Hannah sure is pretty," Dusty said with a half grin on his face.

Chick, with his eyes still closed, nodded and grumbled an agreement. "She seemed to think you were pretty looking too."

"You think so?"

"Either that or she sure had a funny way of lookin' at ya. Now that you mention it, yeah, she was lookin' at you funny. Probably tellin' all her friends about how ya can hardly make a sentence around her or that ya almost blew that cat to kingdom come," Chick said with a chuckle.

"Lookin' back, I admit there were some mistakes made," Dusty said shaking his head slightly.

"Well, you and I will go out on the town tonight, and you won't remember makin' any mistakes in front of that waitress," Chick said.

• • • • • •

ONCE THEY HAD finished with their baths and dressed in clean clothes for a change, Dusty and Chick made their way down Front Street. The saloons and dancehalls were full of people, and it was sure gearing up to be a wild night. There were some gunshots that came down the street from some cowboys declaring their arrival.

"Only a matter of time before that marshal sits those boys down and gives them the talk about their .44's," Dusty said and spit on the ground.

"For the best, I reckon," Chick said. "I once knew a fella that was walking down the street in Abilene, mindin' his own business when a crowd of cowboys came shootin' down the street. They ended up shootin' him full of holes, and just like that, his time on this earth was done."

"Hell of a thing," Dusty said shaking his head slowly.

They headed for the Long Branch Saloon. Tonight was going to be for celebrating the end of the long trail from Texas—for all of those cold, wet nights staying with the cattle, hoping they wouldn't spook into a run, for those hot, sweat filled days with nothing to eat but dust, dust, and more dust.

They passed by the Beatty and Kelley Restaurant, and Dusty could not help but peek his head in the window. He saw Hannah wiping up tables before the next rush of people came in for supper. He walked quickly and caught back up with Chick who had not slowed down to peek in the window.

"You know Chick, I am feelin' mighty hungry all of a sudden. You want to stop and get supper first?"

"You are not hungry, and you know it! You just want to stop in and see that waitress again."

"The hell I ain't hungry!" Dusty replied.

"Save your lyin' for somebody who doesn't know you. I will save a seat for you when you decide to quit romancin' and start drinkin'!" Chick said barely even slowing down to wish his friend luck.

Dusty quickly turned the opposite direction and pushed through the doors of the restaurant.

• • • • • •

STRIKING THE MATCH on the side of the table leg, Chick lit the cigarette dangling from his mouth and took a heavy drag. The smoke that he blew out of his nose and mouth encased his face until it started drifting upwards toward the ceiling of the saloon. His shoulders sagged in relief, and a slight smile creased his face. Nothing like a deep drag on a cigarette, he thought. Taking another drag, he opened his mouth and let the smoke again vacate his lungs.

"You going to play your damn cards or just sit there looking like a chimney?" a voice asked across the table. The man who spoke had a thick blond beard with tobacco stains down the middle.

"My apologies, amigo," Chick replied throwing three chips into the ever-growing pot in the middle of the table. "I call." He reached over and gripped his shot glass, throwing back the warm whiskey.

There were five players around the table. Two had folded, and the remaining players were the impatient bearded man who had just gone all in, a man in a bowler hat who looked like he would be more comfortable in an establishment set up a little more to the east, and Chick.

The bet was to the man with the bowler who looked nervously at his cards. He first looked to the bearded man whose anticipation of the bet was growing by the second and then over to Chick who was fumbling with a bottle, trying to pour more whiskey into his glass. At first the brown liquid splashed a little on the table, and with a little bit of correction on his part, Chick got the liquid into his glass. He filled it to the top, and it took him half a second to realize that it was starting to overflow.

The cowboy clearly had had his fill of whiskey and seemed to forget that there was a poker game going with a substantial pot taking place. Looking at his remaining chips, he realized that this hand was getting too expensive for him to continue, and he quietly folded.

Grunting in dissatisfaction at the bowler man folding, beard stain laid down his cards, three kings. "Lay down cowboy."

Chick realized someone was talking to him.

"Is it my turn again already?" Chick asked, laying down his cards, a flush in spades.

The smile that had slowly crept up on the bearded man's face slowly crept back down at the realization that he had lost.

"Oh, would you look at that," Chick said pulling the chips to his side of the table.

The bearded man slammed his fist down on the table and let out a curse heard across the room.

"You cheated me! There is no way you could have beat my hand!" The bearded man yelled at Chick.

Chick suddenly seeming to sober up quick and said, "How do you figure that, *amigo?*"

"Stop calling me your damn amigo!" the man said getting to his feet and came around to Chick's side of the table.

Chick rose to his feet and eyed the bearded man now standing nose to nose. Chick could smell the tobacco from the stained beard on the man's face.

"You been accusin' me of cheatin', and I will let you know right now, that does *not* set well with me. Now you need to back up."

"And what do you think will happen if I don't?" the bearded man said, poking a finger into Chick's chest.

The bearded man was a good forty pounds heavier than Chick and built like an oak tree. Chick was more on the slimmer side, and it probably would have been smart to let this man's rude demeanor go. However, Chick was never one to back down from a fight, regardless of how bad the odds looked against him.

Letting out a sigh, Chick reeled back his right arm and smashed his fist into the bearded man's face. The bearded man stumbled backwards and fell on the table they were all just playing at. The men around the table moved to the side to miss getting caught in the commotion. As the bearded man fell back against the table, it broke under his weight, and he crashed to the floor.

Chick let out a loud victory yell and declared drinks were on him. The crowd around him cheered and clapped. That was when the bearded man tackled Chick from behind.

• • • • • •

DUSTY AND HANNAH went on a walk after he had finished his supper. They had started talking, and seeing that his time for talking was ending, Dusty had asked her if she would go on a walk on the town with him. To his surprise she accepted his offer.

Dusty tried to stick to talking about things Hannah wanted to talk about. When she started asking him questions about his life, he stuck to the more logistical side of being a cowboy and tried to leave out the more rough-edged stories, though he could not resist telling her the story of the prank him and the boys pulled on Cookie with the fake Indian attack. She had laughed at that story, and from there, their conversation seemed to flow a lot easier.

They had been walking for close to an hour when a loud commotion started coming from Front Street. Walking toward the sound, they saw a large crowd shouting and cheering outside the Long Branch Saloon. Knowing his friend was supposed to be there, Dusty went to see what was going on. When he got there, he was surprised to see Chick slugging it out with a large, bearded man. Both men were bruised and bloody and swaying back and forth. Chick smashed his fist into the bearded man's face, and he went down like a sack of potatoes. Chick threw his arms up in the air, and there was a loud cheer.

Those cheers, however, turned to screams and panic as the bearded man rose to his feet and pulled a six shooter from his coat pocket. Cocking back the hammer, he took aim right at Chick. Dusty tried to push through the crowd to his friend but could not get there in time. As the bearded man started to pull the trigger, the marshal with the steely eyes broke through the crowd and pistol whipped the bearded man, who crumpled to the ground, unconscious.

Getting to Chick, Dusty dragged him through the crowd and away from the saloon. If Chick knew that Dusty was the one dragging him away, he didn't show it, let alone that he understood much of what was going on. Dusty got him to the wagon yard, where they were going to spend the night, and got him situated in his bed roll and saddle. He covered him up with a blanket, and in no time his friend was sleeping.

"You are a good friend," a voice said from behind Dusty. Turning, he saw Hannah standing there.

"I 'm sorry I left you behind back there," Dusty said approaching her.

"No need to be sorry. Watching you take care of a friend in need was heartwarming. Not everyone would do that."

"He's my saddle pard. We have ridden to hell and back together," Dusty said, and realizing he might have offended her he added, "We have ridden a lot together."

She laughed and walked closer to him as well. "You are different, you know. Most cowboys that come here seem to want to get drunk and look for all kinds of mischief."

"I have found my share, but this trip up the trail feels different for some reason." He looked down at his boots.

Hannah stood now right in front of Dusty, and she pushed his hat back off his head, catching it on his neck by the stampede string. She leaned in and stood up on her toes, kissing him. Dusty was caught off guard but only for a second. His hands wrapped around her back, and he pulled her toward him.

They kissed for a moment and then heard a voice from behind them. "Would you two mind doin' that someplace else? Man can't get any sleep around here!" Chick said, rolling on his side and pulling his blanket over his head.

Dusty and Hannah both laughed, and Dusty offered to walk her home. She took his hand, and they left Chick to his drunken slumber.

• • • • • •

THE NEXT MORNING, Chick sat in the Beatty and Kelley with his head on the table, a plate of food next to him. Dusty sat next to him forking big bites of his breakfast into his mouth.

Glancing at Chick's uneaten breakfast he asked, "Chick, you going to eat that?"

Chick only groaned, and Dusty pulled his plate over to him and started in on Chick's breakfast. Shouldn't waste biscuits and gravy, Dusty thought to himself.

The marshal who had pistol whipped the bearded man the night before, walked into the restaurant and walked up to Dusty and Chick's table.

"Boys?" he said setting himself down.

"Please have a seat!" Dusty said with a sarcastic tone that could not be missed. Chick didn't move his head from the table.

"Just wanted to let you both know that I have let Carter out of jail this morning with a warning to get out of town."

"Who the hell is Carter?" Dusty asked.

"He is that *hombre* that your partner here last night whipped and was almost killed by."

"Why did you let him out already?" Dusty asked with some shock in his voice.

"He paid his fines, and we have a limited amount of space in our jail. That being said, I recommend that the both of you hit the trail out of town soon as well. Even though there were no charges against your friend here, he still caused quite a ruckus last night."

"Mind if we finish our meal here first?" Dusty asked.

"By all means. I will see you both when you come to pick up your pistols. Keep in mind that Carter was mad as a wild cat when he left the jail this mornin'.'" The marshal got up from the table. Turning, he tipped his hat at Hannah who had just come from the kitchen. She gave him a slight nod back.

After the marshal was gone, Hannah came over and sat down next to Dusty. She had a coffee pot in one hand and filled a cup for herself.

"Seems like it is time for Chick and me to hit the trail," Dusty said with a heavy sadness in his voice. He looked at Hannah, and she had the same sad look on her face as well.

"Will you be coming back?" Hannah asked, concern in her voice.

"I want to. I don't have much in the way of money though. I wouldn't be worth a whole lot to you," he said dropping his gaze to his coffee cup.

"Dusty Simms, I want you to know something. I do not care about any of that. I had just about given up on this world giving me something worthwhile, and then in you come through that door." She reached out and took his hand.

• • • • • •

ONCE THE MEAL was done, Chick's head seemed to get a little clearer, and he wasn't groaning as much. He wouldn't be much for the beginning of the ride out of town, but at least he could sit a saddle.

Getting their horses from the livery, Chick and Dusty rode over to the Marshal's office to pick up their pistols. The marshal stood out front leaning against the post of the building.

"Sure hate to see you boys go," he said.

"Yeah, I bet you do," Chick said half smiling. "We did have a hell of a time in your town though."

From behind Dusty and Chick, the loud clop of hooves coming to a stop could be heard. As they turned in their saddles, both Dusty and

Chick were caught off guard to see in the cloud of dust, Carter sitting his own horse, a pistol in his hand.

"Cheat me again you son of a bitch!" He yelled and fired two shots.

It was hard to see through the dust and gun smoke, but Dusty saw Chick fall from the saddle to the ground. Carter turned his horse and dug his spurs into his horse's side hard. The horse took off just as quick as it had arrived.

The marshal had pulled his revolver from its holster and started to return fire, but Carter was out of range.

"Take care of Chick!" Dusty yelled, spurring his horse after Carter.

Hannah had just run up to the Marshal's office as Dusty rode off. She yelled his name, but he was gone in an instant. Looking down she saw Chick lying on the ground, blood soaking his shoulder.

"Where's Dusty?" he asked with a painful grimace.

"He went after the man who shot you." She grabbed Chick's bandanna and pressed it into his wound.

"He doesn't have a gun."

Dusty realized in his pursuit that once again his holster was empty, and Carter still had however many bullets in his pistol. He shook that thought out of his head and instead focused on the rider in front of him. He was closing in on him as Carter's horse did not seem as rested as Dusty's. They left the town limits and rode out on the prairie that surrounded Dodge City.

Again, he pushed the thought of getting himself killed out of his mind. He knew that it was damned near impossible to hit a target, at a run, on horseback, let alone shooting backwards.

Carter, realizing he was being followed, fired a quick shot behind him. The bullet went wide to Dusty's right. He was closing the gap, and even though he felt like his logic was sound on the slim chances of being shot, the closer he got, the more that logic seemed to be tested.

Two more shots came his direction. One hit the ground in front of him, and the second clipped his hat.

Knowing time was of the essence, Dusty brought out his rope. Making a loop to the size he needed, he brought the rope above his head and began swinging it. Carter shot another shot as Dusty threw his loop in the air. The loop sailed over Carter and settled down around his midsection. Dusty wrapped the rope around his saddle horn and brought his horse to a sudden stop. The rope cinched tight around Carter, pinning his arms to his sides and ripping him out of the saddle. He hit the ground with a thud, and all the air went out of his lungs. Dusty turned his horse and ran him for about fifty yards before stopping. Carter was wheezing, and his clothes were in tatters when Dusty finally stopped and came over to him. Dusty swung a fist into Carter's face.

"If my friend is dead, so are you," he said pulling Carter to his feet and wrapping the rope around him a couple more times to make sure he could not get free. Dusty got back in the saddle, and with a slight kick to his horse, he led Carter back to town on foot.

•   •   •   •   •

IN THE DODGE House, Chick sat in a bed with his shoulder wrapped up in bandages. Dusty sat in a chair next to the bed.

"So much for leaving town," Chick said.

Dusty nodded, rolling a cigarette and handing it to his friend. He rolled himself one and then struck a match on the wall. Lighting Chick's, he quickly lit his and blew the flame out.

"We sure did paint the town red, didn't we," Chick said with a grin, blowing the smoke out of his lungs.

"We did, but I didn't realize that would be a reality with your own blood," Dusty said shaking his head.

"Ah, it's nothing. I will be up before you know it."

Dusty rose to his feet. "Take your time, pard. I have no reason to hurry back to Texas. Speaking of which, I am going to go get some supper. You want anything?"

"If I waited for you to bring my supper with that waitress there, chances are I would probably never see it."

"Good point." Dusty laughed and closed the door behind him.

—*Since he was a small child, Ben Bailey has been in love with Westerns. He was born and raised in Colorado and in 3rd grade fell in love with the history of the American west. He likes to travel to different historical sites and imagine the brave men and women from all walks of life, who braved the frontier.*

Smoke of a .45 by Charles M. Russell

ONE EYE ᴏʀ TWO?
JD ARNOLD

HOWDY, YA'LL. MY name is Delbert Smith. I was the clean-up man and general helper at the Long Branch. That's the Long Branch Saloon in Dodge City, Kansas. I worked there since it opened in seventy-four before it was the Long Branch and then with Chalky and Bill until Chalky sold his interest to Luke Short. I stayed on with Luke clear through 'til he and Bill sold in eighty-three.

Now, ya'll kin believe me or not. Don't make no never mind to me. But I tell you, I seen 'em all. The gunmen and stone-cold varmints and lawmen even more steely like Wyatt or Wild Bill or Bat. Yer name 'em. I seen 'em. But there's one you might not never heared of. He was the surest shot I ever seen. Even more sure than Wild Bill, and he was so stone-cold fearless his breath was like a frosty north wind. He didn't look right through you like Wyatt would do. He stared at yer and froze your guts. He could stand in front of a hail of bullets and not git hit, like Wyatt but even more cold. And if he took a bead on you, you were dead. I'm talkin' 'bout Texas Jack Vermillion.

He was a feller a little more'n average tall. He had a handlebar mustache just like Wyatt, 'cept he wore a full beard to hide his pox scars. He never bared his teeth in a smile so not many folks knew, like I did, that he had a big gap between his two front teeth. I seen it one time when he sucked a lime with tequila and made a face.

The first time he was 'round these parts was seventy-five. He was a gambler and a gunman. He hardly ever drank. Far as I knew he didn't have no wife or even a woman. He had a few gunfights that weren't no real fights 'cuz he killed 'em right off. 'Cept for one fight when he faced two cowboys right out in the middle of Front Street. They started firin' with both hands, rippin' bullets right through Jack's overcoat. Just as cool as a cucumber, he walks, steady and straight right for 'em, pulls his revolver, takes aim, and shoots 'em both right between the eyes.

Ever'body in town knew about him and steered clear whenever he was 'round. He was a quiet feller and weren't given to temper tantrums like a lot o' the bad men who came through town, but he wouldn't in no way be prodded or accused of wrongdoin'. After a year, I heared he took off down to Texas. Then I heared he was with Wyatt in Tombstone and rode the posse with him. I never seen him agin until he showed up here with Wyatt at the end of May in eighty-three.

I was at the train station to pick up some stock for the saloon. We had to keep it in a locked shed behind the saloon since them reformers kicked Luke out o' town and shut down the Long Branch. I had to take care none of 'em saw me, so I sorta was sneakin' 'round. When the train pulled into the station I was hurryin' to git to the freight car when I dang near ran smack into Wyatt. He was steppin' onto the depot platform from one o' the passenger cars. I stopped and stood back and watched as five men stepped off right behind him. Four o' them I didn't recognize. But I seen and knew right off that the fifth was Texas Jack Vermillion. Him and all the others, 'cludin' Wyatt, carried rifles and pistols and knives as big as my arm. I could tell by the bulge in their coats they was wearin' shoulder holsters, too.

Next thing I seen was ol' Prairie Dog Dave Morrow come up an' start talkin' with Wyatt. He was wearing his special policeman's badge, and it wasn't but a minute when all six men raised their right hands and ol' Dave was sayin' some kind o' oath. When he finished, they picked up their valises and walked into town. I knew why they was there, or least, I thought I knew. Luke prob'ly sent 'em word to come help him take the Long Branch back and git rid o' them reformers for good. There was gonna be a war.

That first night Wyatt and his posse were in the Stock Exchange Saloon owned by mayor Webster. He was one o' the reformer kingpins. I ran down from the Long Branch when I heared they was there, and ever'body was real nervous. I slipped in the front door just in time to see Webster step up to Wyatt and face off. The other four and Jack were set up in different places all over the room and looked alert as eagles. I eased up closer to Wyatt and Webster so's I could hear what they was sayin'. The two o' them were eye to eye. Neither one o' them flinched under the other one's stony cold stare. Webster spoke first.

"What are you doing in town, Wyatt?" he asked real uppity like. He was from New York.

"If it's any o' your business, Alonzo," Wyatt said through clenched teeth. "I'm here on private business."

"We have a vagrancy law in Dodge now. If you can't give evidence of being gainfully employed, we'll have to ask you and all the vermin you brought with you to leave town. Are you gainfully employed?"

"None o' your business."

"Jack!" Webster called to the bartender, Jack Bridges. He was the town marshal too. "Arrest these men on vagrancy charges."

There was a bunch o' chairs scraped back and the sound a folks movin' to safe places against the walls or to where they could toss a table and git behind it, like that. The piano music stopped, and it was quiet.

Texas Jack moved over close to Bridges and just stared at him. Right at him, without ever blinkin'. I guess Bridges's guts froze because he did not move one way or ta other, and he kept his hands on top o' the bar.

Wyatt held his steady gaze on Webster, smiled ever so slightly, and said low and slow, "But since you are so curious, I'll tell you. We've all been appointed city policemen by special city policeman Dave Morrow."

I saw Webster's eyes widen and then narrow as he took in what Wyatt said. He continued to hold Wyatt's stare, but I could tell he was listenin' for anyone to stand up for him. He was no coward, but he weren't no fool. He could see a yellow streak as good as the next guy. Nobody stood up. So, he says, "Is that right? Well, I'll see what Morrow has to say about that. In the meantime, Bridges, cancel that arrest order. Now, if you'll step aside, sir, I'd like to depart these premises."

Wyatt obliged him, and he took a step toward the door when he stopped in his tracks at the call of his name by Texas Jack Vermillion who marched right for him. He turned around and was frozen in place by Jack's stare.

"I think you owe us an apology for callin' us vermin."

"And who are you, sir?"

"John Vermillion."

Webster looked a little puzzled and queried, "Texas Jack Vermillion here in town a few years back?"

"Some people call me that."

Like I said, Webster weren't no fool. He knew 'xactly 'bout Jack's doin's. "Yes, sir. You are right. I did not know about your employment as city policemen. Please accept my apology."

"Jack," Wyatt said in almost a whisper. "Let it go."

Slowly Jack turned his head to look at Wyatt and said, "Apology accepted. Now be on your way."

"Also, just so you know, Webster, Bat is on the way and will be here in a day or two with some more men." This time he broadened his smile at Webster who wheeled and stomped to the back of his saloon.

Wyatt and his posse left the Stock Exchange Saloon and walked on down to the Lady Gay. I followed 'em but not too close. The Lady Gay was owned by Tom Nixon and Brick Bond. They was in cahoots with Webster, and Nixon was an assistant town marshal. Wyatt and the other five city policemen came through the front door of the Lady Gay. I have to say it was purty lively in there. Lot o' cowboys and cattle buyers and gamblers and railroad men. And even a couple of shell games in one o' the corners. The city policemen moved in and looked around at everyone. Many o' the crowd dropped their mouths open and stared at Wyatt and Jack. But Wyatt spotted George Hinkle standin' at the bar and went right for him. He was the sheriff and was watchin' Wyatt and Jack in the mirror. Wyatt walked right up to him and said, "Howdy, George. Been a while."

Hinkle gulped some beer from his mug, wiped his mustache, and said, "I already wired the governor to send troops. So, whatever you and your henchmen are plannin', you better give it up right now."

Wyatt faked looking like a kid caught with his hand in the cookie jar. "Oh, durn it, George. You caught me." Then his brow furrowed, and he looked puzzled. "But what did I do?"

"Reckon you ain't done nuthin' yet, but you're plannin' sumthin'. Bringin' into town all them hard cases armed to the teeth."

Wyatt got serious. "You're damn right we are planning something. We are going to take back what you took from Luke. We can start right now if you'd like." He let his hand drift down to his pistol butt, and he laid a heavy, deadly glare on Hinkle. Ol' George blinked and looked away from Wyatt, but when he did, he ran right into Jack's icy stare. He shrank back and held up his hands like he was holdin' back Jack and Wyatt. Of a sudden it got quiet in this saloon too.

"I ain't doin' nuthin'. You got me outgunned. I'll wait for the troops."

"That's smart, George. In the meantime, you don't mind if we have a beer, do you?" George motioned to a bartender and disappeared in a back room.

The next day we found out the governor weren't sendin' any troops. He was sendin' the Adjutant General to check on things. Wal, that broke ol' Webster's back, and he sent for Wyatt to talk over things.

The war only lasted a week, and never a shot was fired. Wyatt got ever'body to settle peacefully, and then he went to Texas, and Bat left town for New Mexico. But Texas Jack Vermillion hung around. Just between you and me, I think it was Jack who scared the reformers the most, and they gave up. Afterward, customers stayed away because of him. But after a couple of weeks of peace, folks got used to havin' ol' Jack around. We got to know each other cuz he was usually sittin' at a table drinkin' coffee and playin' solitaire long before any o' the other gamblers showed up. We'd talk a little while I was workin' 'round, cleanin' up. Like I said, he didn't talk much, and I did most o' the talkin'.

One time there were a couple o' big herds just came in from Texas, and on Saturday night the Long Branch was full o' cowboys and gamblers and conmen o' all sorts. They was all after the cowboys' money. I was standin' off to the side watchin' Jack play poker. He didn't like nobody standin' behind him where they could see his hand. Three gamblers, three cowboys, and Jack sat at the table. The gamblers were new in town and didn't know 'bout Jack. O' course the cowboys didn't neither. Jack, he just looked like a regular old town feller.

Wal, they'd been playin' for almost three hours, and one o' the gamblers and Jack had purty good size piles o' chips in front of 'em. It came to one hand when Jack called the gambler. The gambler laid down three aces, and Jack did not move. The gambler started to rake in the pot, and Jack slammed an iron grip on his arm. He pinned it to the table and laid down two pair, aces over jacks. "You're cheatin'," Jack said low and slow.

The gambler looked like a scared rabbit for just a second, quickly got his wits back and said, "I ain't cheatin'. You are. I thought I saw you pull that ace from your sleeve."

Jack stared hard at him for about ten seconds. "One eye or two?"

"Huh? Whatta you mean? You talkin' about jacks?" He giggled and tried to wrench his arm free but couldn't. Jack had him pinned good. I could see that gambler was gittin' a little nervous. It was prob'ly his gun hand Jack had pinned. Then he tried to get all brave and rake in the pot with his free hand.

"I mean do you want me to shoot out one o' your eyes or both?"

The gambler stiffened and growled, "All right. That's 'bout enough o' this. I ain't cheatin' and you better—"

Faster'n a striking' rattler, Jack pulled a .32 he had in his shoulder holster and shot that gambler right through his left eye. The gambler stayed at the table after he was shot cuz Jack still had his arm pinned, but his head flopped back like a dead pheasant. He was kilt dead. Jack let his arm go, and the body fell to the floor. He gave the crowd in the place a look around, raked the pot and his pile into his hat, stood, put on his coat, and walked out the door.

I never seen him ag'in. I heard he hightailed it to Texas and down to Hermosillo, Mexico. There was a reward out for him. Long about April o' eighty-eight I was readin' an article in the Kansas Western Farmer that a feller was seen in Coronado who they said was a very

bad man and who they called "Shoot-your-eye-out-Jack." I said to myself, "Well now, ol' Texas Jack's got his self a new nickname. And I
seen it all happen right here in Dodge City."

—*Back in the day, when Jeff was a kid, he watched plenty of westerns on TV,
read a few books, and always wanted to be a rancher. As it turned out, he
never got there. Instead, he is a veteran combat Army aviator, former deputy
sheriff, death investigator, and longtime CPA. Now he sort of lives a rancher's life vicariously through the stories he writes.*

CLOWNS FOR BANDITS

BROCK POULSEN

HATTIE AND BENJAMIN were praying, kneeling on the floor in a tiny chapel, when the shooting started. It was all outside the church, in terms of its origins, but one of the main things about bullets is their tendency to travel and break things. Some folks might have said that bullets are like cowboys in that respect. There were, at the time of this story, an awful lot of both bullets and cowboys in Montana, though that detail may not narrow it down so much. To be clear, it was a bullet that crashed through a window of the church and toppled a candelabra, setting fire to a pew.

The boy froze, tilting his head toward the sound, his eyes unfocused, and pointed at his knees. More bullets punched through the windows. Hattie took hold of her son's hand and pulled him lower to the floor, moving him slowly, trying to keep herself calm, until they were underneath the pew. Benjamin rarely needed calming at the times when you would expect a person to need it and occasionally required quite a lot of it when you would not expect it. Such was the case with the fire. It spread, climbing greedily up the curtains and brachiating along the bare rafters of the ceiling. But the gunshots continued outside, and Hattie and Benjamin cowered in their shelter until both had run their course.

Over the next hour, the screams from the town outside resolved themselves, replaced by the cruel laughter of the men who'd arrived so suddenly with blood on their minds. The fire only burned up part of the roof before a fortuitous rain put it out. It had been storming all day, off and on, and luckily a downpour moved over town before the whole building went up. Hattie kept still on the hard church floor, listening to rain leaking in through the damaged part of the roof and wondering why in hell she'd picked this miserable little town. She repented damned fast for the curse and the ingratitude and focused on Benjamin. He hadn't let go of her hand. He'd soothed himself the way he often did, by running his thumb over her fingernail. Ever since he was a young boy, Benjamin had been of a different sort. Other folks in town called him "touched" if they were being polite or "stupid" or "mule-kicked" if they weren't in danger of being overheard, but Hattie just knew her boy was special. He hardly spoke, only wanted to eat roasted carrots and eggs over-easy and wouldn't hardly look you in the eye. He wouldn't abide even a fleck of black pepper on his eggs, and he would have an absolute conniption if his socks got twisted. When he turned six years old, then seven, and then eight, and still the schoolmarm didn't inquire after his attendance, it was clear that no one in town had much faith in Benjamin.

But Hattie knew. A mother knows her son.

More time passed beneath the pew. Benjamin focused on her thumbnail while Hattie tried to keep her crying silent. Occasionally the boy made little exhalations, hardly loud enough for Hattie to hear, that eventually she realized were his recreations of the sounds of gunfire. *Pow,* he said. *Pow. Pow.*

The men were still out in the town, loud and destructive. At the saloon, Hattie guessed based on how they were carrying on. She shifted on her hip, moving her weight to the other side, trying to ignore her aching bladder. It was less of a concern than bullets or the beam overhead that was still smoldering, but she knew it would be an issue sooner than later. If she pissed herself, or if Benjamin did, it'd be all the more miserable hidden under a church pew.

"Let me go for a spell, Benji," she whispered, gently freeing her hand from his. But before she was halfway out, she heard footsteps, heavy boots slapping on muddy earth.

"I'm telling you," a voice said from just outside the chapel, "I heard something in here."

"Probably just the rain." Another voice, nasal and chiding. "Look, the roof's burned out. Come on, I'm aching for a drink."

More footsteps, clicking on the chapel floor, coming closer. "I'm still fixing to look around. You go on back to the saloon if you're so anxious for it."

The man walked up the aisle, taking his time, his jingle bobs making noise with each step. He liked the way they sounded, never mind that some of the other men made jokes. None of them were smart enough to think of checking in the church. Could be some kind of valuables hereabouts. He reached Hattie and Benjamin's pew and sauntered right past without even a hint of curiosity. Hattie could see his shoulders dip with each step, his thumbs hooked in his belt, his elbows pointed out. For being party to the murder of a whole town, she thought, he seemed mighty relaxed.

"Stinks in here," he muttered as he reached the rostrum. There was nothing of value in sight, though he looked, and nothing secreted away anywhere, nor anywhere to hide it. The man spent another few moments walking the chapel when his stroll was interrupted by shouting.

"Lookee here!" There was a shout from outside the church, followed by the sounds of horses and war whoops. The man rushed outside to see what the commotion was about, leaving Hattie to release a held breath. Benjamin carried on with her thumbnail, oblivious to the world around him.

Outside in the sunlight between storms, the wagons of a traveling carnival had arrived. They were on schedule, stopping in to ply their trade for miners and farmers in want of a bit of distraction. Their timing, though, they very quickly surmised, could scarcely have been worse.

Fay, the troupe's director and the woman at the reins, tried to turn around and make an escape as soon as she took stock of the town—bodies in the street and a group of men not at all in mourning. Unfortunately, a carnival wagon isn't built for desperate getaways, and one of the outlaws quickly interceded.

He was a sneering man with a stringy beard, the leader who went by Lawrence, who tugged the horses aside. "Turn aroun'!"

There were more than enough guns pointed at the driver to be convincing, so she led the horses back into town and stopped in front of the saloon. She put her hands over her head as the men formed a circle around the wagon.

"What in the hell is this?" asked Lawrence. "Some kind of traveling show?"

Fay glared at the man. "Traveling show. We was just passin' through."

Someone hooted, and a few others laughed. A big man, taller than the rest of the group, smiled a yellow grin. "Well, your timing is just perfect, ain't it? We're in the mood for a show."

A group of men like them were rarely in the mood for anything decent, but it wouldn't have done any good to point it out. The woman tried to talk them out of the notion and get her troupe out of town, but they wouldn't hear of it. The biggest wagon was steered to the shadow of the saloon, with the small one right behind it.

Lawrence's eyes surveyed the town, all smoke and ruined buildings, until they landed on the church. "You all start bringing out pews from the chapel. We'll set them up right here in the road, and we'll take in our show right here."

Fay and her troupe thought better of arguing, owing to the persuasive nature of Lawrence and his ornery-looking men. Instead, they filed inside the church and set to work moving the benches.

As she lifted one end of a pew, Fay spotted something in the dim light. The corner of a straw-colored dress peeked out from under the bench.

"Hello?" she whispered, still holding up her end. "Someone there?" She didn't want to find a body hidden in the church and was relieved— for a moment—when the dress moved and the woman slipped out.

Hattie's blonde hair was matted and damp from being on the floor, and her face was smeared with dirt and ash. She looked at Fay with bloodshot eyes, wide with fear.

"Please," she whispered, and her voice rasped out of her throat like wind through a dry riverbed. "They'll kill us."

Fay, to her credit, kept hold of her end of the bench. She decided that finding a live woman was better than finding a dead woman but only just. And then she saw the little boy.

"Two of you?" The man holding the other end of the bench, a lanky fellow named Beau, hissed out a long string of curse words in French.

"I don't—just—hold on for a second and let me think." The rest of the troupe looked to Fay for a level head in times of crisis, but never had they seen a crisis like the present one. Another pair of performers—the White Pines sisters—had paused in the aisle when they saw Hattie and were waiting for Fay to come up with a solution.

After a minute, during which the roof continued to drip with rainwater, Fay shook her head. "We need to move these pews, or we'll all end up shot." She looked at Hattie. "We're going to figure this out. I'll be back."

They moved the first set of benches outside—the twins Annie and Beth in the lead, next Fay and Beau, and finally Dysa and her husband Avit, the magician. Three pews would have been enough to fit the bandits, but they insisted on more being brought, so they could "get comfortable."

Hattie and Benjamin waited under their pew for Fay to return with her promised solution. Every moment that passed she was sure they'd be found out.

Inside the church, it was easy for Fay and the rest of the troupe to pretend that the crumpled shapes were just piles of clothes. But back outside, with the sun shining on a whole murdered town, the truth was too apparent—the fate that was in store for Hattie if these men found her. Fay tried not to think of the dead all around them, the funerals that would never happen. The thought gave her an idea.

"I need our tools," she said to Beau as they set their pew in place. He gave her a puzzled look as she turned to Lawrence, who was milling around by the saloon door, leering at each of the women in the troupe.

"Some of them pews are fixing to break," Fay said to him as his eyes took her in from tip to tail. "Reckon I can fix it, just need to fetch something from the wagon."

Lawrence chewed his tongue, running it over yellow teeth, and finally he snorted and spat on the ground. "Be quick about it. We're gettin' restless."

A leather pouch held the few tools the troupe kept around for wagon repairs and stagecraft. What she was after were the hammer and a handful of nails, and after finding them she hurried back to the chapel.

"I'm back," she whispered, and Hattie poked her head out just a hair. "I have an idea for how to get you out. It's only half an idea, but it'll have to do for now. What's your name dear?"

"H—Hattie."

Fay hadn't been lying when she told Lawrence that some of the pews were in bad shape. The gunfire and a collapsed roof had splintered several of the planks forming the backrests, leaving them hanging like broken fences. Fay used the hammer to remove a few that seemed in better shape and brought them to Hattie's pew. She took a deep breath, looking over the pile of wood at her feet before she started explaining her plan.

"I'm going to seal you up under the pew, and we'll carry you out like that." She tried to make her face seem optimistic and hoped the dim light would hide her doubt.

Hattie's face twisted, and she recoiled back into the darkness under the seat. "You can't be serious. Can't we just hide out here until night? We could sneak to your wagon before you leave."

Fay shook her head. "The wagons are clear across the town, and the church is about to be empty, so you won't have nowhere to hide. No telling when one of them might check in here. One way or another, you all are bound to be spotted, and we'll all get killed. This way we get you close to the wagon, and when the time is right, we sneak you in. But you're gonna have to sit tight until we get our chance."

Hattie's eyes narrowed, two white spots in the darkness. "Sit tight under a church pew, surrounded by murderers, you mean?"

"I ain't got a better idea, and it's not much different than what you've been doing anyway. We're running out of time. Can you do this?" Fay held out her hand, and after a couple heartbeats Hattie reached and took it.

As quiet as they were able, they pried more wood from damaged pews, nailing it along the legs and supports of one of the sturdier ones. It took shape quick enough, looking far too much like a coffin for any of their comfort. They tried not to think about it as Fay nailed in the last few boards, sealing Hattie and Benjamin inside and leaving only a few gaps.

The finished product wobbled slightly, but Fay was more worried about the boards holding the weight of two people than their being a little crooked.

The sound of Hattie's breathing sped up, getting ragged and panicked. "I don't know if I can do this," she whispered.

Fay set down the hammer and knelt on the floor, getting close to the slats. Hattie had all but disappeared in the blackness under the pew, so Fay started taking slow breaths, trying to get her to match the tempo. "You can do it, Hattie. Take a deep breath, slow down. You need to be strong. For your boy."

Hattie squeezed her eyes shut, and it was hardly different from when they were wide open. She nodded to herself and let her breath come easier.

"Okay, Benji," she said finally, the panic mostly gone from her voice. "We're going for a little ride. We need to stay extra quiet, okay?" Having him with her was a special kind of terrible, but she had a feeling that Benjamin would take it in stride. A mother knows her son.

Fay took a step back to examine the bench. The job was ugly, but at least it hid them from view. The rest of the troupe had come back, and Fay looked around to see the only other pews remaining were the ones they'd broken for planks.

With a nod, Beau and Avit lifted the pew, grunting from the

extra weight. The wood creaked and strained, and after a tense moment, it held, and the men headed for the exit. Fay slipped her arm
through Dysa's, leaning on her as the fear started to weaken her legs.
She still held the hammer, and her hand still seemed to vibrate from
striking the nails.

"Right up front!" Lawrence shouted, and Beau and Avit maneu-
vered the pew to the position closest to the wagon. The plan had
worked so far, but Fay hadn't worked out what the next part would
be. And then three of the largest men settled onto the pew, making
themselves comfortable just a few inches above Hattie and Benjamin's
heads. Fay could only watch, imagining a scream that would happen
any second as Hattie finally lost herself to the fear.

But there was nothing she could do for the moment.

They had a show to put on.

• • • • • •

THE MEN SETTLED on the pews, clearly getting irritated with the
wait. Fay stood behind the wagon, trying to steady her hand long
enough to apply lipstick. Annie leaned against the wagon nearby, a
cigarette hanging from her lips as she adjusted her costume. It was a
dress she wore for her first three scenes. First, she would be Ophelia
from Hamlet. Next, she portrayed a wealthy woman being swindled
out of her fortune. Lastly, as the title character for an aria from La
Sonnambula. It was classier than this crowd had any right to—even
the bits that were crass or stupid—and Fay felt her bile rising just to
think about them. They'd be hooting and staring, she knew, and her
girls would have to carry on like it was any other performance.

"You reckon we'll be able to pull this off?" she asked quietly.

"It's just an audience," Fay said, and the angry set of her face became more determined. "We'll worry about everything else when the show is done."

"'Everything else' is what I'm worried about." Annie smoothed the front of her dress with gloved hands. "I've performed for worse crowds than this. Remember Boulder, Colorado? When all those prospectors were belly sick?"

"If these folk get belly sick, I'd count it a blessing. I don't reckon getting away from here is going to be that easy, though."

A drumroll from Avit signaled the start of the show. His instruments stood beside the stage, a little tin drum and collection of horns. His music was simple compared to some traveling shows, but it served its purpose well enough.

Annie walked onstage to hoots and whistles and began her monologue as Ophelia. Fay tried to listen, but her attention kept drifting to the crowd and the pew hiding Hattie and Benjamin. She got so caught up in the panic of imagining them under there, she nearly missed her cue for the second scene.

Fay's role was one that she'd written with Beau—something of a villain, using trickery and fancy speech to convince Annie's character to give up her material wealth for a cure-all elixir. The character promised her eternal youth and perpetual romantic attention for only a small initial investment in her product. Annie's knack for voices and physical comedy never failed to win over a crowd, and this night was no exception. The gang's ire turned on Fay as she tried to swindle their already beloved Annie White Pines. Even with talc powder graying her and hasty wrinkles drawn on, Annie was captivating.

It was much to the gang's delight when Annie turned the tables on the duplicitous vendor. With a bit of fancy talk of her own, the old woman revealed herself to be more savvy than the villain suspected and ended up owning the whole operation, including the elixir's secret formula. It wasn't Shakespeare, but it was entertaining, and under normal circumstances, Fay would have been proud to hear it met with applause.

She squinted into the front row, tried to see through the gaps in the boards beneath Lawrence's pew without making herself too obvious. It was too dark, of course, to see anything, which she thought should have been comforting, since it meant that Hattie and Benjamin wouldn't be spotted by anyone. The scene finished with Fay's character realizing her mistake and storming offstage to Beau playing an up-tempo rhythm on his horn.

The gang clapped and shouted as the curtain closed. Fay collapsed against Dysa as soon as she reached her, squeezing her eyes shut against tears.

"I don't have any ideas," she whispered.

"It's okay." Dysa's words were confident, and Fay was grateful for her taking a turn as the hopeful one. "We'll think of something."

The next performance gave Fay a chance to think. Beau and Avit presented a scene adapted from a poet called Poe. Beau played a man who'd just murdered his housemate and hidden his body under the floor. The police came to investigate, and slowly the guilt drove the man insane when he started hearing the housemate's heart beating under the floor. Beth took over Beau's instruments, adding the sound of the heart on the drums to sell the effect.

The piece did nothing for anyone's nerves. Fay watched from the front of the wagon, still wrapped in Dysa's arms, sometimes watching the crowd and sometimes her fellow actors. None of it led her to any solution.

Beth sat next to the women, hidden from the gang in the shadows. Her eyes were hard, and her throaty whisper was almost lost on the breeze.

"We have to leave them."

Fay went stiff, tried to recoil from the words, but Dysa held her fast. She shook her head, trying to force words out of her throat.

Dysa spoke in low tones. "The rest of us discussed it, and it's a real honorable thing you did for those folks. But we don't owe them nothing. All we're liable to get done is getting those two killed and us along with them."

"There has to be a way," Fay finally managed, but Dysa gently shushed her.

"Ain't no way we get our own hides out of here along with two more bodies. We have a chance to just get ourselves out coming up soon, but we have to move quick."

Fay looked at her in alarm. "What's the chance?"

Beth's hand settled on Fay's like too many blankets on a bed. "As soon as Beau and Avit finish their piece, they're fixing to take their bows, then draw up the stage. Then Annie'll spur the horses and take us out of town. We need to get in the wagon, and quick."

Their faces beamed, eyes pleading, willing Fay to see the light. "I can see the wisdom in it," she said, nodding. "It kills me to know how close we were. I just wanted to help."

After a moment she released her hold, and the women crept around the far side of the wagon, opposite the stage, and made their way to the rear door. Their timing went along with Beau's character beginning to confess on stage, his voice rising to almost a shriek as he cursed the vulture-eyed man beneath the floor. Beth and Dysa climbed inside, and Fay paused to glance at the crowd. Some of the men were nodding off, and she felt her bile rise to see them sleeping through one of her best productions.

Instead of climbing the stairs, Fay dashed around just as Beau and Avit started to close the stage, pulling it up into the side of the wagon. It should have been their best chance to escape, but instead Fay stopped in the space where the stage had just been.

"Howdy, y'all!" she said, loud enough that a few men startled awake. The troupe whispered angrily from inside the wagon. "I wanna thank you all for being such a great audience. Them folks are just getting ready for the next piece."

She spread her arms wide, projecting her voice to the back row. "From the Bard himself, Mr. William Shakespeare, a scene from King Lear. This one's a long and beautiful monologue, some of Shakespeare's finest work, if you ask me. Now don't fall asleep, we're just getting to the good stuff here!"

Most of the gang grumbled to one another, looking around for somewhere else to be. The pews started to empty out, men leaving for the ransacked saloon or in search of a proper bed.

Fay continued with a wide smile. "It's beautiful out, ain't it? Last time we performed in Montana, it was a chilly night like this one, and some folk just curled right up, and the show lasted near until dawn."

Another two members of the gang got up and left, so there were only a few men left. Lawrence stayed put, sitting on Hattie and Benjamin's pew, and looking more alert than most. He watched Fay with a smirk at the corner of his mouth, his eyes fixed on her even as he took a swig from a bottle at his side.

"King Lear, you might like to know, was one of Shakespeare's best loved tragedies. It tells of King Lear, nearing the end of his life, and dividing up his fortunes and lands among his three daughters." Shuffling sounds rattled inside the wagon, including the latch to lower the stage. "Things do not go well for dang near anyone, just like you might expect for one of these tragedies. Well, folks, I reckon you can see it for yourself. I present to you, King Lear."

Fay stepped aside as the wagon opened once again, revealing a frustrated Annie and Avit. Their demeanor changed as soon as the dwindling audience was revealed, and they started into a dull scene. It was half-improvised, partly from snippets of Shakespeare, sometimes just lists of places and things that sounded English.

Dysa took Fay by the arm as soon as she was out of sight. "What are you thinking? We could have been gone."

"This plan is going to work," Fay said, hoping to turn it into truth by force of will. "We'll send them all back to the saloon to sleep, or they'll pass out right on the pews. Once they do, we sneak Hattie and Benjamin into the wagon, and we slip out of town."

They leaned around the wagon to see the crowd getting sparse under the lamplight. A few men were already resting their heads on the wooden seats, snoring gently. The dull droning of improvised drama filled the silence for the next half hour at least as more heads became heavy with sleep.

Finally, Lawrence was the last man left conscious. It became obvious that Avit and Annie had reached the limits of their material, so Fay decided to make one last effort.

She marched to the edge of the stage and made a signal for the scene to end. The actors took an abrupt bow and disappeared into the shallow privacy allowed within the open wagon. The stage closed back up like a drawbridge, leaving Fay stranded on the outside.

"And that, my dear gentlemen," she said, keeping her voice low. "Is the end of this evening's entertainment. With your blessing, we will be on our way."

Without waiting for a response, she took her own bow and headed for the steps.

"Hold on," Lawrence said, slapping his knees as he stood. "I ain't finished with y'all."

Fay braced herself, but as the man came closer, she could see tears on his cheeks, reflecting the shaking lantern flames. "That piece was a thing of beauty. You all have to stick around for another show," and here he drew a shuddering breath, raw with crying.

Before he could continue, there was a dull thud, and Lawrence's eyes went glassy. His shoulders and knees went limp, and he fell in the road.

"Let's go." Beau brandished the hammer. "This time for real, girl."

"Beau," Fay whispered. "What are you doing? He was fixing to let us go!"

He looked at her with his brow furrowed, offering the hammer. "Weren't that the plan? You keep his attention. I bash his head in? Even if no, it worked very well."

"Come on, then." Dysa was standing inside the wagon, ready to pull Fay up the stairs.

Fay took the hammer from Beau, not looking at the bloody end or the man lying in the dirt at her feet.

"Hattie, Benjamin. Let's go!" She set to work on the pew, prying the boards loose enough so they could crawl out. They were on their feet and following within a moment, headed for the wagon. Benjamin stumbled, falling face down beside Lawrence's still body and quickly scrambled away. When he came to his feet, his hand was heavy with Lawrence's gun.

"What you got there, son?" Beau said. "Gon' get hurt with a shooting iron like that. You give that to your momma."

Benjamin's eyes dropped to his hand, as if he was surprised to find the gun there, and he took a step away from the wagon.

"Come on, Benji, we need to hurry! Bring me the gun now." Hattie waited at the base of the stairs, one hand reaching for her son.

Like a cruel reversal of his fall, Lawrence rose to his feet between them, propping his body up with some difficulty.

He snatched Hattie by the wrist and pulled her down, bringing his face close to hers.

"I thought I smelled piss under me. You scared, woman?"

The wound on his head wept down the back of his neck, and his eyes twitched and darted as he tried to keep his balance. He had Hattie by the arm and the neck, keeping her between him and the boy.

"Ain't gonna shoot me, boy, not while I have your mama."

Benjamin's eyes stayed down, but his arm rose, unshaking, to aim the weapon. Everyone drew and held a breath, watching the little boy with the big gun.

A shot rang out, loud enough to wake the lone man sleeping on a pew. Lawrence flinched away, but Benjamin's finger hadn't moved.

Hattie shoved Lawrence aside and ran to Benjamin, easing the gun from his grip. Sure as any shootist, she spun and laid Lawrence and the other bandit low with two squeezes on the trigger. Each shot was echoed by a perfect replication from Benjamin's mouth. *Pow. Pow.*

They climbed into the wagons, an acting troupe and two extra passengers, and lit out of town. They pushed the horses hard, aiming for the wildfire horizon, and the only sound for miles was wheels and hooves.

Fay looked at Hattie with worry on her face and ran a hand through her hair. "How'd you know he wouldn't shoot?"

Hattie just smiled and held Benjamin's hand. A mother knows her son.

—*Brock Poulsen is a genre writer living in Boise, Idaho, in a house full of kids and stories. He writes to capture what it feels like to be human, to love, to want, to struggle. His work has appeared in the recent* Weird Wasatch *and* Night Terrors #21 *collections, as well as other online magazines. Follow him at brockpoulsen.com.*

THE GREAT BURRO REVOLT

P.A. O'NEIL

GRAND PRIZE WINNER OF THE 2023 *SADDLEBAG DISPATCHES*
MUSTANG AWARD FOR FLASH FICTION

BILLY WOKE TO his brother's foot in his face. This wasn't unusual, as he was one of four little boys who slept in the wide bed. Billy, Richard, and their cousins, Sam and David, all lived at their *abuelo's hacienda.*

Their mothers were sisters who had married brothers, and they all now lived at their father-in-law's ranch, the *El Molino.* The women split their duties, one rearing the children, the other tending to household management.

The bedroom doors to the *porche* were already open to catch an early breeze as *Tia* Fina pulled back the covers to find the tangle of arms and legs she found every morning. She ordered all to wash their faces and dress, so she could do their hair before breakfast. Billy, only six, was usually the last. Dressed in a smock and knee pants, he stood with his back to her as she undid his shoulder-length braid, then dragged a brush through his curly locks before pinning them all up into a bun.

"Ouch, you're hurting me!"

"Cállate!" Tia Fina's response was as sharp as the stroke of the brush.

After breakfast each day, the boys bolted out the door to wander around the *El Molino,* mostly unsupervised, as long as they stayed out of the way of the *ranchero's peones.*

This day, though, Billy doubled back and found his mother as she helped one of the Pima women, hired servants, hanging up the laundry. He relished time spent with her, even just watching her hang sheets on the line.

Billy had waited until she reached down to face the basket before speaking, "Mama. Why does *Tia* Fina hate me?"

"She doesn't hate you, *mijo,"* she replied as she hung another sheet. "Why do you say that?"

"She always yells at me when she does my hair. Last night, she called me *criado con los indios,* and it hurts when she pulls the burrs out.

"Mama, why do we have to wear our hair like this, and how come we have to wear these dresses?"

His mother knelt down and took his hand. *"Mijo,* it's 1898, almost the turn of a new century. Our family has worked for years to help bring civilization to this part of Arizona. Little boys back East dress like this, and have long hair, until they are almost ten."

"Ten! I don't know if I'll live that long."

He stumbled off to find the others petting a lone burro through the rail fence.

Richard asked eagerly, "What did Mama say?"

"She says we have to look like this until we're ten."

The collective groans drowned out the burro's little bray.

"I wonder why this colt is by himself?" David asked.

Sam scratched the burro's ears under the halter. "He's recently weaned. His mama is one of the ones they use on the mill wheel. He's too small, I guess."

Billy's attention wasn't on the animal. "I wish there was something we could do to make *Tia* Fina stop picking on us."

"Oh, I know how to knock her down a few pegs." Sam smirked.

"Sam, I don't want to hurt Mama," David cautioned.

Sam's face lit up. "Richard, hold on to this burro. David, help me get this rail fence down."

Billy giggled. "What can I do?"

"Run ahead to see if my mama is near our bedroom, and make sure the outer doors are open," Sam said.

Richard stepped over the downed rails into the pen. "What do you have in mind, Sam?"

"David, link your hand with mine so we make a kind of sling behind the burro's rear. Careful, we have to stay close, so he doesn't kick us. Richard, lead him toward the *hacienda.*"

Billy came running back to the others as they crossed the yard. "I couldn't see her, and the doors are still open." He softly clapped his hands and giggled. "What else can I do?"

Sam and David gently persuaded the colt from the rear while Richard tugged, holding the halter close under the burro's jaw. "When we get to the *porche,* pull down the blankets on the bed."

Billy's eyebrows rose, and his jaw dropped, but silently, he trotted away to complete his mission. As the others approached their room, he made one last check that Fina wasn't in the hall, then he pulled down the blankets on their large bed. His chest expanded with the thought that if he were caught before the others came, it would be worth her wrath.

The boys whispered to one another as they led the burro through the doors and toward the naked bed. Richard stepped up, pulling the animal behind him, while the others tried to lift as they pushed. Billy covered his mouth with his hands as he watched them push it down upon the white linen. Then, they got off, pulling the covers up over the colt.

Everybody did their best to hide behind doors and furniture.

It wasn't long before *Tia* Fina arrived. "Haven't I told you boys not to play Hide-n-Seek in the house?" She pulled back the covers with a force.

The scream echoed throughout the *hacienda* and yard. Others came running, only to find a confusion of boys chasing a braying burro around the room and Fina yelling in Spanish that she wished she had a strap.

The others returned the burro to his pen, while the boys sat with their noses in the room's four corners. No one was allowed to talk, and each was sure more punishment would come.

It seemed like hours before the women returned. With solemn voices, they called their children to them.

Billy and Richard approached Mama with downcast eyes. Her face was stern as she took each by the shoulders and turned them around. Billy squeezed his eyes, prepared for a spanking but popped them open when he heard the snipping sound of her shears cutting the bun off his head.

—P.A. O'Neil's stories have been featured in over forty anthologies, on-line journals, and magazines. She and her husband reside in Thurston County, Washington. A collection of her stories, Witness Testimony and Other Tales, is available on Amazon. Her article, "Northwest Passage," about the Ellensburg, Washington Rodeo from the Summer 2022 issue of Saddlebag Dispatches is currently a finalist for the 2023 Will Rogers Medallion Award. For links to books which feature her stories, please visit her Amazon author page: P.A. O'Neil.

THE MYSTERY
OF
THE ONE
RALPH GRECO, JR.

RIFF FRENTZ WAS the black rider. The youngest of his three-brother clan, he was acknowledged with curt nods or whispered curses—the quintessential "black sheep." It was assumed by all who knew them that Riff would someday be the downfall of the Frentz family. But Riff would prove to be their savior, as well as everybody else's in Little Arc, with the McBlade brothers currently in town.

● ● ● ● ● ●

EFFIN AND MACLEN McBlade were twin brothers with nary a black heart between them. Born mute, Effin was the brawn to his brother's more than caustic bite. Surely, both men were precise and merciless shots, but their nasty reputations had been earned by Effin's ability to render men limbless with his bare hands and Maclen's bragging of the attack later. They were cattle rustlers by trade, but as of late, were looking for a permanent home, a privilege denied them from their less than harmonious orphaned background and their years scrambling together as far from it as they could get.

Effin and Maclen came to Little Arc on the brine wind of that October Thursday morning, invading the house of farmer, Seaston Baint. Seaston's wife's brother ran with a rather nasty crowd and had had occasion to brag to the McBlade brothers about his hardworking brother-in-law's prosperous farm, and for all intents and purposes, this double-dealing degenerate gambler enslaved his sister's two-child family.

Riff smelled the McBlade brothers' foul stench of the wind at the beginning of that quiet October week. Rendering a quick and reluctant decision to extend his visit home, the youngest Frentz son determined to place the foul odor he could pretty much taste. When true evil was within a two-mile radius, the lanky, brown-eyed man knew it, and his curiosity as well as his caution piqued that day.

Men like Riff Frentz didn't smell their own kind that often... at least not above ground.

"Not too much jerky there little brother," Cecil Frentz remarked, literally walking into Riff who was coming from Hackey's that Saturday afternoon. "Thought you be takin' more seein' you is leaving."

Cecil was talking more for his own confirmation than to remind his baby brother of their daddy's wishes. Riff was welcomed to visit, as much as he wanted, but the older man had made it clear that he never wanted his bad-seed son around much longer than a night or two. Not that the old man wasn't happy to see his son. The elder Frentz just knew that where Riff managed his strong self, trouble was sure to follow. It was rumored that the older man had seen plenty enough trouble in his day and had lived his later years avoiding the same, so he knew well his son's reputation and could suspect fully well how he came by it.

For Riff, this had been a perfectly amicable agreement. He had no need for his family. He respected his father to be sure, he even loved the balding sixty-seven-year-old man when he ever actually thought about it, but he could never understand his father or his brothers' lives. How a man could work land for years and reap so few rewards, Riff couldn't rightly rationalize, let alone would wish on himself. He knew deep down his father boiled with passion and honor, but Riff never saw the old man get his dander up for anything 'cept his books or the memory of their mother. In a way, maybe his father's single-minded intent was like his. Riff did love his rifles and Night, his horse. Still Riff knew he would never take to farm life as his two brothers and daddy had.

Riff had left the farm at fourteen, making his way fighting the law and fellow outlaws from here to the California coast.

"Not leavin' just yet," Riff growled to his sandy-haired, boxy kin.

The youngest Frentz brother could have just kept quiet about his plans, as was his manner, but he was in a testy mood. Prices at the store were climbing, and a half-full saddle bag he held reminded him of the not-so-good season he had had roping. And with this twitch of sour smell in the air, Riff was more than ever in a terse mood over his brother's pressing remarks.

Unlike the respect Riff felt for his father, he held little for his two brothers... especially when they got on him as Cecil was doing now.

"Brother, you test us all." That was all Cecil could offer as he walked past Riff and into Hackey's.

Securing his pack over the horse's black side, then mounting Night, he spied Maclen securing his chocolate mare, actually young John Baint's mare, from across the eastern side of the pitted dirt main street. Riff knew that horse well, as he did how much thirteen-year-old John loved it. No one, but no one had ridden that horse since the boy received it from his father on his tenth birthday. Now, this big ugly with the stubbly face and bleary black eyes was tying it to a post outside the tavern?

It's hard enough for most men to explain their motivations. So many feelings coil inside us daily, feelings we neither acknowledge nor understand. Feelings that often times push us to foolhardy action. But unknown, misguided, and misunderstood motivations didn't enter into Riff's psyche. He knew where his destiny would lead him, as he knew he had to leave Night then, walk across the muddy main street, and follow after that ugly bastard who had ridden in on little John Baint's horse.

His intentions clear as a lake in late June, Riff swung the saloon doors open in and walked right up to the long wooden bar, leaning a spot right next to the ugly man.

"Hey," Thomas Fetch, the beanpole barman said to Riff. "Comin' in or goin' out?"

The old man didn't mean anything, Riff knew, but it was damn annoying how interested everyone was in his travel plans. Riff knew he just damned-well made folks nervous, and somewhere deep inside himself, if he searched long enough, he knew he would find that he wished this wasn't the case. But he really couldn't do a thing about how folks felt about him, and even if he could, this certainly wasn't the time to try.

"Just need a shot of whiskey," Riff sighed, and the old barman took his cue to fetch the drink as the ugly guy turned full to Riff.

There's as much something in the sound of a voice as there is in a smell, Riff thought.

"Nice horse you rode up on," Riff offered just as Fetch slid a small glass of amber-colored liquid down the bar at him. Riff kept his body turned full to the bar, not managing even a turn of his head to the ugly man beside him. "One just like it out at the Baint place."

"Yeah?" the ugly guy spat.

"Yup," Riff continued after sipping his whiskey. "The kid I know got one, never lets it out of his sight."

"That so?" Maclen asked. "You see that kid lately?"

"Not for a bit." Riff placed his glass on the bar and straightened up.

"Might stay that way... for a while," the man offered.

"I really wouldn't like that much," Riff said, at last turning to face the ugly man. "Got a soft spot for that family."

"Do ya now?"

"Sometimes you can surprise even yourself with who you come to care about and which folks you regularly check up on."

"Like that with me and my brother. I take care of him. He takes care of me."

"Good to have close kin."

But sweet Jesus, this guy was ugly, Riff thought as he stared at the wide face and dead eyes that were attempting to stare him down. The guy had yellow teeth, what there were of them, and a jowly mouth. But his eyes were deep and intelligent as if not a flitter of a mosquito passed by his sharp nose without his notice.

"Got to keep an eye out," Riff added.

"Yeah," the man agreed, allowing a tight smile to stain his dark face.

Riff turned back to the bar, downed his whiskey, stood up fully, turned to the man, tipped his black hat, then left the bar.

On the way back to the family farm Riff thought over what he had learned about the ugly man.

First of all, the man had taken to Riff's challenge of knowing the horse was stolen by warning he might not see little John ever again if he pursued his questioning. Then, there was the acknowledgment that the ugly guy knew Riff for what he was. The "wouldn't have thought you'd have one" jab about Riff's soft spot indicated that the ugly guy knew full well that Riff was a fellow outlaw… maybe not as pure evil and dumb but a "fringer" as Cecil had taken to calling Riff and his friends. In turn, the guy had let slip, certainly as a threat, a most crucial piece of information, that he was not working alone, he had a brother, maybe even a gang up there at the Baint farm.

As he flew through the gate of his family estate, Riff headed for the main house. After tying Night, he walked to his father's spacious cherry wood and glass study.

"You do know your brothers ain't none too happy," the eldest Frentz said, standing up from his red cushioned reading-chair when his youngest walked into the room.

"Something's up, Daddy," Riff said, throwing-off the mention of his brother's trivial concern as he moved around the room.

"Always is with you," the squat man said, moving across the shiny floor to the high bookshelf to the right of his son. He tapped at the row of leather-bound hardcovers over his head, keeping his slightly stooped back to his youngest.

"The way you came in here, I thought the back forty were on fire."

"Fire is at the Baints," Riff said, walking to the side of his father to catch the older man's tinny blue eyes. "And it's a blaze."

"Stay out o' trouble son," the older man offered, stopping his search of his books to turn and look straight at his son's square chin.

"Can't…." the son said to his father. "Family's in trouble, Pa."

"We'll call on Sheriff Bransen. You stay clear."

"Pa," Riff pleaded, the only time his low voice ever cracked was when he attempted these heart-to-hearts with this old man, probably the only living soul who really loved him.

"Sheriff'll get those folks killed," Riff explained as his father walked round to sit in his chair again. "I've seen the man that's got them holed up. I know men like that."

"I'm sure you do," the old man said, not a hint of mocking or malice in his voice.

A minute of silence passed the cavernous room as the late afternoon sunlight lit the gilded windows behind the older man's desk. Riff stared at his father, the wide shiny head, the tiny blue eyes, the handsome, yet rugged face, and tried to burn the picture into a memory to last him all his days. The old man looked so regal, holding his book, erect in his chair, resplendent against the backdrop of the amber sun setting off the high fields beyond the windows. A solitary figure of poised elegance. A man to make a son aspire.

"Take your brother Lane...." his father offered but then looked away for a second, indicating that he knew how foolish a suggestion this was.

"I'll be back soon. I'm gonna take the big gun," Riff said, as if in confirmation of why he had come to the house in the first place. "Then we'll go into town and get the sheriff."

"Why always you?" the elder Frentz nearly whispered as his son turned to go.

"Pa, you find the answer to that one in these fancy books, and I'll bronze the sucker's leather cover!" Riff said, then left the house.

•   •   •   •   •

A TEN-MINUTE ride and Riff was at the south path to the Baint's massive spread. Seaston Baint was a quiet man, a man with money but not one to spend or show it. He and Riff had barely had two sentences between them over the years, but Seaston kept to himself anyway. His wife, Hubby, baked pies for the church group and his sons, John and Brant, kept good grades.

A well-to-do gentleman-farmer currently being held hostage in his own home.

Riff liked this scene he was coming into it, the sun just dusking as he left the south gate. He took the rest of the way up the gravel path to the big utility barn that fronted this side of the property. Cocking his father's heavy rifle to his side, aiming for the mass of peach trees to his right, Riff fired a few rounds to warn the occupants of the main house that he had come to visit.

"Come to see that boy?" said a voice to the quick resounding silence.

The man had appeared from the side of the utility barn. Riff had known the ugly guy was there all the while, as much as he knew this guy wouldn't be the kind to shoot him until they laid eyes on each other.

Twisted as it could be, there was an honor among these men.

"This ain't your business," Maclen offered the speckled night. "You should just ride off now."

"Can't do that anymore than you'll let me," Riff said. He was standing not ten yards from the man.

"Reckon so," Maclen said, and suddenly Riff saw a shadow appear on the porch of the Baint house.

Momentarily distracted, Riff stared hard and long at the mountain that stood in the doorway—the ugly man's brother. But what unnerved him most was the twisting figure in the man's embrace.

It was the sprite, yet terrified, John Baint.

"See the boy now?" the ugly man taunted.

Maclen had moved into full view, knowing he was safe from any rifle blast Riff could attempt. As long as John was held as he was, Riff would not be making any sudden moves.

"Now go," Maclen spat with an uneasy chuckle.

Riff didn't move, but he felt something. It was a tremor he had experienced many times in his career, and he blessed God for it now as he had in the past. The odds against him, a seeming life-threatening danger before him, with darkness descending, who-knew-what-horror about to unfold, Riff felt the single cold touch of an advantage he could not name but understood all the same. If he searched long enough, he knew it was a tickle on his back he realized was destined to be here. In the ugly man's dismissal, in the silent tension passing between the big bear of a man on the porch and his mouth-piece brother here on the ground, Riff felt the brothers' fear. As he had countless times before, Riff knew his singular purpose, his standing alone with nary an advantage in sight, his solo cast of easy blackness to the space around him allowed him a mystique of skill, a potential of purpose, the mystery of the one, even when it might not be so.

Riff knew he'd have to meter his words very carefully, indeed, to maintain this edge.

"I do not wish to leave," Riff answered. He was calm, resolute, but not demanding—treating this all as if he was asking for a visit he was not prepared to be denied.

"I don't care what you wish," Maclen said, now stepping out full into the light and staring his ugly face into Riff's. "You got to know my brother'll snap that boy's neck I so's much as look in his direction."

"I don't doubt it," Riff agreed. His hand was itchy on the rifle, but he could not let one second of a muscle jump.

"So go!" Maclen said as if banishing a spirit.

Just a little longer, Riff thought. Just an inch more of the night, then he could make full split-second use of his advantage.

"You don't listen real good," the man before him said and raised a six-shooter to Riff's chest.

There it is, Riff thought. I was waiting for you to show me.

"Leave," Maclen said, accentuating his command by pointing his pistol at Riff and fingering the trigger. "Or die."

"I'm not going to do either." A shot rang out to fell Maclen.

The second shot, the first from Riff's rifle, hit dead square center of Effin McBlade's forehead. John Baint fell to the porch floor with not a scar or scratch as his family rushed from the kitchen in the commotion. Riff turned to his daddy, the older man holding the second of his two big rifles across his lap, steadying the horse he sat on.

"Well, shit, Daddy...." Riff smiled as the older man came trotting down the path on his best mare. "Took you damn well long enough."

"I was waitin' on your sign," the old man lightly protested, smiling down at his son. "You okay?"

"Fine," Riff agreed. "You best go see about Hubby. Maybe she'll bake ya a pie for this."

"Son, you doubtin' your old man's motivations?" the elder Frentz asked as he turned his mount to trot up to the main house.

In the quiet middle distance, Riff could just hear, sense actually, the sheriff on his way with either Lane or Cecil who had been sent to fetch him. Riff's father might have been cunning as a fox, could ride and sit in shadow, could shoot from a distance like nobody else, but he would rely on propriety now that the danger to this farm had been alleviated.

Riff turned down the gravel path, past the high hedges, to Night who was grazing softly at the edge of the farm property. The mystery of the one is that the one always knows when it is best to be solo or best to just appear to be. Riff could never have asked his father for help, but he knew how close his daddy was with the farmers in this town and especially how fond he was of the Baints. Riff's seemingly lone crusade had prompted what he had hoped of the older man. It was a risk to raise Maclen's ire like he had, push the man to the point where he showed his gun and his murderous brother, but Riff had been counting on the mystery of the one.

One man like his father.

—*Ralph Greco, Jr. is a professional writer and musician. His poetry, articles, fiction, and scripts have been published in eight countries. Ralph's one-acts have been produced across the U.S. and his songs performed in venues in the U.S., U.K., and Italy. He lives in the wilds of suburban New Jersey.*

Singing Cowboy by Thomas Eakins

PIANO PLAYER
JAMES A. TWEEDIE

CURLY MORGAN'S DREAM of a good life was nearly in his grasp when Buck Kelly turned his dream into a nightmare—a moment of horror from which he feared he would never awaken. But all that comes later. A story, after all, is a story, and if it is to be a good story, it should start at the beginning and not at the end.

Curly was given his nickname by his grandparents when he was just a pup, but his parents preferred to call him by his given name, which was Ulysses—a name bestowed in honor of the Union general under whom Curly's father was serving at the time the boy was born. To their dismay, the name "Curly" stuck and was still sticking in 1879 when the only curls the balding eighteen-year-old had left were to be found in the soft tangle of unshaven chin hairs he someday hoped to cultivate into a beard.

Curly found his calling early in life when his mother started him on piano lessons. It wasn't long before he was playing Sunday morning hymns on the Estey pump organ in the local Methodist church.

When he turned thirteen, he was abruptly relieved of his organist position when it was discovered he was moonlighting by playing the piano and collecting tips at a saloon in the next town over.

"Mama," he said, "if'n they don't want me playin' in church no more, then I'll not be goin' there agin. The saloon folks hain't kicked me out yet for playin' at church so I figure them's more Christian-like than them sorry folks singin' hymns under the steeple."

Curly was as good as his word and never set foot in a church again—at least not on a Sunday morning. But it wasn't long before he began to sour on the saloon, too, for he got tired of counting the pennies, nickels, and dimes that found their way into his hat each night. He began dreaming of silver mines in Colorado and cattle drives in Kansas where he imagined himself playing the piano in boomtown dance halls where miners and cowboys filled his hat with silver dollars, double-eagles, and gold nuggets.

At sixteen he left Indiana and headed West on a two-year pilgrimage that led him to Dodge City, Kansas.

On the afternoon of April 5, 1879, when Curly walked into the Long Branch Saloon for the first time, the only thing that caught his eye was the piano. As he began tickling the ivories, the old upright started singing and dancing in a way that set spurs jangling as the toes of cowboy boots began to tap.

"Play it, boy!" he heard a man yell, and before he finished pounding out "Arkansas Traveler," someone's gnarled hand had already placed a silver dollar on top of the piano.

Chalkley Beeson, who co-owned the place, led a five-piece orchestra each evening but needed a piano player to fill-in whenever the band took a break. Curly didn't hesitate to take the job when it was offered.

The Long Branch may have had its share of gamblers, drovers, and desperados, but Beeson kept the place as genteel as possible. By the time Curly arrived in town, it catered to wives as well as husbands and had long since sent the painted ladies to ply their trade at the town's less reputable establishments.

Unlike the cowboys and gamblers who rode into town with six-shooters on their hips, Curly didn't see the point in owning a gun. After all, Dodge City, along with most frontier settlements, required everyone to check their guns at the Sheriff's office as soon as they rode in. Dodge even had a sign in the middle of the street that spelled it out in no uncertain terms.

THE CARRYING OF FIRE ARMS IS STRICTLY PROHIBITED.

When Curly arrived in Dodge the rule was being enforced by former Sheriff and now town Marshal Charlie Bassett along with Deputy Marshall Wyatt Earp and the new Sheriff, Bat Masterson. But as Curly discovered his first night on the job, not everyone chose to read the sign.

It was getting on near 8:00 in the evening, and as the band settled into their seats to begin the concert, Curly was serenading the clientele with a sentimental rendering of "The Ballad of Lilly Dale."

Through the smoke and din of the crowded saloon, Curly heard the sound of a table being shoved across the floor.

"Levi, you son of a bitch, you've gone too far. My wife's honor demands you offer both her and myself an apology, after which you will leave this place and crawl back into the...."

"Sit down, Frank, and shut up," shouted a second voice. "I meant no harm by it, but I'll not apologize unless it's over your dead body."

"So, you threaten me! Here in front of the whole town! Then show your gun and let's get at it."

The shouts and screams began before the four gunshots set Curly's ears to ringing.

When the smoke cleared, Levi Richardson lay dying on the floor with three bullets in his chest while Frank Loving, who believed Richardson had made advances toward his wife, stood tall with a pistol held by a hand bleeding from where it had been grazed by a bullet from the gun wielded by Richardson.

By the time Marshal Bassett arrived, Richardson was as dead as "sweet Lilly, dear Lilly Dale."

Loving was reprimanded for carrying a gun in town, but when witnesses testified that Richardson had drawn first, both Bassett and Masterson decided Loving had acted in self-defense and let him go.

Beeson told the orchestra to go home and then shut the place down early. As he shuffled the last group of patrons through the front door, Curly turned to him with a question.

"Is it like this every evening?"

Beeson answered by silently and sadly shaking his head, "No."

Over time, Curly became as much a part of the Long Branch Saloon as Chalk Beeson—to the point where nearly as many folks came to hear him play the piano as came for the orchestra.

One of his admirers was Emma Peacock, the niece of Alfred Peacock who had opened the first Long Branch Saloon in 1872 in partnership with Charlie Bassett.

Half or more of the young men in Dodge would have eagerly snapped up the brown-eyed Emma as their wife or girlfriend if they'd had the chance but, with one exception, the possibility was something they could only dream about.

The exception was Buck Kelly, a ruffian, bully, and street fighter who had grown up alongside Emma and was as sweet with her as he was sour with near everyone else.

Three years earlier, when she was sixteen, Emma made the mistake of letting Buck kiss her, and she had been trying to keep him at arm's length ever since. For his part, Buck made sure that any man that set his eyes on Emma in a way that showed interest soon found himself with a bloody nose and a clear understanding that Emma Peacock was Buck's property, and no trespassing was allowed.

Emma felt as trapped as a bronco being broken in a corral and desperately wanted to find a way to escape the fawning, grasping control of Buck.

The man she chose to rescue her was Curly Morgan.

Curly knew Emma and would have asked to go for a walk or some such thing if it wasn't for the fear of Buck punching him in the face.

What Curly didn't know was that Emma had convinced herself that she had fallen in love with him—bald head and all. At night when she was in bed, she dreamed they were lovers, and in the evenings before going to bed, she would walk over to the Long Branch Saloon and sit as close to the piano as she could and watch Curly play.

Wherever she went Buck hovered over her like a thundercloud—dark, grim, and threatening.

"I've seen you sparkling your eyes at that piano player," Buck growled one night as he walked Emma home from the Saloon. "It's got to stop. It's got to stop... now!"

Emma stopped dead in her tracks, thinking that maybe the time had come for her to finally break off with Buck and move on. The thought of being free and as far away from him as possible filled her with a sense of purpose and power that welled up inside like a flash flood about to explode from the mouth of an arroyo.

"Buck," she began as quietly and gently as her pounding heart would allow. "What if I do? What if my eyes do shoot sparks when I'm looking at Curly Morgan? They're my eyes, aren't they, Buck?

And I can do whatever I want with them. You don't own them, and you don't own me. So, what are you going to do about it? Are you going to hit me in the face like you did that poor cowboy last week? I swear I didn't even know he was there, but you sent him to the doctor without giving him a chance to defend himself. There's something wrong with you, Buck. I know you try to be sweet, but sometimes you scare me, and I can't go on letting you think I'm your girl because I'm not—and to tell you the truth, I never was. So, I'm asking you to let me go and leave me be. You hear me, Buck?

Buck stood in the dimly lit street like a frozen, ghostly shadow and said nothing.

"And don't you take it out on Curly, either!" she added with a fierce glare that Buck couldn't see. "He's got no idea that I even exist. You hear me, Buck? Don't go near him or I'll...."

Buck cut her off with a voice steaming with anger.

"Or you'll do what?" he roared. "Give me a beating?"

The thought of Emma swinging her small fist into his face struck him as funny. He burst out laughing so maniacally that Emma's feet began moving her away from him—slowly at first, and then after three faster backward steps, she turned and disappeared into the darkness running as fast as her tight, short-heeled shoes would allow.

Buck didn't follow.

Instead, he headed back the way he and Emma had just come— back to the Long Branch Saloon where Curly Morgan was playing his final piece before the orchestra started in.

Buck's temper was hot, and whatever sense of reason or common sense he possessed was so dulled by rage that he gave no thought to the fact that Chalk Beeson and forty-five people enjoying an evening out were watching as he stormed across the saloon and slammed the piano cover down over the keys.

The music stopped, the room went silent, and Curly was so startled he almost fell off the piano bench backwards.

"You bastard!" Buck screamed. "Stealin' my Emma from behind my back!"

With his foot he kicked Curly off the bench and onto the floor while at the same time drawing a knife from under his shirt.

"I'm gonna slit your throat like a stuck pig, and I don't care if they hang me for it, 'cause without Emma I got no reason to live no how."

The people at the surrounding tables stood up and stepped away leaving the two men facing each other like gladiators in an arena.

Curly jumped to his feet and, as Buck lunged at him with the knife, turned and ran for his life.

Curly was fast, but Buck was faster.

The room was crowded, and after a few steps Curly found his way blocked by tables, chairs, and a wall of people trying to get out of the way.

Buck caught Curly from behind and with his free hand grabbed him by the collar at the back of his neck, spun him around, and paused for a moment to stare into his eyes.

It crossed Curly's mind that if this were a nightmare, he wasn't going to live long enough to wake up from it.

"Die like a pig!" Buck rasped as he reached his knife across his body with the blade facing toward Curly's neck.

As the saloon erupted in a roar, Curly closed his eyes and was surprised to find that his final thought was of Emma, sitting at the table closest to the piano with a smile on her face and her shining eyes locked on his.

As if from a great distance he heard something that sounded like a "thud" followed by a moan—sounds that were immediately swallowed up by a collective gasp from the crowd.

When he opened his eyes, he saw Chalk Beeson standing in front of him looking down at the floor where Buck Kelly was stretched out cold with his knife still in his hand.

As Curly tried to take in what had happened, he saw Beeson lift his arm and stare with sad eyes at the crushed remains of what only a moment before had been his prized cornet.

At this point in the story—if it were an ordinary story—you would expect it to wind down to a happy ending, but that's not how things played out.

After some cold water was splashed on Buck's face, and after Chalk Beeson had slapped him a few times with more energy than necessary, he got up and staggered out of the saloon swearing and vowing that next time he was going to finish what he'd started, which was to send Curly's soul to heaven ahead of schedule.

Curly couldn't hide the fact that he had wet his pants, but no one held it against him because every man in the saloon figured they'd have done the same if Buck had come after *them* the way he just had with Curly.

In spite of Buck's threats, Curly might have stayed in Dodge simply for the love of Emma Peacock. But once she found herself cut loose from Buck's sinister shadow, Emma fell out of being in love with Curly just as fast as she had fallen into it.

With Buck still coming after him and with Emma moving in the opposite direction, Curly thanked Beeson for giving him a job and for saving his life, and when he was done with that, he up and quit.

Beeson said he didn't want Curly to leave but also said he understood why he had to go.

Six weeks later, Curly Morgan walked into the silver boomtown of Leadville, Colorado, and was hired to play piano at the rough and tumble Silver Dollar Saloon. In the following months, after dodging a few stray bullets, he put up a sign asking would-be shooters to kindly aim in any direction but his.

In 1882 the famed Irish playwright Oscar Wilde paid a visit to Leadville as part of his lecture tour of the American West. While drinking one night at the Silver Dollar Saloon he took note of Curly's sign, and upon his return to the British Isles, shared it with a wider audience.

According to Wilde, the sign read as follows. *"Please do not shoot the pianist. He is doing his best."*

A year later, Bat Masterson stopped by the saloon, and he and Curly had a good time swapping tall tales both true and otherwise.

Not unlike the one you've just read.

—*James A. Tweedie has lived in California, Utah, Scotland, Australia, Hawaii, and presently next to a Pacific Ocean beach in southwest Washington. He has published six novels, three collections of poetry, and one collection of short stories with Dunecrest Press. His western stories and poetry have appeared in both print and online media. He claims to be an optimist.*

In Without Knocking by Charles M. Russell

ON ᴛʜᴇ RIO GRANDE
WILL AMES

ROLAND BRANDT SPURRED the stolen bay through the dust and scrub, ignoring its rolling eyes and sweat-flecked lips. There were only a handful of miles to cross before he hit the muddy Rio Grande, but it felt like half of Texas stretched between him and freedom, and he was itching to be across. There was a real blowout of a soiree brewing down south, and if he'd played his hand right, he'd be the guest of honor.

He reached back for the hundredth time, felt the solid weight of the bulging saddle bags, and breathed a sigh of relief.

His life's worth was in those bags, one way or another.

A hundred miles behind him was a Wells Fargo and Co. bank that stood twenty thousand dollars lighter, and the only thing between him and a life of luxury in Old Mexico was some scrub brush and a river.

• • • • • •

THE LAST FLAMES of the dying sun glinted on the Rio Grande, not a hundred yards away beyond the last of the chaparral and down a shallow bank. He let out a deep breath. He'd made it.

Two sharp clicks shattered the twilight stillness.

"Don't even twitch."

Roland's scalp tingled. Damn. He was so close. He didn't twitch, and despite himself he half smiled. "I knew a fella once," he said without turning. "Had an ol' Navy Colt sounded just like that. Never made the switch to cartridges." He flicked his eyes from side to side searching for a way out, but there was nothing but low creosote and sage between them and the stumpy mesquite and cottonwoods that grew thick along the riverbanks. Damn. "Yessir," he continued, "said cap and ball was good enough for him. Heard he threw down on another fella, and it blew up in his face."

The voice snorted. "Hell, if he was a friend of yours, it was probably so dirty it just chain fired on him."

Roland grinned. "Some things never change. Can I turn around?"

"Like molasses in winter."

He eased the bay around until his back was to the river and found a U.S. Deputy Marshal staring him down over the barrel of a well-worn Navy six. He glanced over his shoulder at the sparkling water.

"You'd never make it," said the marshal.

Roland grinned. He couldn't help it. "Just admiring the view," he said. He turned back. "I hear Mexico sure is pretty at night."

"Guess you'll just have to find out some other time." The pistol didn't waver.

Roland squinted at the marshal in the dying light. He hadn't changed much in three years. A little gray stuck out from beneath the sweat-stained Stetson, but the mustache was full, and the deep-set blue eyes were still clear and bright.

"Been a long time, Heck."

"Yes, it has."

"You look good."

The mustache twitched at one side. "You look good, too," said Hector Langdon, "for about twenty years breakin' rocks up at Huntsville."

"Why, Heck," said Roland, "here I was thinkin' you'd come all this way to catch up with an ol' pard. Say, you remember that time we were up on the Llano—"

"Don't play dumb, Roland." Heck cut him off with a wave of the pistol. "You knew I'd be the one."

"I don't know what you're talkin' about, hoss. I just came down here to have some mezcal and dance with the señoritas. Ain't no law against that, surely." The West Texas gloom was setting in, and Heck's heavy duster was starting to blend with the scrub brush. If he could just keep him talking a little longer....

"It is when you're totin' twenty thousand Yankee greenbacks from the Wells Fargo in Pecos," said Heck.

"Pecos?" Roland raised a brow. "Shoot, I ain't been up there in a coon's age, hoss. Last time I was, I lost my whole stake at cards. Left a bad taste in my mouth." He smiled. "Ain't been back since."

There was still enough light for him to see the mustache twitch again. "You were there less than a week ago when you busted into the bank and stripped it clean." Heck raised an eyebrow. "And you been ridin' hell for leather south ever since. I oughta know. I'm the one been eatin' your dust."

"I never," said Roland.

"Half the town was able to identify you, Roland." The whites of Heck's teeth shone pale in the twilight. "To say nothin' of the fella who's mouth you busted with your pistol when he tried to block you gettin' in that safe."

Roland smiled and shrugged. "Never could abide a banker man. Say, you remember that ol' Mex pistolero we bagged down around these parts when I caught that slug for you?"

Heck's smile faded. "A man don't forget somethin' like that, and you know it, Roland. You got somethin' to say, spit it out."

Roland smiled again. "We sure rode the river a time to two, didn't we, hoss?"

"You know we did."

Roland spread his hands slowly. "So, what do you say?"

Heck's stained silverbelly was a pale shape that shook from side to side in the gloom. "You walked out on me, Roland. Not the other way around. Any debts between us are finished."

Roland shook his head. "Same old Heck. Still a hard case. Life ain't all black and white, you know, hoss." And then he smiled because the sky's deep purple had blurred the chaparral shapeless and now was his chance. "By the way, how's Libby?" he asked.

"Libby?" asked Heck. The Stetson cocked to one side. "What's—"

Roland rammed his spurs back and hoped the bay wasn't so blown it would balk, but the big gelding squealed and danced into a rearing start. He ducked low and held tight as it took off in a dead run straight at Heck. The marshal swore, there was a flash and boom, and he felt the wind as lead zipped by his ear, but it was too dark, and Heck was too late. Two more strides and he yanked the bay sideways into the brush with a brace of shots snapping dry branches around him.

The Rio Grande was somewhere over his right shoulder, and he drove straight for it. The moon was on the rise, and if he didn't hotfoot it, there might be enough light for a lucky shot while he forded the river. But he still couldn't resist a parting shot for an old friend.

"Gettin soft, hoss!" he called into the darkness. "Maybe next time!"

He hung low over the bay's neck and waited for a shot, but none came. And then there was nothing but darkness clear to Mexico.

•   •   •   •   •

HECK LANGDON SWORE and rammed the Navy home. Smoke hung on the still night air, stinging his nose and eyes. Roland had played him like a damn fiddle. It was a waste of time, but he called out anyway. "What happened to you, Roland? What changed?" His voice floated out over the chaparral.

"Aw, you know me, Heck! Life's too short to take all that serious!"

Roland's voice was closer than he thought, and the Navy jumped into his hand, but he stopped himself. No. No sense wasting lead. *How's Libby....* He shook his head and half smiled in the dark. Slick as a damn whistle. And then he heard it. Somewhere off in the night came the noisy splashes of a tired bay floundering across the Rio Grande into Mexico.

He ground his teeth and spat. It would be impossible to get him now. Even if he did get permission from the rurales to cross the border and hunt Roland, he'd just be wasting his time. Mexico was where folks went to disappear. It was wide, it was strange, and the Mexicans didn't like to cooperate with snooping *blanco* lawmen.

No, it was pointless to try and chase him across Mexico. They both knew it. Time had been they'd hunted men up and down both sides of the border. Lost their fair share, too. Few knew better just how easy a man could get swallowed up by those hot Mexican sands.

He leathered the pistol. There'd be no more need of it tonight. Then he swung the dun's head back north and tried to wash out the taste of dust and failure with a swig from his canteen. The only thing left to do now was wait Roland out. Keep his ears open and wait. No

matter how long it took, they always came back. Always. He wondered if Roland remembered that lesson, too.

It was strange. He never understood it. Why leave a country
where they're as good as safe from any kind of law that mattered for a
place with a price on their hide? Maybe it was too much to resist, the
temptation. Maybe the money ran out. Or maybe they just got home-
sick. Who the hell knew.

But Heck Langdon knew one thing. Roland would come back,
sure as the sunrise. Sooner or later, he'd slip up and cross that line
again. Sooner or later, that damn luck of his would run out. And
when he did, Heck would be waiting with a smile and a gun.

• • •

TWO YEARS OF nothing but mezcal sure made a man thirsty for a
sip of good Texas sour mash. The late afternoon sun lay on Roland
Brandt's left shoulder, drenching the wastes of Chihuahua in gold and
shadows. All those pretty little senoritas and their hot, sultry nights lay
behind him, but he didn't care. It had taken two slow, mezcal soaked
years, but the itch had come just the same. It was time to go home.

• • •

HECK HIT TOWN with the midmorning sun bleaching the sweat
from his stained hat. It had been a long morning, riding since before
the predawn gray misted the chaparral, but the fatigue hadn't set in yet.
He wouldn't let it, not when the man he was hunting was this close.

Jake Mason had been busy in the month since he'd cut his way
down from the Nations. A Butterfield holdup, a string of stolen army
remounts, and a shootout with the Tenth up on the Llano. Some folks

said there were better pickings in Texas than Indian Territory, others figured he was dodging Judge Parker's noose. Heck didn't get paid to worry about the whys.

But even after raising all that hell, Mason could've still disappeared. Texas had swallowed up hundreds just like him and would swallow hundreds more before law and order had its day. But Mason had made a mistake when he'd killed Jim Lynch up in Big Springs, and afterwards his name and description had been wired to every peace officer in the department.

The life of a deputy marshal might not be worth a plugged nickel in the Nations, but Texas marshals took better care of their own, and Mason had gone to ground quicker than a dog town with a badger on the prowl once they'd picked up his trail.

It had taken a week to root him out and ended with Del Anderson laid up waiting to die with lead in his guts, and it had been another two weeks before Heck finally cut his sign again on the southward run.

Now he was three days eating dust, and time was short. With Mason's lead he could already be in Mexico, but Heck made himself move slowly through town, head on a swivel. No sense riding blind into trouble. And he had a hunch Mason would still be there. Nothing but badlands lay across this stretch of the Rio Grande, and if he were smart, Mason would stop just long enough to lay in supplies to see him across the desert, and that might be all the delay Heck needed to get the drop on him.

Looking at the town, he could hardly remember the last time he'd had business in Candelaria. Five, maybe six years. Not much had changed. A few less adobes, a few more cottonwoods, same choking dust and heat.

His mind peeled back the years as he rode the dry-baked streets, remembering. A posse of ranchers had called him in to run down a horse thief, and he'd tracked the man to Candelaria only to find out he'd slipped across the river with the remuda just the day before. Then he'd had to stop the frustrated posse from stringing up a young Tejano they'd decided was in on the rustling.

He squinted down heat shimmered streets, remembering his way. Down one alley a sun-scarred old woman hugged the scant shade of a gnarled cottonwood while she beat out the laundry. As he passed by, she straightened with a hand to her hip and stared. Her eyes were tight lines in the reflected glare of the adobes, turning her face hard and pitiless, and his scalp tingled. He rolled his shoulders and looked away. Just another distraction he didn't need. Then he saw the alley he was looking for and turned into its sparse shade. Time to call on an old friend.

•   •   •   •   •   •

"MANUEL." HECK SMILED and peeled off his hat in the cool of the ramada. The gnarled stump of a man in the tiny adobe's doorway bobbed his gray head.

"*Señor* Langdon, it has been many years." His threadbare white cottons and the gray stubble peppering his leather dark face were the same, but something in the old Tejano's eyes seemed different. Then he started firing off a slapdash mix of Spanish and English and Heck forgot the notion.

"He drinks in the cantina. Ever since he come to town. In the mañana he stay there."

Heck grinned. He'd figured right. No need to ask who the old man was talking about. Mason was taking the breath before his plunge across the badlands.

"He alone?" Mason could've always picked up a few mavericks on the way down.

Manuel shrugged. "Is the cantina ever empty, señor? Some men, nothing better to do."

There it was again, that look. Heck didn't like it. Like the old man was trying hard not to say something, and he wondered if maybe the old Tejano had forgotten his debt after all.

He leaned against one of the rough cedar posts that held the thatched ramada and fished his makings from a vest pocket. He took his time and rolled a quirley, scratching a match on the post, and when he'd dragged it to life, he settled back and eyed the old man over the glowing stub.

"We've come a long way together, you and me, eh, *amigo?* Ever since I stopped them *rancheros* stringin' up your boy as a horse thief?"

He thought the old man looked a shade paler as he bobbed his grizzled head. *"Sí, Señor* Langdon. Long way."

"How is your boy, by the way?" Heck looked around the little adobe, but there was no sign of anyone but Manuel living there. The air in the shade was only a few degrees cooler than in the direct sun, but now it seemed almost chill.

"Bien, señor, bien." Manuel looked down and started turning his frayed sombrero over and over in gnarled hands.

"What's he up to these days?" Heck asked. "I take it he steers clear of them *rancheros* now?" He smiled around a puff of smoke but kept his eyes hard on the old man.

"Manuelito works for a man, *señor,"* Manuel said a little too quickly. He wasn't smiling, just turning that old hat around and around like it was the most interesting thing in the world. *"Pequeños trabajos,* but he stay busy."

Heck took a long drag, rolling the smoke between his fingers, and chewed a loose shred of tobacco. "Good," he said, spitting the shred out. "Good. Around here?"

"Some." The *sombrero* was almost spinning now.

"Good," Heck said again. "Boy should be near his family. Might get into trouble out in the world all by hisself." He flicked the smoke into the dust and snubbed it out, looking sidelong at the old man. "Fall in with the wrong kind of folks." He pushed himself off the cedar and dug in a pocket. Gold flashed in the dappled shade, and he smiled as the old man snatched the eagle out of the air. He'd have to come back later and get Manuel talking straight, see what it was about his boy he didn't want to say. For now, time was wasting. He settled the hat down tight on his sweat slicked head. *"Muchas gracias, amigo.* The saloon?"

"Sí, Señor Langdon." Manuel looked relieved and miserable all at once, but he waved further into town. "That way."

"I know the place." Heck slipped the hammer loop off his pistol, making sure Manuel was watching. He slid the pistol up and down, making sure it moved freely. "Be seein' you, Manuel."

And then he stepped back out into the blistering heat and swung aboard the dun, the little saloon already in his mind's eye. He needed a drink.

●　　●　　●　　●　　●　　●

CANDELARIA WAS SO small the saloon didn't even have a name. It was just a wall of whitewashed clay with a framed opening and a deep ramada shading some rickety tables.

He started to worry when he saw the four big geldings snubbed to the short crossbar out front. Four was a crowd in a piss-ant little town like Candelaria, especially before noon. Then one of the horses shifted and flashed a U.S. army brand on its hip. An old, worn-out McClellan sat on its back, and his scalp tingled. That frayed, old sombrero was spinning around and around in his mind's eye.

He hesitated and then swung down next to a bay sporting a flashy Mexican rig. He fingered one of the shiny conchos, thinking, and shook his head. It didn't matter. Brady Ellis was forty miles away by wire, and the nearest Ranger battalion was busy helping the Tenth track Lipan renegades. And no posse alive would go after Jake Mason. He was alone.

He snubbed the dun and double checked his load. The heavy iron on his hip was comforting, but he wished he'd brought a scattergun. Two loads of buck staring you in the eye made you think. Something else he'd have to do without.

He thought for a minute and then fished a stubby pocket model from his saddlebags, checked the load, and tucked it into the small of his back, flipping his heavy duster in place over it. It wasn't a shotgun, but it was better than nothing. He squared his shoulders and stepped through the doorway.

•　•　•　•　•

HE HAD THE Navy clear and cocked before he'd finished blinking the sunspots from his eyes. There were five—two bellied up to a bar tended by a pinch-faced old-timer, a scrawny Mexican kid shuffling cards on his left, and a drunk in the corner sleeping one off between a half-empty bottle and a hand of solitaire. The pistol's sharp clicks cut across the room like whipcracks, and he drew a bead on the barfly with a brace of turkey feathers sprouting from his hatband.

"Mighty early to be drinkin', ain't it, boys?" he said.

The barroom froze.

•　•　•　•　•

HECK COULD FEEL the Mexican kid's eyes on him. *"Señor* Mason," called the boy, *"El hombre* has a *pistolo* on you."

"Butt out, *amigo,"* snapped Heck, keeping his eyes on the turkey feathers. "Unless you want to share his cell."

The pair at the bar eased around, eyes falling on Heck's pistol. The old barkeep went white as his hair and slid slowly away from the two men. Both wore pistols and had long guns propped beside their knees against the empty whiskey barrels supporting the bar.

"Well, if it ain't Charlie Harris," Heck said, looking the shorter one up and down. "You got fat."

"You." Harris spat, wrinkling up the big purple splotch that marred his cheek. "Bastard."

"Gonna introduce your friend, Charlie?" drawled the man with the turkey feathers. His elbows rested on the bar, a quirley dribbling smoke in one hand.

"He ain't no friend of mine," growled Harris.

Heck grinned. "You keep poor company, Mason. Last time I saw ol' Charlie here, he was three jumps ahead of me and killin' a good horse to keep it that way."

The tall man raised his chin. "Heck Langdon. I heard of you."

Heck snorted. "Anything good?"

"Heard you were a hard man. And fast."

Heck shrugged.

Mason half smiled. "Question is, are you fast enough? The other two thought so."

Heck forced a smile. "Don't reckon we're gonna find out, seein' as I got you eight ways to Sunday. 'Fore long you'll be too busy worryin' about Judge Duval's noose to be thinkin' about much else. I figure folks been waitin' a long time to see Jake Mason dance the gallows jig."

Mason's eyes narrowed, but he didn't answer. He glanced at the pistol again.

"Even you ain't that fast," said Heck.

Mason stood rock still, the quirley forgotten. Beside him Harris licked dry lips, his eyes flicking back and forth between the two.

And then Mason smiled.

Heck felt the hair on his neck prickle. Something was wrong. He twitched the pistol. "Shuck the belts. Now."

Neither moved. Now Harris was smiling, too. Then he realized they were looking past him, and his blood went cold. In the corner of his eye, he saw the Mexican kid's head turn.

He wanted to whip around. His shoulder blades itched like fire, but he forced himself to stay still. A wrong move and it was all over. "I'll drop you where you stand," he warned them. "Hell with a trial." And then something cold and hard pressed into his spine, and he heard two clicks.

• • • • •

"YO' TURN," SAID a deep voice. "Drop it."

"Hot damn," breathed Harris, sagging against the bar. "Took you long enough."

Mason's eyes bored into Heck. He flicked the smoke into the dirt and slouched on the bar, propping a boot against a whiskey barrel. The smile widened. "Your move, Marshal."

Heck's mustache twitched. He didn't move. Maybe if he could….

The gun dug deeper. "Ain't gonna ask again," said the voice.

Heck let out a breath. He eased down the hammer and let the pistol dangle from one finger.

Mason's eyes narrowed. "You heard him. The belt."

Heck ground his teeth. He tugged one-handed at his buckle, and the rig snaked down into a heap at his feet.

A tall, lean black man sidled around him, his long Army Colt waist high, and tucked the dangling pistol into his own waistband.

"Wondered when you'd show," said Mason. He rubbed big hands together. "Barkeep, get over—" But the old man was gone, disappeared through a door along the back wall. Mason shook his head and leaned over, snagging a fresh bottle from behind the bar. "Chickenshit."

Heck stared at the black man. He still wore his faded blue army trousers tucked into high boots and a backward facing flap holster rode his hip. "Ike Prichard," he guessed.

"I don't know you," said the black man as he backed over to the bar, keeping a bead on Heck the whole time.

"Ain't too many deserters I know of wearin' sergeant's stripes," said Heck. The Army's barrel looked wide as a howitzer's muzzle.

"Think you're damn smart," growled Prichard. He looked at Mason. "I reckon he's alone. I circled town once fo' I came in. Didn't see but one set of fresh tracks."

Heck jerked his chin at Prichard and Harris. "You're startin' a gang," he said to Mason.

Mason showed his teeth. He handed Prichard a glass and pulled his own pistol while the black man tossed the shot back. "Yessir," he said, "I figured you for a smart one. Me and the boys here are moving in. Speakin' of that,"—he looked at Prichard—"where's J.D.? I sent word to you two a month ago."

Prichard spat. "He ain't comin'. Fool got hisself shot by the rurales when we was comin' up from Durango."

"No shit?" asked Mason.

"Damn," said Harris. "What do we do now?"

Mason rolled his eyes. "Sit here and wait for the waddies to get smart and send a posse. What the hell do you think?" He waggled his pistol at Heck. "I shoot the marshal here and we get on with the plan. And now J.D.'s dead we only gotta split things five ways."

"Four and a half," said Prichard, eyeing the kid. "He ain't earned a full share yet."

"We'll handle that later," said Mason. He looked at the kid and nodded to the corner. "Manuelito, get over there and throw a bucket of water on that lazy bastard."

The Mexican's palm slapped down on the table, and he half rose, cheeks flushed and scowling. "My name is Manuel," he said, and his hand fell to a flashy nickel-plated Remington peeking out of a tooled holster. "We agreed. One full share each."

Mason's face darkened, and the pistol swung over. "You'll answer to what I damn well call you. Chico. And you'll take what share you're given. Unless you think you're good enough to ramrod this outfit."

Heck should've made his play then, while they were all distracted, but he couldn't make himself move. Manuelito? He'd been played. Old Manuel had known the whole time his boy was riding for Jake Mason. Had all but said it. And he'd missed it.

Manuelito stared at Mason's gun as heartbeats passed. His fingers twitched, but then he looked away. He kicked the chair back and spun on his heel, stomping over to the drunk in the corner.

"Four and a half," said Mason, and Prichard nodded. "Hey, *chico*." Manuelito stiffened and half turned, his face dark red but not meeting Mason's eyes. "We ain't got all day. Use the bottle if he don't move." Manuelito left off shaking the drunk and popped the cork on the half empty bottle.

Mason swung back to Heck. "I'll say this for you, Langdon, you're game as a banty rooster. I been bird-dogged by some good ones, but they never had the grit to come this far. Too bad you fell short."

Heck tensed. This was it. It was now or never.

Then a shout came from the corner, and something crashed to the floor, and everyone wheeled.

Manuelito was on the floor, and Roland Brandt was staggering up from the upended table, swaying and blazing away with a pistol.

His first shot went wide, but the second caught Charlie Harris square in his fat belly and dropped him like a sack of potatoes. He tried a third, but the kid yanked out his nickel Remington and snapped one off from the floor just as Heck snatched his belly gun from the small of his back, twisted, and fired.

Jake Mason was a heartbeat too slow. Heck caught him mid-spin, just before he could level his pistol. There was just enough time for his eyes to widen before Heck put a ball in his chest, so close the powder blackened the man's dirty vest. Heck kept turning and fanned two more shots into Ike Prichard before the deserter could finish tugging his pistol from under the army holster's flap.

Harris was on his knees, clutching his belly with red fingers, so Heck spun back to the corner where Roland and the kid were. Two bodies sprawled in the dirt.

Roland lay on top of the kid. Heck pulled him off and saw the powder burns blackening Manuelito's fancy outfit, and he wondered what he was going to tell Manuel. Then he shook his head. The old man had known the score from the get-go.

Then Roland groaned.

Heck knelt and propped up his head. Blood frothed at his lips and more covered his chest, and he was surprised to see how much older Roland looked with flushed cheeks and twenty extra pounds. Bloody lips twitched, and the breath rattled in his chest.

"Don't talk," said Heck. "You're lung shot."

Roland's head rolled to one side. "We get 'em?" he wheezed.

Heck looked around. Blood pounded in his ears, and smoke clouded the low ceiling. Harris was slumped over, curled up in a ball and moaning. Mason, Prichard, and Manuelito were slack mouthed and still.

Three dead in ten seconds. And two more on the way.

"Yeah, Roland. We got 'em."

Roland coughed, and more blood bubbled at the corner of his mouth. "Just like old times," he rasped. And then he smiled.

Heck wanted to ask him what he was doing here. Wanted to ask why he'd helped against Mason. Most of all he wanted to ask why he'd left the safety of Mexico just to die in some piss-ant little border town. But he didn't.

—A tradesman by day, Will Ames spends his free time pursuing his innumerable hobbies, the most satisfying of which is finding the right words to breathe life into his stories. A proud and lifelong Alabamian, he hopes to one day see firsthand the big sky country that haunts his dreams. "On the Rio Grande" is his first published work.

Riding the Range by William Dunton

THE
HANGING DAY
GRANT EAGER

IT WAS A beautiful spring morning in Dodge City, a sleepy town in western Kansas. Sarah stood alongside a man and a teenage boy. In front of them was a gallows built out of scraps of old barn wood and whatever else they could cobble together.

The young lady with long coal-black hair and ice-blue eyes moved her hands to try and get some circulation back into them. Deputy Broom had tied Sarah's wrists tight. She frowned. Seeing a lady go to the gallows was a rare and wondrous occurrence. Broom, a large redheaded deputy whose shirt did not cover his belly, had even hinted he would let her escape for the right offer, but she was not tempted. This, however, had given her an idea, and she suggested the same to the well-boned Sheriff Parker and had been declined. She regretted killing her husband, but well, no buts. She did the deed and must now suffer the penalty.

The deputy gestured to the crowd of several hundred onlookers wearing their finest clothes with festive hats and parasols. Kids ran through the crowd with streamers and pinwheels being chased by dogs. Broom said, "Ladies and gentlemen let us begin the proceedings, please back away from the miscreants. We'll not tolerate anyone interfering with a lawful hanging."

The crowd ignored him, jostling for a prime viewing spot. The sheriff raised his hands and yelled, "Quiet while I read the judgments!" He explored his coat pockets and pulled out several crumpled-up sheets of parchment. He straightened the papers and then climbed onto the gallows. He felt in his shirt pocket and retrieved a pair of spectacles. He glanced at the prisoners. "When I call your name step forward while I read the judge's decision. Akondo Silver-Chief, please step forward." When a tall boy with braids in his late teens did not move, the deputy shoved him forward. He sprawled onto the ground, and the deputy brusquely pulled him to his feet.

Sarah said, "Show him some respect, there is no need to treat someone so."

Broom snorted. "Why does it matter, he'll be dangling from a rope soon enough."

Parker cleared his throat. "That will be enough. It would not hurt to show the culprits some compassion before we put them in the noose. Now, Akondo, you've been found guilty of horse thieving, resisting arrest, and assaulting my deputy. The judge sentenced you to be hung until you are dead. Go ahead and step back. Jacob Jacoby, please step forward. You have been charged with cheating at cards, stealing the tithing from the poor box, grave robbery, lying, adultery, bigamy, rape, public intoxication, and kicking a dog. The judge sentenced you to hang until you have drawn your last breath."

After Jacob stepped back, the deputy gave Sarah a shove and said, "Miss, it's your turn."

She stepped forward and looked at the sheriff. He cleared his throat and read," Sarah Anne Sanchez, you've been convicted of poisoning your husband, a Mister John Angus Sanchez, as well as bribery and soliciting prostitution. You have been sentenced to hang."

She said, "I hadn't meant to kill John, the rat poison bottle said a tablespoon could kill a man, so I thought a teaspoon would just make him ill." She offered a sheepish look, "Well... it sounded right when I planned it. Is it my fault he had such a weak constitution? Since he had been unfaithful... again, I figured this would be my way of showing my displeasure. He was a lecherous swine. God rest his soul."

The Sheriff said, "That will be enough."

She stepped back and glanced at the crowd who were chanting, *"Hang her! Hang her! Hang her!"*

She scowled and spoke up, "That is getting annoying. I felt the charge of prostitution was a bit harsh. I just asked the sheriff if he would look the other way concerning the poisoning thing, I'd be willing to offer him some of my time. How is that prostitution? I could make him some bread or mend his socks. I didn't say anything about having sex with him. Now everyone thinks I'm a tramp. And right here in front of all my neighbors."

A lady in the crowd said, "That sounds a lot like soliciting prostitution to me."

"I said that is enough," said Sheriff Parker.

The crowd continued to laugh and jeer at her. Even though the community was highly religious, it had never been tolerant. She regarded the throng.

Should they be tolerant of me poisoning my husband? The pious folk sure did enjoy a good hanging.

After reading the verdicts, the sheriff asked, "Do any of you have any final words or confessions? I'm sure clearing the air will be good for the soul."

Akondo, the Cheyenne boy, stepped forward and sang a song of mourning with his head held high. Several dozen Indians in the audience sang along with him. When he finished, he bowed his head.

Jacob, a short redheaded man in his thirties said, "I have a few things I would like to get off my chest. I'll have you know I had intimate relations with Molly, the minister's wife, five different times, Jenny, the mayor's wife, four times, and Anne, the sheriff's wife, twice! I call her Sweet Anne." There were screams of protest from the women mentioned, and the minister's middle-aged wife fainted dead away.

Sarah said, "Jacob, you're despicable."

He sneered, then gestured at Sarah. "One of these is true. I'll leave it to you to figure out which one. Now I had relations with this fine lady twelve times, she couldn't get enough of me." At this Sarah kicked him in the groin, and he bent over. She kneed him in the face busting his nose, and he collapsed onto the ground. After a minute the deputy helped him back to his feet. "The miserable witch wounded me. Sheriff Parker, you can't hang me like this. Please give me time to heal."

Parker pulled a pencil out of his pocket and wrote on the paper. "Jacob, I'm adding defaming the character of honorable women to your offenses."

Sarah asked, "And me?"

"Okay, I'll add assaulting a gentleman to your list, and I'll remove the prostitution bit."

She gave him the thumbs up the best she was able. "That sounds much better."

The minister came forward, bible in hand. "Let me read a scripture in Matthew. 'And shall cast them into a furnace of fire. There shall be wailing and gnashing of teeth.' God have mercy on your blackened souls. As you burn in hell may you recollect all your dark deeds, feel sorrow for the evil you have done, and have the desire to change." He then offered a long and fervent prayer on behalf of the unfortunate hell-bound souls and then turned to go.

Sarah said, "Reverend Thatcher. Could you put a good word in for me. I was in the church choir, and I even sang a solo. I haven't missed a sermon in three years."

Thatcher asked, "What did your husband say when he learned he had been poisoned?"

"Okay, he wasn't very happy. He cursed me good before he gave up the ghost, but I don't deserve to hang." Thatcher raised an eyebrow. "At least not first."

Jacob said, "Hang the witch, hang the witch, I want to see her drop before I go. It will be great sport."

The sheriff glanced at his wife, and she shook her head. He said, "We all know who is going first."

Jacob was led up to the gallows by the deputy. "Sheriff, you have no sense of humor. You know I was just joking about having sex with your wife." A noose was put over his head, a lever pulled, and the floor fell from below him. He thrashed and kicked, then finally hung still swinging back and forth. This was accompanied by wild cheering and applause from the crowd. Sarah gasped and closed her eyes, then opened them, regarded him, and felt ill. Did he deserve this for cheating in a card game? There were also the charges of rape and stealing that could not be overlooked. Even though Jacob was a degenerate, it was painful to see him go. She, however, did deserve this fate. She had killed someone. She thought of her husband, and despite the doctor's best efforts, John finally passed after two hours of suffering.

After Jacob had been cut down and his body laid into a pine box coffin, Sarah was led up onto the stand and the noose slipped over her head. She offered a silent prayer. "God, I know I deserve a good hanging, but it wasn't my intention to kill John, just make him as miserable as I felt. I truly am sorry, well mostly. There is a small amount of wicked joy in my heart. Please root that out of me."

Before the deputy could cinch up the rope, the town warning bell rang, and off in the distance there could be seen one hundred Cheyenne braves on horseback racing toward them. The sheriff said, "Shit! We should've hung Akondo first. It appears his kin are here to intervene. Everyone, run for cover!"

He didn't need to say this. The townsfolk had already scattered.

The deputy kicked at the drop lever right before running off, and the floor only partially collapsed. Sarah had one foot on the edge and the other dangling in space.

God, is this your best effort to save my life? Well, you're not doing a very good job of it. Finally, the trap door gave way, and Sarah was hanging in space with one toe on the edge of the opening and the other kicking out in space with her arms tied behind her. Fortunately for her, the noose had not been cinched up.

When the Cheyenne entered the town, there was no one outside, just the two prisoners. The chief came forward and cuffed his son upside the head, then cut the ropes that held his son's hands. Sarah offered in a strangled voice, "You can't leave me like this! Take me with you. I would make a fine squaw. I love the Cheyenne. At the very least cut me loose." The chief spoke angrily to Akondo in his native tongue, and she interrupted them, "Could you please cut me down first, then scold your boy."

Akondo turned to her. "We cannot help you. You must make your own path. We do not get involved in white man's affairs. Tell the sheriff we're leaving two horses here to account for the horse I stole. May good fortune guide you." The Cheyenne then mounted their horses, and Akondo added, "I suggest having the sheriff repeat your charges."

"What good will that do?"

He shrugged. "It may surprise you." He rode away.

"You are the most worthless Cheyenne I ever saw. A pox on you!" After several tries, she caught the edge of the opening with her other foot, and standing up straight, she lifted a leg and pulled a slipknot, and the rope was released. She fell headlong through the opening in the floor onto the ground. Sarah gasped for air. *Finally free!*

She lay there for a while and finally sat up and noticed the sheriff squatting, looking down at her. "Young lady, you have more lives than a stray cat." He climbed into the pit, helped her to her feet, and led her back onto the stand.

What Akondo said came back to her. "Sheriff, before you hang me again could you please read my sentence one more time."

"Sarah, you just want to delay the inevitable." He turned to where the deputy was hiding. "Deputy! They're gone now. Come out from underneath the porch and help me finish the hanging."

The deputy crawled out from under the porch and climbed the gallows and reset the trap floor. Sarah offered the sheriff a bright smile. "Please, sir, could you read it one more time? It will only take a minute. I think it would kind of reset the mood since we were interrupted. The townspeople are returning. I think they would appreciate it."

The sheriff scowled, reached into his pocket, and fished out the parchment. He read, "Sarah Anne Sanchez, you've been convicted of poisoning your husband, a Mister John Angus Sanchez, as well as bribery, and assaulting a gentleman. You have been sentenced to hang." He turned to her, "we have heard this before, why the need to repeat it?"

She smirked. "It did not say to hang me until I was dead, just to hang me. I have already been hung. I admit it was not a great hanging but a hanging nonetheless."

The sheriff frowned and cursed several times. "I should have caught that. Now, what am I supposed to do?"

The judge who was out in the crowd came forward. "Sorry, Parker, that was an oversight on my part. Even though it did not say to hang her until she was dead that was implied. I'd say go ahead and hang her again."

"Your honor, I think you realized it was just a misunderstanding and you were hoping that I would survive. Think of this as serendipity. I have been given another chance at life. Do you really want to take that away from me?"

The crowd began chanting again. "Hang her. Hang her."

The Judge snorted. "You are not helping your defense. The only misunderstanding is how much poison you gave your husband." He sighed, "Miss Sanchez, I must admit you are correct, you have been hung after a fashion, so you are now free to go." He turned to the clerk, "Let it be known that justice has been served, and Miss Sanchez has been dutifully hung." This news was accompanied by boos and hisses from the crowd.

A little girl in a blue paisley dress came forward and said, "Judge, I missed the first hanging. Everyone was blocking the view. Could you go ahead and hang her anyway?"

"Janie! Shame on you. I was your Sunday school teacher. Is that the thanks I get?" asked Sarah.

Parker said, "I'm sorry folks but she has been hung. The show is over. Now calm down and go home." He untied her hands and turned to go.

"Oh, Sheriff, by the way, the Cheyenne left two horses tied up over yonder to account for the horse the boy stole. I guess they think you're square now."

The sheriff shrugged and untied the horses. "I guess this will have to do." He led the horses away.

—*Grant Eagar is a Spaceship Design Engineer. He is married to Becky and has eight children— one girl and seven boys. He enjoys gardening, and most of his plants survive. He calls Tehachapi, CA, home. His love of storytelling began when he would tell his children stories at bedtime. His forthcoming novel is* Angelica: The Caged Bird Sings.

The Flight: A Sagebrush Pioneer by Frederic Remington

SHOOT, SHOVEL, AND SHUT UP
DAVID BIRDSALL

ST. CLAIR, MISSOURI
SUNDOWN
OCTOBER 15, 1884

"Happy birthday to me," I said while I wiped the sweat from my face with the back of my sleeve. It wasn't particularly hot for mid-October, but digging graves in Missouri rock will cause you to break a sweat in the middle of a snowstorm. I wish I could say this was the first birthday I spent digging graves. Hell, twenty years ago to the day I spent my birthday digging graves.

Two decades ago, it was graves for the combatants at Glasgow, Missouri. I was in the Army of the Confederate States of America under the command of Major General Sterling Price. I turned eighteen that day. We were following our former governor and now general on a campaign to liberate our state from the Union occupiers during the War of the Rebellion. We won that battle but lost the war. It feels like a lifetime since the war ended, but the fighting certainly hasn't stopped.

I learned quite a bit during that time of my life. Much I still use today. I can control a team of mules and use them to haul loads. I can shoot straight, use dynamite to turn a big thing into a bunch of small things, and dig graves. Dynamite helps with that last one in Missouri, too.

• • • • • •

ST. CLAIR, MISSOURI
AFTERNOON
MAY 25, 1866

I arrived in St. Clair, Missouri on May 25, 1866, after the war ended. They had been mining lead, barite, and iron in the hills here. I figured I could find work since I knew a bit about dynamite. At first, I stayed in a boarding house in town near the Missouri Pacific Railroad station, but I didn't care much for all the people. I don't know for sure, but I just don't think we're meant to be bunched up. Everyone was wanting to fight. There was still a lot of bad blood about things done during the war here in Missouri. It was truly kin fighting kin. Jayhawkers were hurting Rebels and their families, and Bushwhackers were doing the same to Loyalists. There had been a lot done that any God-fearing man should be ashamed of. For me, I'd gotten my belly full of it all and ended up getting myself a "special discharge."

After what I'd seen during the war, I wasn't about to stand aside when a couple of bad eggs tried to have their way with a young lady just outside of town. It was the Carl brothers. They weren't blood or nothing, but they were both named Carl, and they were never far apart, normally causing some sort of trouble. I tried scaring them off by shooting both barrels of my shotgun in the air. When that didn't work, I cleaned their plows with the butt of my shotgun. Unfortunately, my shotgun stock broke. I regretted that. I really miss the way that shotgun handled for hunting.

A few weeks later the Carl brothers stopped me on the road to the mine with their shooting irons pulled. For average folks that could've been all they needed. Unfortunately for them, stepping in front of an old cavalry Bushwhacker riding a big Missouri mule bred from solid stock wasn't the best idea. I gave a rebel yell while pulling my Arkansas toothpick, and we charged them. They even helped us by bunching close together. Another thing I've learned is why cavalry charges are so effective. Most people freeze when a huge animal is barreling toward them. I reckon it's fear shutting their brain down, and they can't think. We zig zagged fast at them like an old racer snake chasing them. Boomer angled toward the left one, and I swung myself over his right side holding even with the ground and reared my arm back for a swing at the one on the right. I felt Boomer connect with the varmint in front of him, followed by the telltale jostling of hooves on flesh. There was a sickening wet pop just before I swung my knife at the other's right arm. The knife was big but still smaller than my old saber. It didn't much matter, I had plenty of practice in the war using both from horseback. It was a good hit. I felt the muscle of his bicep part like a hot knife through butter. There was only the slightest resistance as the edge slid along the bone without biting into it. It may sound cruel, but it was a cut to be proud of.

Boomer whirled back around like we were cutting a calf from the herd for branding when I saw the carnage of the brief fight. One man's broken body lay on his side on the ground. At the top of his shoulders where his head should have been perched was a bloody mass of grey meat and white bone shards. The other one knelt on the ground a few feet away, clutching his outstretched right arm with his left while blood poured through his fingers. I dismounted and cautiously approached the one on his knees from the side, my hand resting on my revolver hanging cross draw at my waist. Without warning the man on his knees roared and reached for his other revolver, but his draw was slow and awkward. Mine wasn't. I drew my 1851 Colt Navy Revolver and shot him. The .32 caliber bullet punched a neat little hole through the side of his head. A stream of blood poured from the bullet hole like someone working a hand pump on a well before he slumped to his side. I winced instinctually as the gun shot echoed across the hills. An eerie howl replied in the distance to the sound of the gunshot.

I could go and tell the sheriff what happened, but it was far from certain how the courts would see this. The rule of the three Ss. Shoot, Shovel, and Shut up was the only option I saw at the time. Their horses were tied to a tree nearby. I quickly loaded their bodies on their horses and led them deep into the woods away from both the town and the mine. Once I got a couple ridges away from the road, I unloaded the bodies and let the horses go. The horses are too well-known in town, and I didn't want to be caught with them. I left their tack on the horses, figuring that when they were found people would think they got loose and wandered off from the brothers. I went ahead and decided to risk keeping their weapons. My plan was to head to Potosi or Washington and try to sell them. Since Boomer and I were heading to the mines, I already had a shovel and pickaxe tied to Boomer's saddle. I went to work digging the graves. It took most of the day. Once night fell, I stashed the weapons in a rock outcropping and headed back to town.

No sooner than I got back into town, I heard the scuttle. Someone had heard the gunshot while heading to the mines. They found the blood on the road but no bodies. Nothing was said about the horses, so I guess they weren't found yet. One fella said he heard an eerie howl and thought the Ozark Howler snatched someone off the road to the mines.

I settled my tab at the boarding house and let it be known that I was going to try and find me a piece of land and build me a homestead. I'd been talking about settling down at a place of my own for a while. This gave me a plausible excuse to not be in town while things cooled down. The next morning, I left before sunrise, retrieved the weapons, and headed to Washington, Missouri.

• • • • • •

WASHINGTON, MISSOURI
AFTERNOON
MAY 26, 1866

Washington was an up-and-coming town like St. Clair. Washington had the Pacific Railroad and Missouri River for river traffic. The benefit to Washington is that they weren't as familiar with the Carl brothers, so I could sell their weapons without notice.

I headed to the cattle yard just off from the railway where they hold cattle that were brought in. I've found the cowboys there will spend their money on things without asking questions if the price is right.

Mistakenly I decided to cross the platform as a train began pulling in. What was an open wooden deck and the quickest way to the corral instantly turned into a sea of humans. People pushed in and past from all directions. Many were getting off the train, many more were trying to get on, and others were going back and forth trying to get luggage and equipment from other cars. Steam bellowed in thick clouds from the engine while emitting an ear-piercing whistle. Horses whinnied as they were being unloaded. Coal dust and smoke blew across the platform.

Suddenly the scene shifted in my mind to flashes from a battlefield. I saw plumes of smoke and smelled the smells of burned coal, powder, horses, and human sweat. Bodies pressed in close. I expected any moment to feel the sharp pain as a bayonet or a knife cut into me. I froze like so many of the combatants I rode down in battle had done. My heart pounded, my breath coming in short shallow gasps. My head swam, and I couldn't think. "This can't be happening again," was all I could say.

Just when I thought I was going to either collapse or start swinging punches at people, I felt a gentle but insistent pull on my arm. Looking down all I could make out was a slender, deep blue velvet sleeved arm and white gloved hand holding my arm and gently pulling me through the crowd. My eyes followed the line of the arm up to see who was leading me. The arm flowed into a deep blue velvet dress concealing slender shoulders. On the top of the shoulders rested an elegant bun of dark brown hair. Although the bun was tight, a few strands of unruly hair had escaped revealing the hair was curly. I couldn't see her face since she was intent on finding a path through the crowd, but I loved the touch on my arm.

Once she had led us to a sheltered area against the wall out of the main flow of people, she turned to face me and grasped me by the shoulders. She said, "Look at me. Now breathe."

Looking at her I could fully appreciate her beauty. She was slightly shorter than me. Her blue velvet dress was modest but still hugged her full figure. She seemed to be about eighteen. Her most striking features were her deep blue eyes. They were like the color sailors described the ocean to be. At that moment I wanted anything to see the ocean for myself with her by my side just so I could compare them. In my heart I knew there was no way the ocean could even come close.

"What's your name?" she asked.

"What?" I stammered.

"Your name?" she asked. "What is it?"

"Oh, oh. My name is Daniel. Danny, I mean. My friends call me Danny. You can call me Danny too. Danny McIntosh." I instantly felt my face flush.

"Well, Danny, are you new in town?"

"How could you tell?"

"You were the only person standing in one place on that platform."

At this point a tall man in a crisp black suit and matching bowler hat emerged from the crowd. "There you are," he said. "I lost sight of you in the crowd." He surely seemed to be a gentleman of the first water.

"Oh, hello, Herm," she said a little startled. "My new friend, Danny here, was caught in the rush. I helped him make his way here."

"Heaven's sake. Where's my manners?" she said while gesturing with her gloved hands. "Danny McIntosh, this is my brother, Herman Barr. Herm, this is my new friend, Danny McIntosh."

Herman took an appraising glance from my head to my boots. Looking back, I must have been quite a sight. I was wearing a tattered charcoal grey, wide brimmed hat. My crash white linen shirt was threadbare. My gray wool pants, with possibly more patches than original fabric, were held up by black suspenders. Four gun belts, all holding shooting irons, draped one over each shoulder and two around my waist. A large Arkansas toothpick was tucked in one of the gun belts at my waist snug against the small of my back. Two Henry repeater rifles, one slung over each shoulder, hung over the gun belts. Finishing it all off were my worn through black boots, all of it covered in road dust, mud, and briar seeds. After taking the quick glance, Herm tipped his bowler while simultaneously pulling my beautiful savior closer to him. "Nice to meet you Danny McIntosh, but we must be going."

Without thinking I pulled my hat from my head with my left hand while reaching with my right hoping for one last touch of the beautiful woman's hand. "Please, miss, may I have your name?"

She stepped back and grasped my hand fully. "It's Julie," she said smiling. "Julie Barr." It was enough to make me squirmy.

"I am truly indebted to you, Miss Julie," I said while staring into those deep blue eyes. "If there's ever anything I can do for you, all you need to do is ask."

• • • • •

ST. CLAIR, MISSOURI
AFTERNOON
JULY 1, 1866

I used the money from selling the Carl brothers' guns to buy my first cartridge revolver. The Smith and Wesson Model 1 was a .22 caliber double action rimfire cartridge firearm. It proved a little more acceptable to carry in the polite company found in town.

The remainder of the money I used to stay in Washington and proceeded to court the lovely Miss Julie Barr. After a month, I asked her father, Mr. Herman Barr Sr., for his blessing to marry his daughter. Mr. Barr, being a practical man of means said, "Young man, when you return here with proof of your ability to care for my daughter properly and respectably, I'll give you my blessing."

I thanked her father, bid Miss Julie a fond farewell, and promised both I would return once I got myself established. Then I made my way back to St. Clair. I only stopped briefly in town when I returned to buy a saw and feed for Boomer and myself. We headed back into the wilds to find a secluded place to set up my homestead. Boomer and I found a tall ridge off the river with three steep sides. It gave us plenty of solitude and a pretty good view of the only reasonable way to get to us.

We cleared just enough trees for the cabin and a spot for Boomer to graze. Since we were having to skid the logs across the ground anyway, I decided to take the extras to town and sell them. That's how we found out that some townsfolk suspected someone had killed the Carl brothers.

The brothers' horses stumbled back into town a few days after I left for Washington. Turns out the sheriff was smarter than I thought he was and figured out that the blood on the brothers' horses must have come from limp bodies and not from an animal attack. Some folks knew about the beating I gave the brothers for attacking the girl, and the sheriff put the two together. Sheriff Hicks stopped me at the sawmill when I was selling the logs and questioned me about the incident. To make the story short I wouldn't tell him anything, and he made sure I knew he was watching me.

•   •   •   •   •

ST. CLAIR, MISSOURI
MORNING
JULY 1, 1868

Water slung from my long unkempt hair as I jerked my head from the rain barrel sitting under the short overhang of my porch. The day was already hot and muggy. I walked over and sat down on the edge of the porch in the shade.

I looked over to Boomer in his corral and said, "Well, it's been two years since I promised to return to Julie and marry her." With a little chuckle I sighed. "Turns out it's hard to get established when people think you're a murderer." The mines won't hire me anymore since no one wants to be in the dark with a possible murderer. At least the sawmill will still buy the logs we skid down to them. Of course, they only pay us half of what the wood is worth since, after all, who else will buy from me.

I scratched at my shaggy beard. How I wished I could get a shave and a haircut. The last time I tried the barber whispered in my ear while holding the razor over my face, "I should slit your throat like you probably did to those boys."

Folks forgot how bad the brothers were after their families held those candlelight vigils in town. The last reminder of how the brothers really were left when the girl I saved got married and moved out of town.

I know Miss Julie is doing well. She came to town last year to see me. Unfortunately, the sheriff got to her first and told her about what he thought happened to the brothers. She rode all the way out here to confront me with the sheriff about the brothers. I still remember it like yesterday.

"Don't lie to me," she said. "Did you kill those men?"

"I won't lie to you, Miss Julie," I whispered. All I could do was stare at my feet. I couldn't look into those beautiful eyes. The silence hung in the air like a curtain.

Then it turned into a wall.

"Well." Miss Julie's voice was hard as ice. "That's all I need to know." She strode back to her horse and mounted it with the help of the sheriff. "Good day, Mister McIntosh. I hope you can find a way to live with yourself, because I won't *ever* be living with you." With that she rode down the ridge and out of my life. She sure gave me the mittens that day.

I thought about leaving then, but I had made a promise to Miss Julie that if she ever needed my help all she had to do was ask. At least now I knew she knew how to find me.

•   •   •   •   •

ST. CLAIR, MISSOURI
EARLY MORNING
OCTOBER 15, 1884

"Happy birthday to me," I groaned as I stepped through the front door while stretching. I breathed in the chilled October air. It was an odd experience to have chilled air that was still so thick that it felt like trying to breathe through a wet bandana. After nearly two decades of living on this ridge, you'd have thought I'd be used to how the air feels.

I was thirty-eight years old. That's longer than I figured I would've lived and far longer than I deserved.

As the sky brightened with the dawn, the blues spread around the tree branches. It reminded me of Miss Julie's eyes. My memory and my eyesight weren't as sharp as they used to be. The blue sky was the only thing I had that was blue, so it reminded me of her. I still loved her, and I reckoned I always would.

I knew Miss Julie was doing all right. Far better than if she and I had gotten married. I couldn't imagine her living up here on Murder Ridge.

That's what folks had gone and named my place. They called me the old hermit that lives up on Murder Ridge. I've heard some of the stories they tell. I killed and ate the Carl brothers. I cursed the mines causing them to nearly dry up. I turned into the Ozark Howler and prowled the county looking for travelers to eat.

Miss Julie went and got married to a respectable miner. They used his wages from the mine to get themselves set up on a ranch outside of St. Clair. She got herself two kids, a girl and a boy. The eldest was the girl, probably going on fifteen now, and the boy I figured was about twelve.

I could hear my mule, Boomer, stomping in the corral to the left of the cabin. It wasn't the same Boomer that helped me carve this place out of the ridge. He was from the same good solid working stock though, and the name just felt right.

With a yawn I walked out to the wood pile. I grabbed an armload of limbs to rekindle the fire in the cast iron cook stove in the cabin. Just as I started to step through the door with the wood, I heard Boomer bray.

"That's odd," I said. "We haven't had any visitors in years."

Once inside, I put on my cross-draw gun belt with my old Colt Navy revolver in it, then tucked my trusty Arkansas toothpick into my belt in the small of my back. Lastly, I loaded my hunting double-barrel shotgun and leaned it against the door frame, out of sight, just inside the door.

When I heard Boomer bray again, I stepped to the window and carefully pulled the curtain back just enough to see down the path leading to the river. A small lone figure quickly cantered up the path on horseback. To my surprise the rider was a child, by the clothes most likely a boy, probably about twelve years old.

Once he came to a stop just outside the cabin, the boy gasped, "Anyone home?"

"How can I help you?" I replied.

"Are you the killer, Danny McIntosh?"

I learned back in the war that a bullet fired from a gun held by a boy killed just the same as when fired by a grown man, so I reached down and got a grip of the shotgun. "Why are you looking for him?"

"I don't got time for no games, mister. Are you Danny McIntosh or not?"

"This is no game, boy. Tell me straight why you're here and who sent you."

"My ma always said if we ever got in trouble, then we needed to find Danny McIntosh. The townsfolk told me he's a killer and lives

up here on this ridge." Tears starting to stream down his dirty face.
"Please, mister, if you aren't the killer, Danny McIntosh, then tell me
where to find him."

With a heavy sigh I stepped through the doorway and outside.
"You found me, boy."

"Don't you want to know who my ma is?"

"Boy, I only made that promise to one person on God's green
Earth," I said. "I'm going to keep that promise no matter what."

• • • • •

ST. CLAIR, MISSOURI
MID-DAY
OCTOBER 15, 1884

"Mister McIntosh, you sure this will work?" Miss Julie's son,
Kurt, asked.

"Nope," I replied.

On the ride from my cabin, Kurt explained that his pa died six
months ago with the fever. His ma got sick with the fever now, too.
Doc said he thinks she'll pull through, but a month ago he took her to
her brother's place in Washington to be cared for.

Two men from Kansas City named Joe Pritchet and Bill Leeder rode into town two weeks ago and convinced the family to hire
them as waddies to help tend the cattle while Ma was sick. They
turned out to be a couple real curly wolves. Kurt and his older sister Annette overheard their plan to brand over their cattle so they
can steal them. Annette told Sheriff Hicks about what was going
on, but the varmints killed the sheriff and dumped his body in the
river. Before they left for Potosi to get the counterfeit iron made,
Pritchet and Leeder locked Kurt and Annette in the root cellar by

looping a chain through the handles. Before leaving, the scoundrels yelled, "Too bad about you two being caught in the accidental fire your place is going to have when we get back." Kurt was thin and managed to squeeze through the gap the doors made when the two kids leaned against the doors. He took his horse and headed to me like his ma always said to do.

Kurt and I rode to the top of a high ridge overlooking the road from Potosi. We used the old Negretti and Zambra spy glass I had from the war to spot the men on the road and planned the best place to confront them.

Now, at mid-day, Kurt and I stood in the middle of the road that led from St. Clair to Potosi. A small wooden box sat at my feet with a tee handle sticking out of it.

"Your plan kind of seems like cheating, Mister McIntosh."

"Boy, if you aren't cheating, you really aren't trying to win."

"Why did you want to do it here and not just wait for them back at the ranch?"

"Midday casts less shadows, and no matter how I need to move in the fight the sun won't be in my eyes."

"You're going to kill them, right?"

"I'm going to give them a chance to turn back and leave you all alone first."

"I don't think they will let you talk."

"You know how to shoot?"

"Yes, sir. Pa showed me before he got sick."

I handed Kurt the small Smith and Wesson Model 1 I bought all those years ago and a key. "Take these and Boomer. Use Boomer and that logging chain on his saddle and bust your sis out of the root cellar. Get your sis and head for my place on Murder Ridge. If this works, I'll come get you there and take you two to your ma. If I'm not there by dawn, take the money in the strong box under the bed and get a ticket on the stagecoach going to Washington."

"No!" Kurt exclaimed. "I can shoot. I want to fight and kill them."

"You listen to me, and you listen good, boy," I said while grabbing Kurt by the ear. "There's more to killing than shooting and a good deal more to fighting than killing. Don't be no Ten-Cent Man. If this don't work, your sister's going to need you to keep her safe. Now get."

After letting go of his ear Kurt climbed on his horse. I handed him Boomer's lead rope. Kurt glanced one more time at me, nodded, and they burned the breeze down the road toward their ranch.

The two men approached the end of the wooded patch a hundred yards in front of where I was standing in the road. I waved for them to stop and dismount, but Kurt was right. They dug for their cannons and charged me. I quickly pushed the plunger on the box, and the dynamite charge buried on the side of the road exploded alongside them. The man farther back and his horse disappeared in a cloud of dirt and gravel. The lead man barely escaped the explosion, but his horse bucked him off causing him to chew gravel.

Instinctually, I rushed forward to close the distance. When the man on the ground in the road rose, he still had his shooting iron in his hand, and he swung it toward me. I swung the sawed-off shotgun up from under my coat. Since the stock was damaged all those years ago, I decided to cut the barrels down, cut the stock down to a pistol grip, and wired the triggers together so both barrels fire at once. It swings a little different than before, but it has proven itself for con-versation distances when you have bad eyes. I fired on the man. The twelve-gauge buckshot loads struck him in the chest toppling him back into the grass.

As I started reloading the shotgun, I heard the sickening click of a hammer being thumbed from under the downed horse. I whirled, but then a tiny report stopped me mid-swing. Scanning the area I saw Kurt atop his horse, a few yards to the side of the downed horse holding the little Model 1 outstretched in his shaking hand. The second man lay pinned under his dead horse gripping a revolver pointed at me. There was a single .22 caliber hole in the side of his head.

After Kurt dismounted, we stood in the middle of the carnage.

"What now?" Kurt asked shakenly, still unable to take his eyes off the man he had shot.

"You done the shoot part of the three Ss," I said. "Now you learn about the shovel part. Last will be to shut up. I hope it goes better for you than it did for me."

—David Birdsall has lived his entire life in Missouri. For enjoyment, he turns to writing, camping, horseback riding, canoeing, sailing, and reading. When reading and writing he's pulled toward science fiction, fantasy, historical works, and, of course, westerns. He lives in central Missouri with his wife of 25 years, daughter, three cats, and three dogs.

VIGILANCE
COMMITTEE
BENJAMIN THOMAS

HENRY RAYMOND SHOOK out his heavy leather coat, trying to get the last of the dust out of the folds and creases. His friend, George Cox, the proprietor of the Dodge House Hotel, wouldn't appreciate the mess, but after a month out on the hunt, Henry felt an unerring need to be clean again.

June of 1873, he noted to himself. Hard to believe it was getting on into the hot months already. Again. The yearning for change was creeping up his spine once more.

Obtaining one of the thirty-eight rooms at the hotel had been a stroke of luck, even if he did have to share with a couple of young skinners. For a moment, he'd felt bad for using his friendship as a bargaining chip... but only for a moment. As a veteran buffalo hunter of six consecutive seasons, he'd earned the right to quality accommodations rather than his usual haunts. Charles Rath had moved to town last September and had soon begun hunting, freighting, and marketing the hides. Henry admired the man but was wary of him, too. Rath had only recently formed the Rath Mercantile Company, and his yard was said to be filled with as many as 80,000 hides at a time. It was Rath that had insisted on the two skinners sharing the room. How long should a man work so hard merely to fill another man's pockets?

Henry's thoughts were jolted by a thunderous boom that shook the floorboards. The unmistakable sound of a shotgun fired in a confined space. One of his roommates stirred in his sleep. The other was evidently too drunk for the sound to register.

Pulling on his boots, Henry crossed to the door in two steps, yanked it open, and stopped. Better to be armed, he decided, so he grabbed his Colt revolver, stuffed it into the waist of his denim pants, and charged out the door.

Running along the balcony that overlooked the hotel lobby, he ignored the other hotel guests who poked their heads out of doorways. They seemed content to stay put. The sound of gunfire was not a rare occurrence here in this new town called Dodge City, but it was mostly heard in the night hours when the alcohol flowed and games of chance went wild. By the aroma coming from the kitchen, Henry judged it to be close to noon. Who would be shooting it up at this time of day?

Reaching the bottom of the stairs, he followed the moans of an injured man to the saloon that had recently been tacked onto the side of the hotel. He was not the first to arrive, judging by the batwings that still pivoted open and shut, but he'd been fast enough to still see the smoke drifting from Tom Sherman's shotgun which now lay crossways on the top of the sloping bar. The saloonkeeper had switched to a high caliber revolver, his knuckles white with tension as he pointed it at the downed man. His round face was marred by a pair of bushy eyebrows jutting down in anger. Before Henry could respond, Sherman began emptying the revolver into the prone body as it lay before him, despite the obvious lack of life now left in it.

"There! That'll teach him," Sherman's voice was harsh, but his face was already beginning to relax. He glanced about at the small group of men in the saloon, meeting their eyes with confidence. "That Burns fellow... he kilt a friend of mine. And me being on the Vigilance Committee, well, he shoulda known better." Henry saw two of the men shrug and move toward the body preparing to cart it away.

"No don't. Just leave him there. He'll serve as an advertisement to other such varmints." With that, Sherman moved back behind the bar and began scrubbing his hands in a large bowl of water.

The sound of kid boots clicking on the floorboards to his right caught Henry's ear, and when he turned to look, a smile spread across his newly shaven face. Lucy stalked away, toward a side door, her flame-red hair restrained by a green scarf but still bouncing along behind. Henry chased after her, catching up just as her hand reached for the door latch.

"Hold up there, Lucy. What're you doing over here? And dressed like a housekeeper? Tired of all the dancing at the Peacock?"

Lucy spun around, glaring at Henry for a moment before softening. Henry's smile grew wider at the sight of her fawnlike brown eyes and long lashes.

"I'm doing a favor for Mister Cox. He's worked it with Mister Hendricks over at the Peacock so I can fill in at the hotel. Cleaning, mostly." Then the fierce look returned to her eyes as she glanced back at the dead man lying on the dry, dusty floor. "But I'll be damned if I'm going to clean up that mess!"

"Don't blame you a bit. What did that man do to deserve getting a shotgun blast in the belly, anyway?"

Lucy smirked. "Who knows? Mister Sherman claims he killed a friend of his by shooting him in the back. But I doubt anybody knows the real story." She turned back to the door, unlatched it, and moved on through, Henry following closely. "Truth is it's that Vigilance Committee. Things have really gotten out of hand."

"What do you mean? I thought they were put in place to address all the violence that's come to this place."

They began to stroll down a short lane that folks were beginning to call "Front Street." Henry was amazed at the changes to the little town in just the past two months while he'd been out on the hunt. Many of the tents and dugouts were being replaced by sturdy wood-framed buildings. As he awaited Lucy's response, he sidestepped a puddle of rainwater, then realized it probably wasn't rainwater.

"Well, that may have been the intent and a worthy cause, I dare say. But the idea of the town's prominent citizens banding together to rid the town of some of the rougher elements had turned rapidly into an unlawful wielding of their own power. You've been gone quite a while, Henry, but that poor Mister Burns back there is hardly the first in recent weeks to be the target of that Committee."

"So, you're saying Burns hadn't necessarily killed a friend of Sherman but may have simply been a rival of some kind?"

"Exactly. Members of the Committee believe in swift justice, whether it's deserved or not. But there's nothing anybody can do about it without risking their own necks."

They walked on for a minute, slowly, each alone with their thoughts. Buffalo hides towered along their path, stinking in the mid-day air, awaiting shipment. The street ended, and they had to turn back, leading Lucy to say, "I'm sorry, Henry. I haven't been the best of company to welcome you back home."

Smiling down at her, he nudged her gently with an elbow. "That's all right, Lucy. I've got some business to take care of this afternoon, but I'll plan to stop by the Peacock and get a dance or two with you."

"Oh, that would be wonderful, Henry. But I can't. Not tonight.

I and several other Peacock girls have been hired to attend a dance at Fort Dodge. We'll be transported by wagon, leaving about eight o'clock this evening."

"I see," Henry said, trying to keep the disappointment out of his voice. "Sounds like fun."

Lucy was quiet for a moment but then said, "I'm not so sure. I'm worried they'll think we are more than just dance girls."

"Soiled doves? Surely not."

"You'd be surprised. It happens at the Peacock all the time. I start dancing with a man, get him to buy a whiskey or three, and then he tries to get me to go upstairs. I explain that there are other girls for that sort of thing and that's usually sufficient. I keep my little dagger handy, of course, in case things go sour. But I can usually rely on one of the boys that work there to keep me safe. But at this Fort Dodge dance, there won't be any chaperones at all—none trustworthy, at any rate."

"I see." They had reached the hotel once again, and Lucy told him she needed to return to her cleaning. Duties first, then back to the Peacock to clean up and prepare her frilly skirts and petticoats before that evening's event. Lace and fringe had to be smoothed and straightened, and she would likely need to add more sequins.

As Lucy left him standing there in the street, Henry made a decision. He couldn't directly accompany the girls to the Fort Dodge dance, but he would do his best to keep an eye on them.

• • • • • •

HENRY LEANED CASUALLY against a sturdy beam that supported the roof of the livery stables, breathing in the pungent aromas of sweet hay and fresh horse shit. He had saddled his mare, prepared to follow Lucy and the girls to the Fort, but as the time drew closer, he wasn't sure if that was such a good idea. He doubted he would be welcome inside Fort Dodge, and he didn't much fancy waiting around outside all night for the dance to conclude.

Nighttime came late this time of year, but the sun had already sunk beyond the horizon by the time the wagon arrived. Across the way, a gaggle of finely dressed girls had been waiting along with several rough looking men, most of whom were clearly drunk. Henry recognized the wagon driver, a large negro named William Taylor whom he'd often seen carting buffalo hides in from the field. One of the men harshly scolded Taylor, using words not normally spoken in front of a lady.

Lucy was there amidst the other girls, looking just as pretty as could be. He watched as one of the men boosted one girl after another into the wagon where they found seats upon several mounds of hay. Soon, it was evident that the wagon wasn't nearly large enough to handle all the girls though, so more coarse words were directed at Taylor as he was told to move out and return for the rest as fast as possible. Taylor simply nodded his understanding and climbed up on the wagon seat. More time passed as he worked to get his two mules moving, but, slowly, the wagon began its journey to the fort.

Henry reckoned it would take upwards of an hour for the wagon to make the eight-mile round trip to Fort Dodge and back, if not more. Lucy was among those girls still waiting in front of the Peacock, but any ideas that he might get to have a dance with her in the interim were quickly dashed. The man who seemed to be in charge, the same one who had given Taylor his instructions, issued new orders to the waiting group. They were to wait right where they were until the wagon's return.

That next hour passed slow as a tortoise. Henry didn't want to be seen observing the group, but he found a way to mosey across the street and sidle up to the front corner of the Peacock. The sounds of drinking and frivolous laughter poured out from the front of the saloon, making it difficult to eavesdrop, but he did learn the leader's name was Bill Hicks. The man's thin lips were fixed in a perpetual smile, reminding Henry of the man who'd tried to sell him some crowbait disguised as a horse last year. Hicks was a talker, seemingly incapable of letting a stretch of silence last more than three seconds. John Scott, another one of the rougher men present, was obviously partnered with Hicks. Scott was the meaner looking of the pair though, with heavily lidded eyes that darted around like angry bees. They were certainly alike in their impatience as well as their profanity. Henry's heart sank when he heard them bragging to the other men about being members of the Vigilance Committee. Apparently, they were there to ensure the girls were protected from any bad men that might happen along. The accompanying laughter curled the hair on the back of Henry's neck. Now, more than ever, he was determined to follow them all the way to Fort Dodge.

Eventually, Taylor returned with the empty wagon, and the rest of the girls began to be hustled aboard. However, clearly, they still wouldn't be able to cram them all in, much less the remainder of the accompanying men.

"They're all going to fit in there even if they have to sit on each other's laps!" Hick's voice held an edge even while Taylor began to protest. The other leader, John Scott pulled a gun from his holster and started to casually wave it around.

"Now, sir," began Taylor from where he sat on the driver's bench, "I only gots the two mules, sir. Ain't no way they can pull the wagon and all them girls too. They're plum tired enough as it is."

Hicks's eyes widened as he looked up at the negro. "I promised eighteen girls for the dance, and eighteen girls is what they're going to get," he barked. Sticking his chest out, he took two steps toward Taylor. "Now you get them mules to understand that or else you'll have the Vigilance Committee to deal with."

Taylor, to his credit, did not seem intimidated in the least. His eyes bore into Hicks for a moment, and he seemed to come to a decision. Dropping the leather leads, he climbed down to stand before Hicks, towering over him by at least six inches. He planted both his meaty fists on his hips and said, "You hired me and my wagon for one round trip to Fort Dodge. I done that task, so now I want my money. Then me and my mules are goin' to rest a spell." Even from Henry's vantage point, he could see the muscles rippling in the big man's shoulders. "After that, if you want to hire us again, then I'll entertain the notion. If that don't suit, feel free to hire yourselves another wagon and driver." Turning his broad back on the men, he started to climb back up to the driver's seat.

A brief moment of stunned silence was broken by the sharp note of a gun firing. One of the mules slumped in its harness, half its head missing, blood spray covering the companion mule.

Taylor turned in mid-step and glared daggers at the gunman, John Scott. Dropping back to the ground, he swiveled his gaze from Hicks to Scott and took one aggressive step forward. He looked ready to tear both men limb from limb. But before taking a second step, both Scott and Hicks fired lead into the big man's chest, dropping him to the hard packed dirt.

Henry was incredulous. He started forward, not sure of his own intent but determined to do something. Pandemonium surrounded the wagon as he drew his revolver, the women running in several directions, mostly toward the entrance to the Peacock. Hicks started yelling about how the Vigilance Committee had protected the girls from a bad man while Scott took the opportunity to fire another shot into the prone negro's inert torso.

Henry wasn't sure what the best course of action should be, but that decision was taken from him as several of the other men moved into his path, hands held out to prevent any interference. Over their heads, he could see both Hicks and Scott scampering off in opposite directions.

•   •   •   •   •

"THIS IS BAD business," said the man in the blue Army uniform. He was rail thin and sported a prominent Adam's apple, which kept Henry amused. Major Richard Sanderson leaned his head back and downed the entire shot of whiskey in one gulp before repeating once again, "Bad business."

They sat across from one another at a small table in the corner of the Peacock saloon. It was nearing supper time on the day following the shooting of William Taylor.

"Major," Henry tried again, "your outrage over the incident is entirely understandable, but I've told you all I can about what happened. I'm not sure what else I can do for you."

"Well, it's like this. I've got my men on regular patrols, scouring the area for threats. Indians, mostly. As I'm sure you know, we're charged with protecting the U.S. mail as well as emigrant wagon trains on the Santa Fe Trail. Now, speaking as the commander of the Fort, and the Third Infantry, that ties up all my men. Frankly, I need more than I have. I can't spare a single man to chase down those killers. That's where I need your help."

"But Major, I'm just a buffalo hunter. I'm no sheriff."

"Well, that's just it, isn't it. You all don't have a sheriff around here. Just that so-called Vigilance Committee. From what I hear, they're actually the root of the problem." He put down his whiskey glass and stared hard at Henry. "So... I need somebody who's not on the Committee to round up a posse and track down that pair. Bring 'em into the fort for justice."

Henry sat quietly for a moment, looking down at his own shot glass and thinking. He did have a few days to spare between hunts. He had been there last night and could easily identify both Hicks and Scott. Any stranger to the situation would likely consider him a good choice to lead a posse to capture the two men. As much as he'd shied away from such things in the past, the truth of the matter was that he was as filled with outrage as he'd ever been before. Men, supposedly in authority, who had sworn to protect the innocent citizens of the town, had instead bullied their way into getting whatever they wanted. And they'd killed an innocent man just for standing in their way.

"All right, Major. I'll help you out. I'll gather some men and see if we can figure out where those two have holed up or if they've gone on the run. But you'll answer one question for me first."

"Shoot."

"Well, you know shootings and killings are happening here all the time. Just yesterday morning, the very same day as Taylor was shot down, the hotel bartender shot a man for supposedly having killed a friend of his. Nothing's being done about that. No trial or nobody even speaking up for the dead man. It happens damn near every day. So why is the Taylor shooting so important to you?"

Major Sanderson sat back in his seat, stretched that long neck, and said, "Taylor was my personal cook."

• • • • • •

IT ONLY TOOK an hour before Henry had a group of men ready to help him track down the two killers. Several fellow hunters readily joined him, but he felt it was important to make sure his group didn't look like some kind of buffalo hunter revenge gang. There needed to be representation from other townsfolk as well. At Lucy's suggestion, he asked her boss, Alfred Peacock, for some names of some stout-hearted men and was surprised that he and his business partner Charlie Bassett added their own names to the list.

The first fugitive was surprisingly easy to snatch. That same evening, Bill Hicks was found in the hotel, openly bragging about the killing to a small crowd gathered around him. Tom Sherman, the bartender, was smiling in approval, but that smile quickly disappeared when Charlie Bassett barked out orders that dismissed the crowd. He proceeded to grab Hicks by the shoulders and push him to the ground. Henry rapidly tied both arms together behind his back, attaching them to his ankles, effectively neutralizing the threat.

"Nice work, Henry," said Charlie. "That should make for easy transport back to the Fort." He looked down at the man lying on the floorboards. "Hogtieing a man has a way of shutting down any and all arrogance."

Henry nodded in agreement. "Now, if finding and hogtieing his partner would be as easy, we could all go have a beer."

•   • •   •   •

TWO HOURS LATER, there had been no sign of John Scott. During the Taylor shooting, he had been much quieter than Hicks, preferring to let his guns do the talking, so it was no surprise that he would be the stealthy one. Also, the deadlier one, to Henry's way of thinking. It was now quite late, and full darkness had settled over the town, bringing with it a cool wind. Henry had called off the hunt for the day, telling his men they would resume at first light.

"I don't know," Henry said, frowning. He looked down at Lucy as they danced. "I think Scott has left town. He's surely heard of Hicks's capture, so has to know this place isn't safe for him."

"Maybe so, but I have a feeling he's still somewhere around. Hiding. I get a shiver up my neck every time I think about him."

Henry grinned. "That might just be my fingers. You have a beautiful neck, and they seem to have a mind of their own."

She giggled and smiled up at him, then rested her head against his chest. Henry was happy to finally get this dance, only wishing it was during a more relaxing time.

All too soon, the dance ended, and Lucy left him for another fellow. Henry made his way to a table where Charlie Bassett sat with two of the buffalo hunters. They talked for a bit about where Scott might be holed up, but Henry's eyes kept pivoting over to watch Lucy work. She was a marvelous dancer, but her true skill lay in convincing her partners to buy another whiskey. Of course, they would invariably buy one for her as well, but Henry knew hers was only cold tea or colored water. As he watched her now, he noticed her partner was getting a little too worked up and starting to let his hands wander too far afield. Henry sat up straighter in his seat, amused. He knew Lucy could handle such behavior but wanted to see just how she did it. Distantly, he heard somebody from behind the bar complaining about being out of ice.

"I'll get some from the back," Lucy called out, taking advantage of the opportunity to disengage from her current handsy partner. Satisfied, Henry swiveled his head back toward Charlie Bassett who had just suggested getting a poker game started.

Shaking his head, Henry said, "No thanks. I'm beat. I'm going to turn in and get some shuteye. Tomorrow will be...."

Suddenly a shriek erupted from the back room. *Lucy!* Henry stood up so fast his chair fell over backwards. Charging toward the back room without a second thought, he tore through the door. He pulled up short, eyes darting about, taking in Lucy who stood in the middle of the room and John Scott who loomed behind her. One arm wrapped around her chest, pinning her against him. The other arm held a gun against her side.

"He was hiding in the ice box," Lucy managed to say before Scott's gun jabbed her in the ribs.

"Shut up, girl." Those heavily lidded eyes bored into Henry's even as two other men entered the room through the same door and immediately stopped. Scott had lost his frock coat somewhere and stood in his shirt sleeves, white streaks of ice dust coating his torso.

"Game's over, Scott," Henry said. "There's nowhere to run." He felt a surge sweep through his body but managed to keep any waver out of his voice. Chagrined, he realized he had stupidly forgotten to draw his gun before bursting in on the scene.

"For you, yes. And for this little lady, too if she don't stand still." A moment passed when nobody moved, nobody spoke. Henry tried to figure out a way to get to his gun before Scott could use his. He looked in Lucy's eyes and saw fear there. But something else as well. A sort of gleam that suggested she was thinking. Plotting.

"John Scott, is it?" Lucy said, her voice dripping with venom. "Couldn't afford a last name so had to have two first names, is that it?"

A deep growl was the only response, but Henry understood what she was trying to do. If they could get Scott angry, then he might make a mistake.

"Well, he *is* part of the Vigilance Committee, as I understand it," Henry said. "And we all know what a 'committee' is, don't we?"

"Yep." Lucy smiled. "It's when the unwilling is appointed by the unfit to do the unnecessary." Then she couldn't help laughing.

"Stay still, I said!" Scott was angry now.

"That's funny, Lucy. I've heard there's a lot of committees in Congress, so you know they're not exactly competent."

"I've heard tell," Lucy responded, "that a committee is something designed by many people but with no unifying plan or vision. That sounds like a perfect organization for a man who never planned on a last name."

Scott's face turned a dark shade of crimson. His eyebrows jutted down, and his jaw was clenched so tight he was liable to burst an artery. "Now see here...."

Lucy's patience had worn out. Henry kept his eyes glued to Scott's even as he detected her right hand snaking through the slit in her dress and grasping the little dagger hidden there. Wasting no time, she yanked it out and swung her arm across her chest, slamming the knife into Scott's forearm. The one holding the gun. The blade sank in deep, angled to slice between the bones, right up to the hilt.

Henry charged forward, reaching Scott even before the dropped gun hit the floor. He hauled back his arm, clenched his hand into a fist built from six years of hunting and skinning and fueled with all his gathered rage, and let loose.

The smack of his knuckles against Scott's jaw sounded like a block of cement crashing to the floor. Scott's head slammed sideways, jaw sagging, eyes rolling back in his head. He didn't collapse so much as fall straight back like a tree felled by an ax.

Lucy looked at Henry and burst out in laughter. "Oh, Henry, you should see the look on your face! Like the cat who ate the canary. Kind of righteous, I'd say."

Henry looked down at the prone form of John Scott, slow to register what Lucy had just said. Then he looked up at her and grinned. Flexing the fingers on his hand, he said, "Well, he deserved it. But now my hand tingles something fierce." He bent down and scooped up Scott's gun.

"I'll take that," said Charlie Bassett, one of the two men who had entered the room after him and witnessed the unfolding events. "Boys, help me drag this slab of meat out of here. We'll lock him in the same closet as Hicks." He glanced at Henry and Lucy before adding, "Looks like we may need a proper jail around here if we're going to keep eliminating trash like this." The toe of his boot nudged the unconscious body of John Scott, none too gently.

• • • • • •

LATE AFTERNOON THE following day, Henry strolled along the boardwalk in front of the Peacock, arm in arm with Lucy. She was about to begin her shift and was already dressed in her fringed skirt over a ruffled petticoat. There was a new embellishment this time though. Hidden among the sequins and lace was a purple thread, hanging from her belt. At the bottom of the thread were two teeth, tied together and dangling innocently. Lucy had shown them to Henry earlier, and he had winked at her.

"I hear they're planning to appoint a sheriff here," she said. "The Vigilance Committee has proved to be ineffective, so I think it's a good idea."

"I agree. The committee will still be around for a while I expect, but I think their bite has lessened. Bullies don't make for good leaders."

They walked on for a bit more before Lucy spoke again, "They wanted you, Henry, to be the sheriff. Why didn't you take the job?"

Henry took a moment to consider his answer. Finally, he said, "That's just not for me, Lucy. Charlie Basset will make for a fine sheriff. And besides, I have my sights set on other things."

"Other things?"

"Yes. My buffalo hunting days are almost over. That's a young man's business. I've been watching the Texas cattle industry and what's been happening east of here in Abilene, Newton, and Ellsworth. The quarantine line's moving west. Those Longhorns are coming through Wichita now, and I think Dodge is next. I think cattle's where my future lies. Right here in Dodge City."

"I see." Her voice was quiet. "Is that all you see in your future?"

He stopped, took her by the waist, and smiled down at her. "Well, there's a gal in town that I'm hoping to have a few dances with in the future as well. Maybe something more. If she don't mind a man like me with two first names."

Her soft smile turned into a grin. "Something more, hmmm? Why Henry Raymond, we'll just have to see."

• • • • • •

Author's Note: This story is based on real historical events in Dodge City history. All named places and characters, with the exception of Lucy, are based on historical figures. Charlie Bassett was one of the founders of the Long Branch Saloon in Dodge City, served as the first sheriff of Ford County, Kansas, as well as city marshal of Dodge City. His deputies included Wyatt Earp and Bat Masterson.

—*Benjamin Thomas is a retired US Air Force medic and author of published short stories in numerous genres as well as a science fiction time travel novel and a western whodunnit. A native of New Mexico, Benjamin has always been a "westerner" at heart, currently enjoying life with his family in Colorado Springs at the foot of Pikes Peak.*

ONE AND FIFTEEN MORE

KEN SNYDER

FELINA REYES RODE into Cuetzalalco, taking a pinch of polvo de tumba between her thumb and forefinger from the inside pocket of her black duster. Eyes followed her warily from porch steps, and mothers pulled their children into their houses. She couldn't blame them. There probably hadn't been another Taranzencoatl Ahwik in this part of the world in centuries. The war between the two clans had gone on longer than the history books were written to tell about it. An old woman rocking in her chair on the front porch made the forked sign for evil at her with her hands. Felina grinned at her and spit onto the ground in her direction.

Felina's dark skin and dreadlocks were dead giveaways of who she was. She sniffed the powder between her fingers and couldn't help but grin as the residents scattered from her path like chaff on the wind. Felina's holsters slapped against her hips as her Sagrada revolvers rose and fell with the motion of Guapo's confident yet somehow fancy gait. The silvery muscle-bound Azteca always had a flair for the dramatic.

Felina had trailed the two brothers across three territories over the Sangre Serpiente mountains and spent the last three days crossing the Desechos desert. Nothing would stop her from bringing Javier and Raul Ortega to justice for what they did to that little girl in San Sebastion.

Nothing.

Felina stopped outside Luna's *cantina* and tied Guapo's reins to the hitching post. She pulled a length of chain with two manacles at the ends and affixed them to Guapo's saddle. If everything went to plan, Raul Ortega would find himself attached to the chains, and she would give the son of a bitch a ride he would never forget.

The porch creaked under her boots. She shook her dreads over her shoulder and sniffed back the remnants of the *polva de tumba* left in her nose. A single grain the size of a pinhead could render a normal man unconscious, but such a small amount wouldn't affect her in the slightest. The *polva de tumba* was the only thing that kept her going. The dark green powder, ground from the root of a strange flowering cactus with bright purple flowers, dulled her chattering mind to a bearable level. Though the substance slowed her reactions slightly, she needed it to function. The last time she tried to quit the stuff, she ended up in a run-down brothel on the borderlands with her pistol pressed against her head. Maybe after this, she would try to quit again, but this deep in Ortega territory, she needed her fix.

Felina stepped through the batwing doors into Luna's cantina. The *polva de tumba* slithered through her veins like a warm liquid serpent, wriggling from the crown of her head to the tips of her toes, taking away her pain and silencing her racing mind. Every muscle relaxed, sending a shiver through her body like an echo. Her vision doubled for a brief moment, a minor side effect she'd experienced with the latest batch she bought from Malrojo, but it would fade. It was pretty stupid to get high before walking into a den of rattlesnakes. She could have made it another couple of hours before the sickness took her, but Gods, she felt truly alive under the effects of the powder.

Felina spotted Javier over the batwing doors. He sat at a table with two other *bandoleros.* The fact that there were no Ortega Xutacutlis inside was a sign in her favor. Dealing with the black priest's acolytes, trained in the way of the gun like she was, would have made things much more difficult.

Her presence would eventually draw the attention of Angel Ortega. It was a matter of time. Even though Raul and Javier were only second cousins, Angel wouldn't suffer a Taranzencoatl Ahwik plucking his blood under his nose. And though Felina liked her chances, with Lobocoatl only a fifteen-minute ride north, she needed to deal with the brothers and get back across the border before they could organize a response.

Felina was sure Angel would risk sending a single Xutacutli against her after she killed Eliana Botello the year before. If he sent enough Xutacutlis, in large enough numbers, her chances of making it out alive would be slim. But no matter what happened, the Ortega brothers were going to die. If that meant her end, then so be it. She would gladly walk the endless trail if she took those two bastards with her. Felina didn't have a death wish. She still wanted to find the men who killed her parents and one day become an Alto Sacerdote like her adoptive father. But she would gladly sacrifice it all for retribution. Felina stepped through the door.

Luna's *cantina* looked like a dozen other places. Round wooden tables covered the floor, and there was a long, polished bar near the back wall. A set of uneven stairs led to a row of rooms on the second floor, with seven doors lining the L-shaped balcony.

If Felina were a betting woman, which she wasn't, she would have bet a thousand gold eagles that Raul Ortega was in one of those rooms with a woman who wished she'd chosen a different client.

All eyes turned as the doors swung closed behind her. Glasses clacked on the wooden tables, and hushed murmurs filled the room.

Eleven in total. Seven on the left and four on the right. The way the bartender's left hand flinched makes twelve. A scatter gun under the bar, probably. Three exits, one in the front, one in the back, and a set of stairs from the second story, not counting the windows in the rooms upstairs. Seven rooms on the upper balcony, with four closed doors. Sixteen possible gunmen.

It was a number she could handle. She would have tried her luck with just about any number.

Javier stood up from the table. He was a broad-shouldered man with a square jaw, laughing brown eyes, and slicked greasy black hair. The man's eyes narrowed into calculating slits. His hand hovered over his pistol.

"I'm looking for Raul and Javier Ortega," said Felina to the room. It would give the locals a chance to get out of her way. This was going to end only one way—sangre por sangre.

"I have warrants signed by the *Tlatoani* of the Reyes Clan, Lord Miguel Luis Reyes the Third, Defender of El Reino, Guardian of Castille Caido, and *Alto Sacerdote* of Taranzencoatl."

Javier drew his weapon, and Felina's heavy calibers flashed.

Fluid.

Fast.

Death.

Her movements were automatic, silky, and quick enough that she fired her weapon before her conscious mind gave the go-ahead. The drugs had no effect on this part of her work. Her reflexes were faster than her wakeful mind.

Felina's round punched a hole above Javier's left eye. Her second and third took the two *bandoleros* next to him. The fever shrouded her like a thin sheet of red silk. Her hands were their own masters, and her guns dealt death.

The acrid gun smoke and the wails of bleeding men cut through the ringing din. People scrambled to get out of her way, diving over tables, the bar, and out the doors. The unarmed wouldn't taste lead, but if they took up arms against her, they would face her wrath the same as the others.

The *bandoleros* finally recovered from the surprise of her attack. Bullets ripped the air around her. Tables splintered, and a sharp pain shot up her neck from her left shoulder. Felina raised her gun and was relieved she still had the use of her arm. She spun on her bootheels and cut down three of Javier's men on her left with a quick fan of the hammer. The rest of the men turned and fled. The clatter of dropped weapons hitting the floor was what she'd been waiting to hear. They knew her order forbade killing the unarmed. A pathetic escape from her wrath that she'd seen too many cowards use against her.

Felina reloaded her weapons. Her hands worked without conscious thought, sliding smoking shells from the chambers and loading in fresh lead from her *bandolier*. Felina snapped the cylinders closed and advanced toward the bartender. She found him with his back against the bar, the shaking shotgun held against his chest like an alcoholic clutching a bottle of booze.

"Where is Raul Ortega?" Felina growled.

The barman removed a trembling hand from the shotgun and pointed above him.

Felina didn't want to hurt him, but she couldn't have him finding his cojones while she dealt with Raul, so she did the next best thing. She accelerated her pistol in between the man's eyes. There was a sickening *crack,* and she winced at how hard she'd hit him. Sometimes she forgot how strong she was. She studied him for a brief moment and decided he would live.

"Raul!" Felina yelled. The guttural sound came from deep inside her. She could almost taste the rage on her lips as she spoke his name. She stepped out into the bar. Empty shell casings scattered under her bootheels.

The door in the middle of the balcony crashed open, and Felina fired two rounds. Raul's kneecaps exploded sending a spray of blood and cartilage on the wall behind him. He stumbled a few steps, breaking through the railing, and crashed onto the last remaining table. The cantina shuddered as he landed.

Raul wasn't getting off easy. No simple bullet to the head would do. She wanted to leave her mark on him before he left this world, penance for what he had done.

Felina grabbed Raul by his greasy black hair and dragged him across the floor. He swiped feebly at her hands, and his pleas for mercy fell on deaf ears. Raul yowled as she yanked him off the boardwalk and onto the hardpacked street. Guapo nodded his head at her. Felina slapped the manacles on Raul's ankles, swung her leg over Guapo, and grabbed her *sombrero* off the saddlehorn.

Word would have gotten back to the temple by now. Her time was short. Felina tilted her hat forward to block the sun and spurred Guapo, and the blessed screams from Raul began. She had over a week's ride back to her father's temple ahead of her, and she really hoped that the squealing bastard would last a while. He wouldn't, but she couldn't think of a better riding companion than the dying moans of the son of a bitch behind her. Each plea for mercy was like music to her ears.

Sadly, Raul eventually quieted as the fading light shrouded the dust cloud of the pursuers on her back trail. It didn't take them as long as she thought, but she figured she had an hour's lead judging by the distance of the swirling dust.

Felina reigned in Guapo and walked back to the mangled corpse. She pulled her knife out and cut off his tattered clothes. The skin on his face was a raw, oozing wasteland. The covered places had less visible damage, but when she rolled him over, she couldn't help but grin. Raul's entire back was a bloody mess, from ass to elbows, like a fresh cut of minced beef.

Felina wished she could have taken her sweet time and brought Raul to the edge of hell and let him live there for a while, but in the end, he got off easy. Far too easy.

By the size of the dust cloud, it looked like a pretty large group. Angel Ortega wasn't happy with what she'd done.

They wouldn't catch her, though. Guapo was a good-looking horse but bred for speed. He reminded her of herself in that way. She wasn't ugly—on the outside, anyway. She had curves in all the right places and a skeleton key smile that got her out of more sticky situations than she could count.

The loss of her parents at such a young age had cut her deeply, leaving an open wound in her heart that grew infected as the years passed. The drugs, the recklessness, and the inability to truly care for anyone or anything was a well-worn suit. Her adoptive father, Miguel, took her in, gave her his last name, and taught her to kill. But nothing would fill the void of losing her parents. The worst part was she couldn't even remember their faces anymore. That fact seemed to bother her more than she cared to admit. There was a faint image of her mother's brown eyes, but she couldn't remember anything about her father. Someone had murdered them in cold blood, stolen her life from her, and left her to die. At least that's what Miguel told her had happened.

The bright side was when she snorted vast amounts of *polva de tumba,* the blood and screams in her nightmares weren't so vivid. Only through training, willpower, and a bulging satchel of polva de tumba had she been able to keep her life together. To the public, she was a hard, careless, killing machine. That couldn't have been further from the truth. They had no idea how haunted she truly was.

Felina shook her head. She'd have time on the trail to ponder her problems. For now, she had a job to finish. She drew her blade and cut off the blue dreamcatcher tattoo on his chest above his heart for proof of her kill. The skin was still soft and malleable as she peeled the layers back with deep jagged slashes around the edges. It wasn't like Raul would complain. She put the strip of skin into her pocket, wrapped in a piece of oiled cloth she used to clean her guns.

One more bump for the ride wouldn't hurt.

Felina opened the leather pouch and took a pinch of the brown-ish-green powder. The wind had picked up, sending powerful gusts that blew her dreads out behind her from the direction of home. She had to be careful not to lose the pinch in her fingers or even the entire satchel. It was a twelve-hour ride to the next hub of civilization, and with some digging, she could probably procure another pouch. It would take time and effort, but doing it with a fever and loose bowels from the withdrawal symptoms sounded like a horrible idea.

I deserve more, anyway! I literally just waltzed into Ortega's territory, killed the bastard and his brother, and I'm going to get away with it.

Felina dropped the small bit of powder back into the bag, turning her back to shield it from the winds. She raised the entire pouch and buried her nose in the powder. Alternating nostrils, she inhaled until her face went numb. She leaned back, wiping the remnants from her top lip with the back of her hand. A powerful surge exploded through her body. Every fiber inside her released. All her stresses, hurts, and scars folded in on themselves. Her heart pattered in her ears for a moment, and the world spun. The last thing she remembered thinking was that the batch was the best she'd ever had.

The drum of hooves on the hardpan woke Felina. The wind had picked up to a yowling scream. The satchel had come to rest between the *V* of her outstretched legs, shielding it from the worst of the winds. Some of the powder had spilled when she fell. Felina's heart climbed into the back of her throat as she watched some of the granules disappear into the wind. She scrambled to stuff the powder back into the pouch, scooping it with the palms of her numbed hands. She wasn't doing a very good job of it, and there was far more dirt than *polva* going into the bag. Felina stood on numb legs that felt as if they weren't her own, raising her arms to steady herself.

The party was so close that she could make out the Ortega banners whipping above their ranks. The red wolf on the black background rode at the vanguard. She had a minute at most.

God dammit, why couldn't I wait until I was back across the border! How could I be so stupid!

Dirt popped next to her feet, then a few more rounds landed nearby. The tinny whine of bullets flew all around her. She could barely stand, let alone make it to Guapo. Her only chance was to stand and fight.

Felina's hands dipped to her revolvers, but when she drew, the guns slipped from her hands. She'd lost all control of her numbed fingers. Felina took a step back toward Guapo and fell hard on her ass. Guapo snorted, and she dismissed him with a wave of her arm. The group was almost on top of her. The bullets drummed the terrain around her like the strings of *petardos* the kids of her village lit during festivals.

Felina looked down at the pouch of *polva de tumba* and then back at the group of Ortega men. She sighed and grabbed the bag with the palms of both hands and shook the powder into the wind. A single grain the size of a pin head could incapacitate a grown man, and the brownish-green cloud enveloped most of her pursuers. Horses and men collapsed like she'd set off a *granada* in the middle of the group. Flesh hit ground, and the man carrying the banner at the front of the pack's head hit a rock jutting out of the earth, and a spray of blood squirted toward her, landing in a streaky line on the hardpan a few feet away. The wind, like a divine shield, had saved her from that sickening injustice. A few of the men near the back seemed to be less affected. They stumbled about but still kept their feet. They would recover quickly. She had to take her chance. It was the only one she would get. Felina awkwardly wrestled her pistols back into their holsters and threw herself over the back of Guapo on the third try.

Felina leaned in close and asked for everything Guapo had, and he gave it to her willingly. The desert blurred as Guapo accelerated to a blistering pace. A small dip in the terrain sent her airborne for a brief moment, and her numbed and buzzing hands barely held onto the saddlehorn, saving herself from a nasty spill and an expedient exit from the world at the hands of her pursuers. The men on the edge of the group fired at her, but she was too far away, or they were horrible shots. Either way, she would take it. She had been a fool today and deserved to die. She would procure another pouch of *polva de tumba* when she got back to civilization, but God willing, it would be her last. She would walk through that valley of hell. She'd face pain and sickness, but it was time to see if she would sink or swim without the crutch she'd leaned on for far too long.

Felina wiped the tears from her cheeks and raced into the salmon-colored sunset with the *polva de tumba* coursing through her veins.

—*Ken Snyder lives in northern Utah with his three children and his rambunctious Labrador retriever named Indiana. He currently works as a freelance writer and is working on his fifth novel. Ken is a voracious reader, an avid gamer, and is relentlessly pursuing his dream of becoming a traditionally published novelist.*

Indian Woman on a Horse by Frederic Remington

COMANCHE WOMAN

JOHN O'DONOVAN

AFTER THREE YEARS absence, I have returned to the Oklahoma Indian Reservation to be with my people, to die with them, as I have lived, loved, and suffered. To my surprise and disappointment, there is some excitement going around our camp about the white man's custom they call Christmas.

I tried living with my white relatives, the people of my birth, but I remember not their customs nor their ways. I have relearned to read and write in a simple way and carry a conversation, but it labors me and saps my strength. It casts me into chaos and doubt where I find myself an alien in both worlds.

A small knocking on my door awakens me. Daylight here is short and cold and bites with hunger. Nights are long and black and laced with twisted dreams. Through the tiny, frosted window in the dim gray light of dawn, I can vaguely make out the thermometer in the village square. It reads seventeen below, but I already know how cold it is. This small cabin thrown together from mud, rocks, and timber is narrow like a cave. Wind cries through the cracks. White man's tools and implements stare back at me. A cast iron stove, cold and useless—no wood to burn. A few metal pots and pans but no food to cook. The timbers above and beside, like ribs of a cage, encase me. By my cot on a wooden crate is a white man's picture image of my granddaughter in her best, most beautiful Indian outfit, but she is gone to the spirit world with her father, my only son. My heart yearns to be with them. We are a defeated people, but I'm not quite dead yet. My hope now, only to hold up my head and look the enemy in the eye, that they should remember forever, in their books and revelations, that I am Comanche.

•   •   •   •   •

IT IS THE winter of 1882. With sixty years on Mother Earth, my face is mapped with wrinkles. Cataracts cloud and dim my eyes. My hair, once the color of the sun, is now thin and white like dirty snow and teeth, broken, rotted, worn down. Yet, what people see when they first look at me is my nose, or that is, the lack of it. Where my nose should be are two small holes. When you meet my gaze, you will quickly look away and whisper to your friend, "How remarkable! What's her name? Oh, yes! I've heard of her, down in Texas they say...."

Allow me then, to tell my story. Go deep into the wrinkles, through the years, through the joy and tears to where it all began.

•   •   •   •   •

MY BIRTH NAME was Barbara Rose Baker. I was born the youngest child to Rose Marie and Robert Joseph Baker. I had two brothers, Benjamin and Francis, and a sister, Rebecca. They called me Babsy. We

lived then in the region called "Upper Ohio River Valley." My family
had an adventurous spirit and felt the call of the West. Seven families
and friends, fifty-six human souls in all, first of the white migration to
venture deep into the wilderness. We went forth undaunted with our
wagons, horses, and cattle... and our superior Christian ways.

It was on the day of my seventh birthday, in the year of 1829, we
arrived at our destination to make our first camp on the banks of the
Brazos River in Texas. At that time, Texas was Mexican Territory.
However, Mexico welcomed white settlers, part of their strategy to
uproot and diminish the native Indians.

Beyond the Brazos, westward, lay the vast grasslands of the plains.
We knew there were Indians out there. Savages, we called them. How
many and how savage, we had no idea. My father, a Baptist minister
and an arrogant optimist wasn't in the least worried. "We came to
tame this land. The savages, we shall baptize them and teach them
our civilized Christian ways, but first we must build a fortress. Even
as God is on our side, it is only prudent that we protect ourselves."

Three years passed, dreamlike and peaceful. All worked hard with
willing hands. We prayed together and gave thanks to the Lord. The
cedar post walls of our fortress rose to the sky, eighteen feet high with
a catwalk balcony all around the inside perimeter.

·   ·   ·   ·   ·

IT WAS AT the break of dawn they came on a summer morning. The
two massive timber-frame gates were swung open for the workers to
go to the bountiful fields with teams of mules and horses. My father,
as was his custom, stayed behind to secure the gates closed. Out of nowhere they appeared, as if in a mirage, the rising sun behind them. One
hundred, maybe two hundred savages painted red and black on white

sat motionless on their painted ponies. Black lances, ominous against
the blue sky. He recognized their colors—Comanche. He had seen them
trading horses, pelts, buffalo robes, and he saw these and their ponies
were dripping wet. He knew then they had been hiding in the river. My
father, unarmed, raised his hands in peace. Their leader wore a wolf's
head atop his own, lunged his horse, drove his lance through my father,
and rode over him. The painted ones poured through the open gates
in a river of screaming savages. They took their time. They tortured,
mutilated, butchered, burned, raped, and murdered.

The Comanche went to the fields to finish the others. My two
brothers were tied to a tree, scalped, and left to die, bleeding their
young lives into the dry Texas dirt. There were five girls left standing—myself and my sister Rebecca and three others who were my
cousins. Our lives spared, to be tied and bound to the backs of the
captured horses.

•   •   •   •   •   •

DAY INTO NIGHT, into day and night again, we traveled, relentless,
in the hot summer wind. On the fourth day Wolf-head tied me to his
pony in front of him. My parents, my family, my friends… their scalps
hanging there as trophies. Yes! I was terrified. I knew I was on a journey of life or death, but I knew, somehow, that I would live.

We crossed a river where it was wide and shallow. Trees and
shrubs faded behind us to give way to tall rough prairie grass. Finally,
we reached the camp of our captors in a secluded valley amid rolling
hills. On the banks of a river, hundreds of tipis dotted the landscape.
Children and dogs ran to greet us with great excitement.

That night after our arrival, Rebecca got a rope around her neck
and strangled herself. Wolf-head was very angry. He scalped her and

fed her body to the dogs. A few days later a small band of Mexicans came with horses to trade. They left with my three cousins. I never saw them again.

Alone with the Comanche, I was given over to a wife of Wolf-head, to be her servant, her slave. To be whatever she could make me. Wolf-head was a war chief with many wives. This one, her name was Lame Crow. The first thing she did was strip me of my clothes and burn them. Next, she went to work on my golden hair. She hacked it off with a dull knife, and when it didn't hack, she pulled. Later, she forced me to weave it into her own greasy mop. At that time, I held my nose trying not to smell her. She laughed hysterically as she took the knife and cut off my nose. She pranced about like a pony, my hair bobbing up and down behind her. Some young ones came and joined her, dragging me around with my blood pouring out. They danced and stomped and chanted in their foreign tongue. In that circle of frenzy, something happened inside me. A calmness came, and I became detached from them and from my own body. I floated above looking down at my own self looking up. I saw myself full grown. I was riding with the wind on a gray spotted pony. My golden hair streamed out behind me like the fire of the sun. Around me, the buffalo. Together, we raced over the prairie. We came to the edge of a cliff. Space and time stood still, until I fell into the abyss, back into myself, a little girl cowering naked, drenched in my own blood, my enemies all around me.

Lying helpless on the ground, insects crawling, mosquitoes and flies feeding on my blood, I envied my sister for being dead. But then someone was holding me, wrapping me in a blanket. I was much overjoyed as I was thinking Rebecca had come back for me. I was carried by strong arms and laid down gently inside a tipi, a soothing voice in my ears. There, I first saw her face. It was not my sister. It was Night Eyes... an old woman... my salvation.

•   •   •   •   •

SLEEP CAME THEN, long and deep, the first since my capture. I dreamed I was back in Ohio with my family. We were in the buggy riding to church. The preacher appeared and preached of the end of the world. My father stood up and told him to go to hell. The preacher replied, "We are in hell." The Indians appeared with Wolf-head leading them down from heaven. He spoke to us, and he was then a real wolf. He said, "Follow me and enter the Kingdom of Heaven."

Night Eyes sheltered me for seven days. It was a time of passage, from the old world into the new. She mashed up leaves and roots to make medicine for my nose and my scalp where the hair was ripped out. She fed me strips of roasted meat and mares' milk to drink. Now and then, Lame Crow would show her face and try to drag me out, but Night Eyes drove her away with curses and a big stick.

Night Eyes became my new mother. She taught me with patience and love how to speak in her tongue. By and by, I ventured out and mingled with the others. In time, they accepted me, and I them. My past before my capture became a dreamworld, fading from my memory. Sometimes I felt I was living in a new dream, until I would see my reflection in a pool of water—not a dream but a nightmare.

The one who took my nose taught me, not to help me or better me, but that I might better help her with her daily back-breaking chores—to clean the fat from the hides of the buffalo, the horse, the wolf, and the deer. To wash them in the river. To stake them and stretch them in the sun to dry. To sew garments, tipis, and moccasins with needles made of bone. Dig edible roots. Start fires with stick or stone. Dry meat by fire and sun and wind. Braid rope from the grasses and the dried inner bark of the basswood tree. I watched in silence and learned to build traps for small game, to tell the passage of time

by the seasons and the journey of the sun, moon, and stars. To understand their spirit world entwined with animals and non-living things
and how their ancestors were living in these animals, the rocks, the
rivers, the trees, and the sky.

•   •   •   •   •

THE SEASONS PASSED, and I grew stronger. I moved with the Comanche as they hunted and foraged. We followed the buffalo, sometimes far, sometimes not so far. We camped by the river, the flow of
life, yet the Comanche never ate the fish or waterfowl.

They know themselves as "Nermernuu"—the people who outride
the wind to fight all the time to the end. I became one with them, to
see, to think, to feel, to breathe their way, to live and die.

Around my waist I tied a short hemp rope, to mark the passage of
the seasons. With the coming of the first snow of each winter season I
made a single knot. In the summer of the sixth knot, I was with Lame
Crow as we washed deer hides in the clear spring water that flowed to
the river just beyond. It was around midday, hot and humid. I stood
up to stretch my back and wipe the sweat from my brow. Before us,
coming up through a draw, came five riders, slow and cumbersome,
shod hooves shattering the silent stream. Behind them, three pack
mules loaded heavy with goods. White men had come to trade. Instantly, terror gripped my heart. I turned away to hide myself. Years
later, I would learn that one of those white traders was my uncle who
had survived the massacre at the Baker fort. He was searching for his
captured nieces.

Three days passed with much singing and dancing. Many of the
men were drunk and some women too. On the third night following
the visit by the white traders, a quietness came over the camp, then

suddenly, moaning and heaving and a great stench surrounded us. Indians of all ages stumbled from their tipis to crawl on the ground, defecating and vomiting, begging for water. Five days more and all were dead but a handful. The white men brought more than knives, guns, and whiskey. They brought their murdering magic—cholera.

Wolf-head was dead and so, too, Lame Crow and my loving foster mother, Night Eyes. I held her close to me and wept as she died in my arms. The survivors slouched away, leaving their dead where they lay. I was forbidden to follow. They resented me and suspected white man's magic was at work.

Buzzards appeared, then ravens and wolves to feed on the dead. Quickly, I buried those I could by covering them with rocks. The Comanches believe that a body mutilated will not rest easy in the afterworld. Wolf-head and Night Eyes, I placed together under a pecan tree. Lame Crow also, even after what she did to me. It wasn't right to leave her for the scavengers.

The wolves, satiated, lay about and watched my movements. I was sick and weak with hunger. I too had the white man's magic inside me, but I fought it off. I crawled to the spring and drank. As I lay on the ground, the wolf pack leader, a female, came and sniffed me. I looked into her gray eyes to tell her I was not afraid, before I fell into a deep sleep. When I awoke, the wolves were gone. Under some rocks and wrapped in reeds I found the dried buffalo strips I had hidden away from Lame Crow. I heated them on hot coals to eat—ravenous, like a starving dog.

Alone in the camp of death, I had to decide—go east and back to the whites or go join the Kiowa band. They lived and hunted to the north. I had once exchanged words with them. They were friendly and not affronted by me for being white. There was one, a short stocky brave. He had eyes of kindness and spoke soft words. He told me I could live with them if ever I should choose. "Follow the antelope trail north four days ride, and you will find us, or we will find you."

Deciding then, with my nose gone, no white man would ever want me, except perhaps to be his slave, and I already had my fill of that. First, I had to find a pony. I had learned to ride as a child in the dreamworld, but that was with bridle and saddle. With the Indians I rode bareback on a soft blanket of tanned deer hide. The ponies left behind were scattered loosely about. I cornered one and got close enough to lasso it. It was a female, and she had a slight limp. With my knife I removed a small arrowhead embedded in her left foreleg. I cleaned it and dressed it with oil of cedar bark and pecan leaves tied off with buffalo hide. She would need a few days to heal.

While I waited, I scoured the deserted camp. Lame Crow had some fine garments, some of which I had fashioned myself—deerskin dress, ankle length, embroidered with tiny seeds dyed red, yellow, and green. I took it, but I didn't wear it, yet. Wolf-head had a son about my size. He survived the murdering magic, but he left everything of his possessions. I took his deerskin boots and pants and a pullover top shirt with colored beads of bone and porcupine quill. I wore these, to fit easy with the riding of a horse, realizing they were not a female costume, but now, I answered to no one—I wore what pleased me. I found a steel knife with elk-horn handle and a small axe. The wooden handle had writing on it. It took me a minute to recognize, but then the letters jumped out—B-A-K-E-R. It was my father's axe. His face floated before me, as in a river drowning... and then was gone. In Wolf-head's tipi I retrieved his bow with a quiver of arrows. I was never allowed to shoot, but I watched them practice. For three days I practiced until my pulling fingers were calloused over. I wasn't great, but I felt good enough at close range. I would need this skill to hunt small game.

I checked my pony. She was ready. I filled a waterbag from the spring. A satchel full of dried buffalo strips. A rawhide bag of dried pecan nuts. My hair and skin I darkened with charcoal and tallow, to conceal my true self.

Across the river in the rolling hills the she-wolf howled. I heard her voice to be a sign from the dead Comanche... go this way. Mounting my gray spotted pony, I wheeled her round. With gentle touch of hand and heel, I did feel the world turning beneath me. I felt the Great Spirit embrace me in the rising summer sun. With my face to the warm wind, I began my journey.

Leaving the camp of the Comanche, my people now and forever, their *tipis* flapping empty in the wind, ghosting in agony with mortal defeat, my heart beating to the dance of death, but also to the dance of life, I knew then, as a certainty, who I was—I was Babsy, Comanche Woman—Comanche Mother. I was not completely alone. I carried within me the Wolf-head child.

We rode to meet our destiny.

•   •   •   •   •

WE FOLLOWED THE river north, along the path worn down by the antelope for thousands of years on their annual migration. Surviving by hunting and scavenging, I never did meet up with the Kiowa, but eventually I encountered some stragglers of my own Comanche band, and reluctantly, they accepted me. I moved with them until my baby came, a boy with golden hair. Others joined us until we were a band again, a formidable fighting force, roaming wild and free like the angry prairie wind.

I rode with my people on raids, when the moon was full and the night hawk cried. The wind on my face black with war paint, my yellow hair streaming out behind me like a white man's banner. It was a banner... but not for the whites.

It was the custom for the women to stay in the rear, to watch guard, to care for the children and the horses, to cook and toil at woman's work. That was no longer for me. I had become deadly with the knife, the bow and arrow, and the tomahawk. I was a warrior. I rode up front with the men. I butchered, burned, tortured, murdered. I became more Comanche than the Comanche themselves.

There was a chief amongst us whose name was Spotted Cat. He was by custom allowed to have two wives. When the Bluecoats killed one, he made me his second wife. Him saying to me, "The white man kill my wife. You white woman make replace." He found it fitting that I replace her, I found it fitting that I was wanted by a man. He treated me well enough until one day he became displeased with something I did, so he slapped me. I slapped him back. He tried to hit me once again, but I put my knife through his heart. His other wife was very upset, until I presented her with ten fine horses, and all was well again.

• • • • •

MY SON WITH golden hair grew up fast and became a warrior. On his warrior day he was named Yellow Otter, after he swam the Red River to raid a Blue-coat soldier camp and swam back with three scalps and five horses.

Those times were the best of times, those few short years lived with freedom I cannot describe with words. I could cook my own food, make my own clothes. I could ride and raid and take what I wanted. I was without a permanent mate since Spotted Cat's unfortunate demise, but I would take a mate when I felt that call of nature.

And as quickly, the time of freedom slipped away like a summer

season into winter sorrow. The white settlers became more numerous than the stars in the sky with their towns and garrisons dotting
the prairie landscape. The soldiers and the Texas Rangers pursued
us, relentless. Trapped in a canyon, those who tried to break through
were shot, their bodies stacked and burned with the dead horses.
It was there Yellow Otter and his wife made their last stand. Their
daughter, Crying Dove, was now in my care.

General Mackenzie and his murdering bluecoats herded us north,
like their cattle, until we reached the Oklahoma Territory. Many died
along the way, and many more lost the will to live and died upon arrival. My granddaughter, Crying Dove, was one of them.

The whites soon discovered me, even as I tried to hide myself.
Traced me back to my roots, to Baker Fort. Ripped away once more
from my people, they took me on a many day's journey to put me with
strangers, whites, my relatives.

I lost my will to live. For weeks, maybe months I was bedridden,
barely alive as they tried to shove some disgusting mush down my
throat. Slowly, I recovered and walked again but in a trance. My soul
wished to die, but my body chose to live.

My memory began then to come back in little bits and pieces of
that time before the Comanche raid on Baker fort. My tongue loosened, and some words formed that they could comprehend.

They were not a bad people, but they were not *my* people. And
I told them so. I could see they were deeply disappointed in me and
would never understand what I had become. They looked down on
me with pity and revulsion, as if I were some curse brought upon
them. They tried their laying on of hands by the preacher to remove
the devil inside me. They tried then to whip me. It was nothing to me,
except to sap my strength. Reluctantly, they loosened their grip and
let me go. A first cousin rode with me back to Oklahoma as the first

flurries of snow melted into the earth. He gave me five dollars and told me to have a nice life.

•   •   •   •   •

THE FROZEN SNOW was treacherous outside in the walkways. A young girl had come to walk me to the dining hall. Inside, it was warm. A wood stove in the center radiating heat and comfort, and Indians of all ages gathered around. An Indian Chief talked in the Comanche tongue, a soothing, gentle sound, like a soft warm breeze by the river beneath a shade tree. He was the great Comanche Chief Quanah Parker, whose mother, like me, was a white woman. He was arranging a protest march to the Reservation Headquarters for the stronger ones to act out their unhappiness about the rations. He told them we wanted more beef, flour, corn, more blankets. Fabric for the women to make clothes. Wood for our stoves... and jobs, work for our young men. And then the murmuring voices went quiet as they listened for his final words.

"My people, my time has passed to out-ride the wind, but I am hopeful for you, my children, my grandchildren. You will out-ride the wind. You will fight all the time to the very end." And never once did he mention Christmas. I knew then I was back where I belonged, with my own people—Comanche.

—John O'Donovan was born in Ireland and emigrated to the U.S.A. in 1963 at the age of seventeen. He is a proud Vietnam Veteran of the United States Army, Infantry. Now a retired carpenter, he lives in Southern California with his wife, Vikki, and two dogs. His short stories have appeared in The Chamber Magazine, The Bear Creek Gazette, *and* Mason Street Review.

Sentinel of the Plains by William Dunton

WALTZ TO THE WIND
DUSTY RICHARDS

THE SHARP MARCH wind swept the yellow wildflowers and tossed them like a tempest sea. Standing before a window on the second story of Millie's House of Pleasure, she wrapped the silk duster more tightly around her body. Poor blossoms, so mistreated by the bitter forces, she felt pained for them.

Win-Anne had come to Dodge City in the cold of winter. Anxious to earn the easy money that others spoke of, she joined the girls at Millie's House. The days had begun to lengthen, but business remained slow.

Most of the cowboys were still in Texas gathering cattle. The new green grass would be headed and brown before the vast herds arrived. All the talk about riches was just that—talk.

Like the flowers, she had been tossed about with less than tenderness, and then, someday she, too, would shrivel and die. There was no justice for her kind. Long ago, she had given up the notion of some gallant knight riding up and taking her away from this place or any other parlor house where she worked.

The Texas boys were mostly young and inept but sweet. A few were snakes, cruel, deliberately defeating in their actions toward her. A shudder ran up her arms at the thought of such worthless wags. She closed her eyes and tried to shut out the past pain. Like the flowers scattered across the fresh green carpet, she, too, had been bent, whipped, and slapped.

Three abreast, she saw them come riding. They waved their hats in youthful excitement. Even tried to get their horses to buck and no doubt were laughing as they approached Dodge.

Would they stop at Millie's? Her heart quickened. Sometimes boys that age—her age—were too bashful and first visited the saloons for whisky courage. She hurried down the stairs to be available. In anticipation, her breath caught in her throat when their boot heels clattered on the porch. Her heart quickened at the sound, and no matter how hard she tried, there was no way she could turn down her smile.

Within minutes, she was in the arms of Earl. Belly to belly, they danced around the parlor to the piano player's tinkling melody. His firm embrace drove away all her regrets. This was why she did what she did—his closeness, her knowing he wanted her, idolized her and even loved her for the moment. In this brief span of time, she was the flower out of the wind.

—*Dusty Richards harbored a lifelong dream of becoming a Western novelist. In 1992, that dream became a reality when his first book,* Noble's Way, *was released. In the three intervening decades, he published over 160 more Western novels under his own name and a host of pseudonyms. Sadly, Dusty passed away in early 2018, leaving behind a legion of fans and a legacy of Western writing that will live on for generations.*

THE
FIGHTING EDITOR
MARK MELLON

THE YOUNG MAN set his nib pen down on the dusty desk, eyes focused on the cobwebbed ceiling, in search of the perfect phrase, the mot juste. He tried to block the clamor from his mind, the Gordon Jobber's steady clank as Soames printed the evening edition, and the camp's roar outside—howling livestock, rasping saws, and banging hammers, foulmouthed, drunken arguments, even an out of tune piano's faint tinkle from the sporting house across the street. After much concentration, his unlined face lit up with inspiration.

He reached for his pen, dipped it in the inkwell, and was about to set it to paper when a fusillade outside distracted him.

"How can a fellow get anything done with that racket going on? Sam. Come here, son."

The copy boy stuck his head in the editor's office, uncut black locks kept in place by a square paper cap. "Yes, sir, Mister Siddons?"

"See what the fuss is about. If there's been a shooting, we'll fit in a headline."

"Yes, sir."

Sam returned shortly, once more interrupting the essay, an anxious look in his eyes. "There weren't no shooting, Mister Siddons. Some fellows hoorawed the town riding in. They say they want to talk with you." Sam flashed a significant look. "It's Billy Mulligan with his pals."

"Well, what matter is that, Sam? In any event, don't keep them waiting. It's not polite. Show the gentlemen up."

Heavy feet tromped on the stairs. Three men entered the small room, all big. The one in front wore a long, swallow-tailed frock coat that complemented his drooping mustachios, a narrow brim slouch hat perched over his left eye. Stub-toed boots gleamed from fresh blacking. A heavy dragoon pistol hung from his holster.

"Are you Siddons, the editor of this rag?"

"Yes, I'm Jeffrey Siddons, but I certainly wouldn't call the *Mineral City War Whoop* a rag. I'd offer you gentlemen a seat, but I only have the one."

"Never mind that."

He reached into his coat and threw newsprint onto the desk. "Did you write that?"

Siddons perused the newsprint. "Ah, yesterday's bulldog edition. What article in particular are you referring to, sir?"

A meaty finger jabbed at a column. "This one. Right here! Did you write it or not?"

"Let's see. 'A fire assay from the Sure Thing OK Mine promises rich results according to Assay Office reports. The mine was considered to be a played out wildcat strike. Rich ore was only found when another shaft was sunk a week ago by new owners. With incidents of salted mines rife throughout the region, investors would do well to carefully investigate any such claims.' Yes, that appears to be my work, all right."

"Well, I'm Billy Mulligan, and these are my partners, Farmer Pease and Jack McNabb. We own the Sure Thing OK Mine and come to say you're a goddamned liar. We want you to take back every word you said about the mine."

"In the next paper," Pease said.

"At the very top," McNabb said.

Siddons smiled calmly and evenly. "Gentlemen, that's simply out of the question. *The War Whoop* has a very strict policy of never issuing retractions. We consider it a sign of weakness."

Mulligan slammed his palm on the desk. "By God, you young pup, you *will* take back those lies, or I'll lay you out where you sit. I'm determined to have satisfaction on this, one way or another."

Siddons leaned back in his chair. He thumbed tobacco from a pouch into his pipe, smiling as before.

"Why didn't you say so in the first place? You could have saved us all a good deal of time and trouble. I'm in the middle of writing a very important essay on political economy, you know. Sam!"

"Yes, Mister Siddons?"

"Would you ask Mister Harding to step around if he's free, please?"

Sam's face lit up with mischievous glee. "Yes, sir!"

He dashed down the stairs. Siddons scratched a lucifer and lit his pipe while the three men continued to glare at him.

"You see, gentlemen, I only handle the writing end of the newspaper. I'm thus known as the writing editor. People with complaints like yourselves are referred to the fighting editor."

Mulligan's mustachios hiked as he bared his teeth in derision. "The fighting editor? What sort of guff is that? Either throw down with me or—"

"I might be able to help you, sir."

The quiet, authoritative voice commanded attention. A spare, middle-aged man entered the already crowded office. He smiled, showing tobacco-stained teeth. A minor miracle in a filthy mining camp, everything about him was neat and tidy, from his mud free boots to his black broadcloth suit and well-brushed, gray planter's hat.

"I'm Mister Harding. Do you gentlemen have a dispute with the newspaper? I hope we can work things out amicably."

Farmer Pease eyed Harding uneasily. "Ain't you the one that shot El Dorado Johnny last week at the Chuck-A-Luck?"

"He cheated at cards."

McNabb murmured to Mulligan. "Maybe just leave this be. We already done found a buyer for the claim."

"Yeah, sure," Pease said. "Come on, Billy, let's find a saloon and have the old thing a few times."

They nudged him toward the door. Mulligan drifted with them. Harding and Siddons continued to pleasantly smile. Yet a stray irritable impulse caught Mulligan before he made it out of the office.

"Hell if I crawfish before anyone, even if he *is* on the shoot. God damn you, Mister—"

Mulligan snatched his dragoon pistol free from the holster. He pulled back the hammer. Yet Harding's Philadelphia Derringer was already out, cocked, and aimed. He pulled the trigger. The firing cap detonated.

The gun's report was overwhelming. A .41 caliber ball caught Mulligan square in the forehead. Fired at such short range, his head caved in from the impact. He fell in a heap, dead even before he hit the floor.

Pease and McNabb stared aghast at their slain friend. Harding pulled out another derringer and pointed it at them, placid, smiling, just as before the shooting.

"There are two of you. Make your play and one shall most likely have me although the other will die. Or get your friend out of here. I recommend the latter choice."

Pease eyed McGann who shook his head. Hardened desperadoes, neither still had the stomach for a fight on those terms. Each man took Mulligan by an armpit. They pulled him out of the office. His boot heels rhythmically clopped against the wooden stairs as they dragged him down. Mulligan's body was draped over his horse and led by his friends to the undertaker, already doing a thriving business that particular day with two previous murders and a suicide. He was buried on Boot Hill in the evening in a shallow grave with an unmarked cross.

Harding tucked his derringers away. Siddons waved at the lingering black powder smoke that permeated the room. Sam rushed to fetch a mop to clean the blood from the floor.

"Sorry to have to do business like that in your office, Jeff. The man left me no choice."

"That's quite all right, Mister Harding. I really didn't need to hear from my right ear."

And with that, business as usual at the *Mineral City War Whoop* resumed.

—*Mark Mellon is a novelist who supports his family by working as an attorney. He writes two fisted, hardboiled, blood and guts pulp fiction. Four novels and over eighty short stories have been published in the USA, UK, Ireland, Bulgaria, Canada, and Denmark. Escape From Byzantium won the 2010 Independent Publisher Silver Medal for F/SF.*

One of Geronimo's Braves by William F. Farny

PLAYING ᴛʜᴇ LOOT
KEITH "DOC" RAYMOND

CRAIGMORE LANSING BURST through the train carriage door, his partner, Goldwyn Monk, behind him. He expected two guards, but there were three, and they were not ordinary payroll security but Pinkertons. The gun he carried "just in case" was now essential. Goldwyn attacked the guy on the left while Craigmore went after the guy on the right. The third man was just standing there, waiting to join the fight, when Lansing shot him.

The explosion threw Craigmore's opponent off balance. The shot meant to maim a shoulder instead killed the third man outright. A double jab with his left and a pistol butt to the temple with his other hand allowed Lansing to dispatch the second guy. He turned to see Monk losing against the largest of the three Pinkertons. He cracked the man in the skull, and the third Pinkerton went down.

Goldwyn wiped blood from his nose, while his right eye was already swelling shut. But the strong box was theirs. Both men rifled through the Pinkertons' pockets until they found the keys. A minute later, they lifted the lid and stared down at more cash and gold than either had ever seen in their lives. The train rumbled on, passengers and crew unaware of the theft in progress, as the steam whistle blew.

Lansing and Monk removed their haversacks from their shoulders and filled them with loot. They ignored the men out cold or dead at their feet. It was a month's payroll for a thousand men, cash for the coolies and gold for the line bosses. Their packs were getting heavy as greedy fists filled them.

Lansing noted some loose floorboards on the carriage, the nails poking up. "Wait Goldy, look there. No need to carry the loot when we can stash it beneath the floor and collect it later in the train yard."

"I want my share now!" Monk demanded.

"As you like, my friend. But I can barely lift my pack. We go back to work, and when Carriage 782 lands in the yard, we collect the money at night. Makes our escape easier."

"Well, I reckon we could do that," Monk answered and started wedging open the floorboards to reveal their new hidey hole. Not the brightest bulb, Goldwyn agreed far too quickly.

Within minutes, the two train robbers had the loot stashed and hammered the floorboards back in place. Lansing locked the strongbox after placing sandbags inside to mimic the weight of the gold, to delay the discovery of the robbery, and replaced the keys in the Pinkerton's pocket. Meanwhile, Monk undressed the others and shoved their clothes in the empty money bags.

"What are you doing, Goldy?"

"Slowing them down, my way."

"Time to go," Lansing said, throwing one of the bulging bags over his shoulder and heading to the back of the car.

"See you on the other side, Craig." Goldwyn tipped his cowboy hat and headed toward the front.

One of the Pinkertons regained consciousness and spotted Monk.

He rose shakily and went after him, the wind from the barreling train reviving him, as the robber climbed the ladder on the adjacent car. Monk planned to leap onto the embankment as the train slowed for the approaching tunnel. He was halfway up when he felt the detective's iron grip on his ankle.

"Leggo there!"

"Not so fast, you crook!"

Monk looked down between the cars, seeing the fierce grin of the whiskered detective in his underwear, pulling him back. Trying to kick his way free, Goldwyn was unprepared for the oncoming tunnel. It was the change in air pressure that made him look, and the granite blocks of the tunnel entrance struck him, cutting him in half ending his life.

The Pinkerton would never forget the man's yelp as he died above him. The money bag he carried dropped past him and under the wheels of the train. Still, he clung to Monk's ankle. Recovering his pocket watch from his pants, the Pinkerton noted the engraving that specified the train yard where Goldy worked. This led to Lansing's eventual capture and arrest.

•   •   •   •   •

AFTER CRAIGMORE'S EXECUTION, they turned his personal effects over to the widow. The company never recovered the money from the train robbery. Lansing refused to tell them its location. Besides Goldy's watch, they handed a document containing Craigmore's last will and testament to the grieving widow, unopened. Inside was a second envelope, a dowry for his grandchildren, with instructions for them to open it on their eighteenth birthday.

Lansing's wife never understood why he went bad. She ended up working as a barmaid. A quick draw orphaned her son before he turned sixteen, the bullet going astray. But the boy found the dowry letter from their father and kept it for his own children. Forty-five years would pass before Craigmore's grandchildren would read the contents of that letter.

• • • • •

ROBERTA AND VICTORIA stared at their huge eighteenth birthday cake, candles glowing above white frosting. Their hazel eyes blazed with mischief. Their parents looked around nervously. They had little to offer them on this afternoon in Omaha, Nebraska, in 1918.

The buxom twins with strawberry blonde hair were tomboys since they could run. Roberta hoped for a horse. Victoria hoped for a trip to New York City. Their parents would disappoint them both.

As the wicks cooled, their father placed an envelope in front of them. The script was old-fashioned, the paper inexpensive and stained yellow with age. They stared at the envelope in disgust. Their parents shrugged, embarrassed. Then they reached out, but both kids pulled their hands back. Looking at each other, Roberta took charge and lifted the envelope, turning it over.

"To my grandchildren," she read out loud.

"It's from your granddad Craigmore," replied their father.

"You mean the *criminal*," Victoria said.

Their parents frowned.

"Probably a hacksaw," Roberta said facetiously.

Victoria grabbed the envelope and tore it open, ripping the contents of the letter.

"Hey, slow down there, Vicky!"

The girls put the two parts back together, aligning the edges.

"In Boxcar 782, below the floorboards, you will find your endowment. Spend it wisely. I gave my life to get it for you." Vicky read out loud.

"Anything else?" Roberta asked, taciturn.

Their parents shook their heads, and their father spoke up, "War-time, you know girls. Everything's rationed. We hoped this would suffice. Sorry."

"What was that we read in the paper clipping about the missing payroll? Several thousand dollars plus gold."

"Doesn't matter," said Vicky, "we'll never find that boxcar, even if it still exists."

"But what if we could? Then what? Moldy old bills? Wait a sec...." Roberta's mind was ticking over. Her mother blessed her with an ei-detic memory. "Vicky, you will not believe this, but the 782 is right here in Omaha."

"Where?"

"Now, you definitely won't believe it. It's at the railroad museum."

"Are you sure?"

Roberta frowned at her sister. She knew better. "How could we lift those floorboards and not get caught?"

"That's all we need," said their mother. "Two more Lansings in jail! No, I forbid it. I won't allow you to tear up public property."

"Momma, we're adults now. You can't stop us. Besides, it's our only gift!" Victoria snapped.

"Well, we ain't bailing you out, if'n when you get arrested," said their father.

"But Dad!" both twins whined.

"You're on your own. And you can't use my tools. Adults have their own."

"Fine," Victoria said, pouting and pushing out the screen door, Roberta right behind her.

• • • • • • •

"I DON'T KNOW," said Billy, their skinny lifelong friend, looking outside the boxcar. "This isn't a good idea. We're going to get caught. Especially with you making all that racket, Bobby!"

Night had settled in around the engines and cars at the outdoor museum. The wind blew up a dust devil that dissipated almost immediately. In their imagination, ghost passengers and ghoulish engineers haunted the steel and diesel train yard.

"Place gives me the creeps," Billy went on.

The two sisters were sweating and cursing, as one used a breaker bar and the other worked the floorboard nails with a claw hammer.

"How did Gramps ever get these boards up?" groaned Vicky.

"They're just rusted in place. Darn it!" Roberta shouted as the wood cracked.

"Shh! You sure this is the right boxcar?" Billy cautioned.

Both women froze and gave him a death stare until Billy cowered, then they went back to work. They wedged the first board, then another one up. "Pass that candle over here, Billy."

All three of them looked down using the flickering light. A corner of a gold bar shone beneath the bundles of bills.

"Holy."

"Gee whiz!"

"Have you ever...?"

Victoria whistled in amazement. Treasure, the kind one could only dream about, or read about in stories, awaited them in the hidey hole. The twins shook their long hair in disbelief.

Six arms reached in, and they filled the bags they brought. When they started out, they had little expectation of finding anything. They did it for the adventure, the intrigue, and breaking into the museum at night. That excited them. This was better. Much better!

An hour later, they poured out the loot and counted it in Billy's barn.

"How much is there, ya think?" Billy asked.

"Enough."

"Those bills are too old," Roberta noted.

"Are they any good?" Vicky asked.

They all had to think about it, but it was Roberta that solved the riddle. "They may not be legal tender, but they are precious to collectors! We might just get more than their face value from the numismatists."

"The what?" Billy asked.

"Coin collectors."

"But these aren't coins."

"Even better. They have a history. We just have to divvy them out sparingly. Go from show to show."

"Who will do that?" asked Vicky. "Oh right, it always falls to me to do the dirty work!"

Roberta booked passage on a ship bound for Britain, third class, though she could now afford first. Carrying a load of gold, it is best not to advertise, particularly during wartime. While her sister worked converting old dollars to new, Roberta made her way across occupied France to Switzerland.

• • • • • •

HER BORDER CROSSING came as a bit of a surprise to immigration, as she entered the neutral country as an American and desired asylum and citizenship. They were going to refuse her entry until, out of desperation, she showed to them the hundred plus pounds of gold she was transporting. The Swiss, never ones to refuse wealth, changed their mind and welcomed her with open arms.

From the border, Roberta made her way to Thonon-les-Bains on Lake Geneva and found a villa, a fixer upper, on the water. While she could afford a chateau, she needed a project to fill her time while awaiting Victoria to arrive. She sent a letter to her father asking him to keep his sister apprised of her whereabouts but didn't tell him about their fortune.

While Roberta improved her French, studied interior design, and worked on the villa, she also dated a handsome Swiss worker that helped with its restoration. Meanwhile, Victoria scoured the American countryside seeking men willing to buy their old dollars, which she carted around in two locked chests. The first World War made it difficult, but somehow, the rich always found novel luxury goods to purchase. She counted on their thirst for the rare things and their greed, figuring their investment in old currency would increase with time.

Victoria rarely divulged the source of the bills unless asked. Then, and only then, she told them if pressed by the buyer. First, she would tell them it was a family heirloom, since she had little use for the old currency and needed the cash. The majority accepted this explanation because of rationing, shortages, and the need for purchasing power. Even then, she only sold small lots to avoid attracting attention.

Once she shared the money's origin with the rare few that insisted on knowing the truth, they reveled in delight, and though sworn to secrecy, often leaked it to friends and family. It was just too juicy to keep to themselves, and the knowledge reassured them they had made a worthy purchase, as the bills had historical value. This information created a comet tail behind her that brought Vicky unwanted attention, particularly when discovered by the Pinkerton Detective Agency.

While the Pinkertons involved in the heist were long gone, the agency continued. A little-known group within the agency, known as the Elephant Corps, existed to "manage" cold cases, particularly when the agency suffered from the hands of criminals. The Corps earned their name from the elephants because they never forgot. The Lansing robbery was top on their list, despite the intervening years, because the theft resulted in the deaths of their own.

When word of the serial numbers of the missing cash turned up, rumors spread, and they sought the perpetrators. It didn't matter who was involved in the theft, all that mattered was that their people suffered because of it. The guilty must face justice.

Victoria, being on the move, made the Corps's search more difficult. Perhaps if she knew the Elephant Corps was closing in, she might have gone to ground. Instead, she lived a flamboyant life as her wealth increased. Roberta's letters were ripe with caution, but Victoria, poor for most of her life, could not resist the lifestyle her grandfather's loot afforded.

It was in Albuquerque, New Mexico, in December 1919, while Victoria was staying in the Grand Hotel, that they sprung their trap. The Pinkerton Elephant Corps hid themselves in among President Wilson's Secret Service entourage during his whistle stop in the high desert city. Both military and civilians gathered in the street beneath the balcony of the Grand Hotel when the President gave his speech.

• • • • • •

"ALL IN!" SAID the man with one gold tooth, pushing all his coins into the pot.

"Hmm, okay, I'm all in," said the fat man beside him at the poker table, while the player piano, missing keys, plunked out old cowboy tunes badly.

"Too rich for my blood," said the scrawny soldier across from Gold Tooth, folding.

"How's 'bout you, Little Lady?"

Victoria drummed her fingers on the top of her cards. "No, boys,

I'm out," she said, folding her cards down and pushing back from the table. "I'll leave ya to it."

Disappointed, the men returned to their game as she headed toward the brass cage elevator. Out of the corner of her eye, Victoria noted four men stand to follow her from different parts of the casino. Alarm made the hair on her arms rise, but she kept a poker face.

After gold tooth collected his winnings and the fat man pushed back from the table, he flipped Victoria's cards. "A flush. Well boys, she would have beat us all!"

Clearly Victoria's luck had run out, as the four men wedged into the elevator beside her.

"What floor, ma'am?"

"Fourth floor."

She was only partially relieved when the man pressed the third floor after hers. She sighed when they all stepped out. In fact, they were just making sure she couldn't escape from the floor above, but she didn't know that. She also didn't know that two Pinkertons were waiting for her in her room.

When Victoria opened her door, the room itself was empty. Then again, she planned it that way. Paying for two adjacent rooms, one under her name, the other under an assumed one, added an extra layer of protection. Knowing she had to get out of the hotel quickly, she hastily packed and dragged the two trunks from under the bed. She called for a bellhop to assist her.

"Where would you like this luggage, ma'am?"

"I need to catch the midnight train, so help me get it to the station quickly, please!"

Next door, the Pinkertons waited anxiously, wondering where Miss Lansing could have gotten to after they saw a signal from their men below that she was coming. Perhaps she went to a balcony to hear President Wilson's speech? The man could drone on. Which was when, on the other side of the wall, they heard the bellhop shout, "Right away, ma'am! May I escort you to the station with your bags?"

"Of course, you fool. Who else will lift these heavy trunks into the carriage for me?"

The Elephant Corps men looked at each other, then rose quickly and charged out of the room. As the bellhop was muscling the money-laden trunks through the door, the Pinkertons bowled him over, knocking him to the ground. Breathing heavily, guns drawn, they stared at Victoria Lansing, cowering backwards, looking for an escape route. Seeing the open window, she turned toward it.

"Don't, Miss Lansing. Best you come with us, quietly," said the tall one, gesturing with his pistol.

Ignoring his warning, she stepped out onto the narrow balcony. She looked down on the crowd gathered below listening to the President.

"Stop!" shouted the other Pinkerton, "Or I'll shoot."

Death here or death below hardly mattered. Victoria chose hope over certainty and flung herself into the crowd. The men raced toward the empty balcony. They didn't see her fall, but they saw her dress flung over her head on the ground, a clump of people crushed beneath her. A woman screamed, then others rushed to their aid as shots rang out from the balcony above. People cried out around Victoria as bullets struck them.

She climbed painfully to her feet, pressing down her long dress. Vicky crouched to hide in the crowd from the men still shooting at her. She felt sorry for those she landed on and those that were shot at her expense. President Wilson stopped speaking, seeing the commotion.

Vicky glanced about, looking for an exit through the legs and dresses scattering. She sought an escape route. Hearing a steam whistle, she ran for the train.

"What is the meaning of this!" cried the President. "Cease fire, you!" he commanded, pointing upward.

The men on the balcony hesitated while the Secret Service closed in on Victoria. Before she could take ten steps, the Elephant Corps seized her. She looked up at President Wilson on the dais and pleaded with tear-filled eyes.

"Unhand that young woman!" the President ordered. "What could she possibly have done to deserve such treatment?"

"Mister President, this woman is a criminal!" replied one of the Pinkertons at Victoria's side, squeezing her upper arm even harder.

"I am not!" declared Victoria.

"Sir, she is living off the ill-gotten gains of her grandfather. Her grandfather, Craigmore Lansing, robbed the Union Express."

"And what became of this Lansing?" asked the President.

"They captured, imprisoned, and executed him, but we never recovered the money. Until now...." continued the Pinkerton.

"And what crime, pray tell, has this woman committed?" asked the President.

By now, all eyes volleyed back and forth between the President and the attractive woman being restrained by the Secret Service.

"I have committed no crime, Mister President! My father willed the money to me on his deathbed."

A tense moment held all in suspense. A hush fell over the crowd. They turned to their Commander-in-Chief for a decision. A decision that would change the course of American history.

"Gentlemen, stand down. Release her. She has committed no crime. She will not bear the debt of her grandfather—one he already paid to society. This woman is blameless. I proclaim here and now that no citizen will suffer the debts of their parents on their death. Not the banks, not the courts, and to no man will they be beholden.

Forcing the children to pay for the debt of their fathers when they die is inappropriate and from here on illegal. Miss Lansing, you are free to go."

Hands fell away from her, bruises already forming in Victoria's arms. She was thunderstruck. The men beside her fought against an unrequited anger, faces tight. Vengeance would never be theirs. The Lansing daughters would receive no punishment for their father's crime. Presidential pardon would insure the Pinkertons could never reclaim Lansing's loot. The twins were innocent. And shortly thereafter, legislation would guarantee it for all citizens.

•　•　•　•　•

SEVERAL MONTHS PASSED before Victoria arrived in Thonon-les-Bains with four trunks. Two filled with cash and another two with her clothes and gifts for Bobby. Her sister ran into her arms, and together they cried. Twins reunited at last.

Roberta introduced Victoria to her new husband, Gabriel, a banker. A man she met while doing business. He was tall, slender, and had a twinkle in his brown eyes.

"It's a good thing he's in banking," said Victoria. "We will need a place to store all this money," she said, lifting the two lids of the trunks to the awe of both of them in the newly refurbished villa. Gabriel's eyes sparkled even more.

"Clearly, you fared well in your travels around America, exchanging the old money for new. Tell me how it went?" asked Roberta once she took her eyes from the loot.

"A long story, dear sister, one involving gamblers, cowboys, lawmen, and presidents!"

Gabriel stared at Victoria, his eyes growing even wider. His imagination getting the better of him seeing Roberta's gorgeous sister. Yet his musings would not be far from the truth.

"Come, Vicky, let's celebrate our good fortune. To our Gran'pappy Craigmore!" Bobby toasted a short time later, lifting a gilded champagne glass.

All three of them clinked, sipped, and while they reminisced, the fire crackled in the hearth as snow fell outside.

—Dr. Keith Raymond is a Family and Emergency Physician. He practiced in eight countries in four languages and is currently living in Austria with his wife. When not volunteering his practice skills, he is writing, lecturing, or scuba diving. In 2008, he discovered the wreck of a Bulgarian freighter in the Black Sea. He has multiple medical citations, along with publications in Flash Fiction Magazine, Chicago Literati, Blood Moon Rising, Utopia *Science Fiction magazine, and in Sci-Fi anthologies among others. He is the fiction editor of SavagePlanets magazine.*

MY VOW TO KEEP

VELDA BROTHERTON

ORLEY CRAMER HAILED Hank while they were both at work. Hank was already tired of putting up fence, so he hunkered down to talk to his friend.

Orley pulled up a grass stem, then stuck it in his mouth. "I just found out something I'd bet you might like to know."

"What might that be? We have another mile of this?" He swung an arm sideways.

Orley grinned big. "Shore wish you were right. No, I just heard this from a fella who rode into Wichita from Dodge City. He heard it while drinking beer in the Long Branch."

"Oh, and anything heard like that must be true."

"Nah, you need to hear this. You know how you told me you wished you could find your brother, George? Didn't he work for Clay Allison over in New Mexico?"

"I don't know that for sure. Someone said so."

"Well, it seems Wyatt Earp has a running feud with Allison, and the last time they drove cattle through, George was on Front Street shooting off his gun. Earp and his brother, Morgan, got to shooting back at him, and when he went down, they beat him with their guns. I was told he died right there. Folks said it was mostly 'cause of the feud between Allison and Earp."

If Orley had hit him in the stomach, he couldn't have hurt him worse. When he could speak again, he did. "You sure this is true?"

"Ol' boy swore it was. That the whole place talked about it plenty. I 'member from when we was at Atlanta during the war, you talked about wishing you could find your brother."

"This George's name was Hoyt?"

"Oh, yeah, yeah. Didn't I say it was your brother?"

Hank didn't finish his job that day but lit out for the bunkhouse, hunted down the boss, and asked for his pay.

"Well, sure. You've been a good worker. What's wrong? You look like you stepped on a rattler." The boss led him inside and unlocked the safe. "What's happened, Hank?"

"I've got business in Dodge City, and I'd like to leave out right away." He didn't bother to tell his boss that he was going to Dodge to gun down Wyatt Earp. He'd only try to talk him out of it.

In Wichita, he stopped at the bar for some fortifying before his long ride. A foaming glass in front of him, his reflection in the mirror threw back a ratty-looking fence builder. Maybe he'd change clothes before he went to Dodge City. Could he really bring this about? How would he stage the fight? He'd been a crack marksman during the war. But he couldn't face down a gunfighter like Wyatt Earp carrying a rifle. He wasn't about to pick him off from a rooftop, either. The point wasn't only to kill the man but to shame him and his name for what he had done.

So, best if he didn't get in such a blamed hurry. Earp wasn't going anywhere, so he downed the beer and hustled to the gunsmith's where he spent some of his hard-earned pay for a six-gun and the ammunition he needed to do some practicing. He soon learned the big difference between hitting a target with a rifle or with the Colt. But by the time the sun set, he was pulling and hitting fast and proper. Wasn't so hard, just don't think but do.

He called a halt, got some sleep, then lit out for Dodge in the morning. Several times along the way, he spotted a good target, dismounted, and shot—fast and accurate. He was ready. Earp would pay for killing his older brother, George.

Late the following day, he arrived at the edge of Dodge City and was hailed by a deputy.

How had they found out what he was up to so fast?

"Hey, mister, just to let you know. This is the south edge of town. Carrying your gun here is fine, but north of the railroad yards, you have to check it. Got that? There'll be a deputy there to take your weapon should you ride north on Front Street beyond the deadline."

It was getting near dark when he got there, so he went in search of the Long Branch. Someone there would know where Wyatt Earp might be. All he needed to do was parley with drinkers or gamblers a while. He had the evening and night to prepare.

Not wise to plan a gunfight for after dark. Stupid, in fact. But he could plan real good sitting in the Long Branch with a beer and waiting for the man who would be his target come high noon tomorrow, that being the best time to have a standoff. Then, the sun wouldn't be in his eyes, and Earp couldn't claim he cheated by calling him out to face the bright sun hisself.

Orley said cattle drives were slowing down a lot in Dodge and that Earp and his brothers were talking about leaving town. He'd best finish this chore—shooting Wyatt and getting the hell out of Dodge. Bat Masterson was Sheriff here, and Wyatt's brother Morgan was a deputy. Hank worried the most about them coming after him once Wyatt lay dead on Front Street. He just might need a distraction.

Compared to the bars in Wichita, or the ones he'd been in, the Long Branch was pretty fancy. 'Course it had to be, for everyone knew about the place. Lanterns already burned on either side of the doors. He tied his horse to the rail, gripped the handle of the Colt to make sure it still rode in its holster, then pushed open the swinging doors to the sound of piano music. Midway and up front of the poker tables, three purty girls swung around kicking their legs, shaking their boobs, and twisting their behinds, in that order. He bellied up to the bar, ordered a beer, then turned where he could watch. Only a foolish man ignored purty girls.

He'd drink his beer, inching around the place like he might be hunting a poker game when all he was really doing was looking for Wyatt and his bunch. Next thing he'd do was plan those distractions he'd need to escape without being shot down or caught and tossed in jail or beat to death like his brother had been.

He took a measure of the fella propped on the bar beside him. "Seen Wyatt Earp?"

The fella grunted. "Talkin' to me?"

"Yep." Hank took another sip to keep from letting the man look at his face.

"Usually at his usual table. In the corner, his back to the wall. You know?"

"Yep. So he can see a bullet coming."

"Yep."

"Many want to shoot the good lawman?"

"Ever'body nearly. He watches out."

"Figures, the law being what it is."

"Figures, the town marshal being who he is."

"Yep."

"Met him, have you?"

"Not yet."

"Want to?"

"Not yet." Hank palmed his Colt.

The fella chuckled. "Can't say as I blame you. Clay Allison once rode his horse right through the doors and shot some holes in the ceiling. Made an enemy out of Wyatt Earp with that stunt, and they still fight to this day. So, I wouldn't suggest you pull that fancy looking six-gun and shoot up the bar. Not so good to be an enemy of Wyatt Earp. Hear that growly laugh?"

"That's him?"

"Yep." The fella laughed.

"Think it's funny, mocking me?"

Taking another look at the no-nonsense weapon on Hank's hip, he nodded and moved away.

Carrying his beer, Hank slipped closer to Earp's table. Got a look only at the shadowy faces sitting around. He asked to join a nearby poker game one man short and got hisself invited to play with information about the rules and high/low bids. He nodded, with no notion to win, lose, or draw before he found an excuse to leave.

From his chair, he listened until he placed Earp who was pontificating about the latest arrest in town.

"You betting, mister?" A player across from him raised his voice.

He pulled his thoughts back to the game and the cards in his hand. Tapping the table, he sat and went back to studying Earp. The bunch with him wasn't playing cards. They was discussing something to do with town business.

"It's getting to where there's not much going on here. Soon, the cattle will be going around Dodge. Morgan and I are looking to leaving out soon as that happens. Reckon I'll stay a few weeks longer. Patrol Front Street to keep the law till we leave."

A man at Hank's table leaned forward and spoke quietly. "Won't be the first time they lit out. What was it last time? Looking for gold or something?"

Laughter circled the table.

All Hank really cared about was if the marshal would be on Front Street the next day. The town marshal, that is. Wouldn't do to think of him as a U.S. Marshal. Hopefully, that'd never happen. He was Dodge City Town Marshal. Soon as the lawman sprawled in his own blood on Front Street, Hank's business would be over and done with. Nothing else they were talking about mattered. One ear on Earp, the other on the game, he soon heard what he wanted to hear when Earp bid good night to someone leaving the table. "See you tomorrow right here." Earp went back to his visit.

Hank lost a pot and excused himself. He'd arrived in town on time to do his duty to brother George. Now, to keep his vow.

"Cain't stand to lose, huh, mister?" One of the men at his table eyed him with a squint.

"Nope, just remembered I got someone waiting for me."

"Next time don't interrupt a game, then."

The remark touched a nerve, and he glared down at the speaker but decided to let it go. No sense calling attention to himself now. He moved away and back to the bar where he ordered another beer. He'd wait and get a better look at the town marshal when the group filed out... and figure out a distraction to help him get out of town without being spotted.

· · · · · ·

HANK'S DISTRACTION

Inside and upstairs at the Long Branch, Julie shook herself into a low-cut dress, wiggled the split skirt over her behind, and dropped onto the divan to pull on stockings and slip into her shoes.

The door popped open and Mae stuck her head in. "Time to go on, girl. Hustle your buns now."

Julie played at ignoring her. Thank God this was her last day in this hell hole. She'd come here to get away from something worse. An awful thing she had to forget. Sometimes life turned around and kicked you. All she wanted now was to be rid of this place and mouthy Mae. How could she ever have thought Dodge City would be a good place to hide? It was just another town to run from. Six months and she was ready to shoot the next man who nuzzled her bare skin with his fuzzy beard. There had to be a better life somewhere. Tomorrow she'd escape and never look back. There was enough money stuffed in a drawer to pay for the way outta here. She'd earned it hard.

She peered into the narrow, dark hallway before stepping through the door only to be addressed by her boss.

"Girl, if you don't get your ass down there—" Mae's voice sent her skin crawling. Maybe she'd kill that old sow before the night was over.

Fluffing her long hair, she hurried down the steps into the saloon where the piano player hammered the keys, and three of the girls hopped around on the stage acting like dancers. They looked more like fleas in hot ashes. It would be her turn to go on when the last notes were held for their final leap. She would do a better job.

Cupping her breasts so they plumped from the top of the dress, she threaded her way through the crowd of men up front. Used to a bunch of admirers, she hurried onto the walkway following the call of her name. The hurrah of shouts and pounding on tables greeted her.

To give those closest a quick peek she leaned forward to spill half her breasts and wiggled her behind to make the men whoop and holler.

A sober handsome man stared at her over the rim of his glass. She gave him an extra twist, and men all around shouted and stomped the floor till the room shook. He only smiled. Determined, she sashayed to the very edge of the stage floor, held her dress tail above her knees, so he had a real good view, and raised her voice in song. Everyone said she had a beautiful voice, but it was her body they hired her for, so she offered that, as well.

When the good-looking fellow reacted with pleasure to her efforts, she approached him and sat on his knee, ran her fingers through his long shiny hair.

If he came in with the cattle earlier, he'd taken the time to clean up. She appreciated that. His blue-eyed gaze moved slow-like over her.

Puckering her lips, she leaned down, kissed his cheek, and wiggled against him one more time before breaking into a new verse. "Oh, Susannah, now don't you cry for me. I come from Alabama with my banjo on my knee." Lifting the dress, she gave him a look at one leg.

Mae would stomp her good if she didn't make all the men happy, so in leaving she dragged a hand across a few laps. The good-looking one's fingers found the low-cut neck of her dress. He whispered her name, tilted a glance toward the cribs where girls pleased their men. Nodded. "Later?"

Maybe this night she wouldn't have to put up with a filthy beard. He even remembered her name. She smiled at him and moved on. When she finished for the evening, he was gone from the table.

Must've read him wrong.

•   •   •   •   •   •

HANK'S PLAN

A few die hard drinkers remained after the girls each followed a man toward the cribs. The piano player tinkled out a solo, then moved away. Time finally sent most of the customers home. Having caught a glimpse of his distraction, Hank slipped into the dark shadows in the far corner of the silent room. He needed to talk to the girl who'd made so much over him earlier.

A colored man brought out a bucket of water and mop and scrubbed the floor from under the front windows and door. The bartender rinsed glasses in hot water drawn from the large stove's reservoir. The girl called Julie moved from the shadows toward Hank and returned the smile he'd given her earlier. Without speaking she took his hand and tilted her head toward the darkness behind them. He went with her. Might as well wait there as anyplace.

Later, he led her to a table in the near-empty saloon. Could he trust this girl? For a silent moment he looked her over.

He'd waited as long as he could. "I need to talk to you."

Not sure where to begin, he kept gazing at her. She had been nice to him. Looked awfully young for this life. He probably ought to let her be. Search for another idea. But she admitted she was leaving town the next day. That would work well for him. She had a complaint about men and their fuzzy beards, which made him happy he'd had a shave. She must've took kindly to that.

Seated, she picked at a fingernail. "What do you want?"

"Where are you going? And why?" He wasn't sure he wanted to know, wanted to think of her later, after they both were gone from this place. Something about her would stay with him.

She shrugged. "Don't care, just somewhere away from here."

"Why don't you go home?" He reached for her hand. It was fragile and cool in his callused fingers.

"I can't. Wish I could go get my ma, and we'd go somewhere together. But Pa would kill me if I showed up at their door."

"Oh, surely not." Shock went through him.

"Yes. Just like he got mad at my sister, Sue, and dragged her out into the woods, and we never saw her again." She gripped his hand tighter.

Too dark to see her expression, but he thought she might be crying. He never could say the right things when they cried.

She went on. "Ma got a black eye for asking, and I lit out in the middle of the night. I still feel bad leaving Ma, but she wouldn't come with me, and I had to be somewhere else before Pa took it in his mind to drag me into the woods. But I'm thinking it sure weren't Dodge City."

"A pretty girl like you shouldn't travel alone or work in a place like this. No matter where it was. No telling what could happen to you."

She shrugged again.

"How old are you, Julie?"

"I'm, uh eighteen."

"I'd be glad to take you away from here. Escort you, so to speak."

"Why should you do that? You already had me."

"No, I don't mean that way. The truth is, I need to leave town with someone on my arm. Like we're a couple. So no one notices me—us."

Her gaze hardened, and she pulled away. "What have you done? Who is after you? I'm no fool."

"The truth? No, you aren't a fool. If I tell you, though, please promise you won't say anything. Whether you go with me or not, I need your promise."

"You've been nice to me." She hesitated and nodded toward the cribs. "I mean, in there you treated me as if you really liked me, and it wasn't just for a poke and that's all. I don't often see men like you."

Even as he tried not to speak, he spilled the story, and so she let him. "Wyatt Earp murdered my brother, and no one did anything about it. Him and his deputies. But it was him that did it." His voice broke, and he cupped a hand over his eyes to hide the tears that fell despite his effort to hold back.

She slid tighter against him. Touched the crook of his arm. "Oh, I'm so sorry. But what are you going to do?"

"I'm going to kill the bastard. Oh, I'm sorry. I didn't mean to—"

"No need." She leaned into his shoulder and shivered. "It's nothing I haven't heard from my pa. That's why I'm here. He killed my sister."

Hank kissed her temple. "My God. Did they do anything to him?"

"No, of course not. Just like they did nothing to Wyatt Earp for his killings. Are you wanted?"

He shook his head. "I've never killed no one, except in the war. Nor have I rode with outlaws. I'm gonna kill Earp, though. But, if I'm careful, no one will know I did it. Tomorrow, I need you to buy tickets for the stage out of here. You may have to go early to miss the crowd, but wait for me in the station, and after I shoot him, I'll disappear and join you. With my hat on and a jacket over my shirt, I won't look the same. Just a man and his wife as we board the stage.

"I will do no such thing." She pulled away and stared into his face. "You shouldn't kill him. They will never stop hunting you, and they'll hang you from the nearest tree when they catch you. Besides, no one will ever kill Wyatt Earp. That's crazy." She grabbed his arm. "He'll kill you, that's certain."

"He got away with killing my brother. They shot him and beat him to death out in the street."

For ever so long her gaze remained on his eyes, then she stared out the window of the Long Branch. "Please think very hard about not killing Wyatt Earp. I'm so sorry about your brother. Even if you can draw your gun before he can draw his, and you shoot him, someone will kill you. Because it's happened before here. I've heard some

of the men talk about it. George Hoyt worked for Clay Allison at one
time. Was he your brother?"

"That's my brother. And everyone talks about it? But they do
nothing. Just let Earp get away with it?"

"He's the law. Nobody's going to challenge him."

"Some say Earp and his deputies shot George down because of the
feud between Clay Allison and Wyatt Earp. That way, Earp avoided a
gunfight with Allison, who everyone knows is a shootist. Others say
that isn't so and they made it up. It was really something to do with
Doc Holliday gonna come into town." She shrugged and leaned close
to him. "You know how tales get to going like wildfire till no one ever
knows the truth for sure."

"I know this. Earp and his law killed my brother. Not only shot
him, they beat him over the head after he was down."

He started to go on, but she put two fingers over his lips. He let
them rest there and closed his eyes for a moment. Her touch felt so
good. Her skin smelled like roses. He'd always imagined a woman like
her wanting a man like him.

If only things were different. But they weren't. He owed this to the
brother he loved.

Without saying anything, she continued to sit with him. He waited as long as he could, then eased out of her touch.

"It's okay. You don't have to do it. I'll figger out something else to
get away with it. I don't rightly want to be caught."

"You going to sneak up on him, or what?"

"No. I'm calling him out. I can out-shoot him if I can get him alone
in the street."

Again, her pause, then she blew a strand of hair from her face with
a loud noise. "That is about the dumbest thing I've ever heard in my
life. No way will you outdraw Wyatt Earp, and with the deputies close

by like they're tied together, if you did, they'd shoot you down right quick. You'd never make it to the stage station."

"I can try. Got to do something. Got no family left."

"And so you would be a wanted killer, too. Nice way to wipe out an entire family. You have to care about yourself so you can live. What would your ma and pa say if they were alive? Wouldn't they want you to live?"

"Well, yeah, but they ain't alive."

"So what they might feel isn't worth anything to you? I'd give anything if I could do something to make my ma feel better. It shore wouldn't be killing my pa, though I've wished I could often enough. You said you never hurt no one, so why start now?"

"But I was conscripted into the Confederate Army, and I killed there. George stayed home to look after Pa. When I got back from the war Pa had passed, and George was already gone. And now he's dead, and I'll never get to see him again."

"Well, then. I have an idea." She rose from the chair. "Let's the two of us go down to the station this morning and buy us tickets out of here. Neither one of us will have to think of killing anyone. You're not a killer, I know you aren't."

What did he want? What would George want of him? Did it matter to Ma and Pa? Julie was offering him more than he'd ever had. But did he know her? He stared across the silent saloon.

He nodded and took her hand. It felt fragile and soft. "I'm sorry, Julie. I have to do this. It just ain't right for Earp and his bunch to get away with murder, and they need to pay."

"Maybe it is murder, but you shooting a lawman won't change that." Tears poured from her eyes.

As always, he had no idea what to do. He lay her hands back in her lap, rose, and fitted his hat on firmly. "When Orley told me George'd been killed by that no-good Earp, I made a vow to my dead brother to make this right. I have to do that one thing."

"No, please." She reached for him, but he backed off, shaking his head. He would never forgive himself if he let her talk him out of this. Ma died having him, and he adored George, grew up tagging along with him everywhere he went.

"I'm going to get some sleep. You be on the stage in the morning and go live your life somewhere you'll be happy. Don't worry about me. I'll only be happy if I can keep my vow. I'd rather die in Front Street than not keep my vow to make this right."

Tomorrow he would kill Earp, and so be it if he was cut down later. They could bury him in Boot Hill as the man who outdrew and shot Wyatt Earp.

"I'll outdraw him. Will you wait for me?"

When she didn't answer, he turned around, but she was gone.

• • • • • •

JULIE'S RETURN

Twenty years later, Julie returned to Dodge City. Her son, Hank Jr., stepped from the train and reached up to help her down. Without speaking, she folded her arm through his, guiding him toward Boot Hill. He appeared not to notice her furtive glance. How would he take seeing his own father's grave? Though she'd told him the story when he was old enough, he was so much like his father. What would he do seeing the gravestone? What might be engraved there? She'd never been back in all these years and only came now because Hank wanted to.

He stopped her. "Are you sure he's buried here? I mean you told me you left before, uh, the gunfight. What if Dad won the fight? Or what if he chickened out and rode away? All these years and you've never been back here or tried to find out."

"I chose a life with your grandmother. After your grandfather's accident, she needed me as much as I needed her. Your father chose to die, simple as that. Neither of us knew I carried his child. You. Besides anyone who can read knows Earp moved on from here to Tombstone."

Hank broke away. "There's his stone."

Moving through the wet grass, she joined him. Even after all these years, the fact of Hank's death chiseled on that stone made her heart ache. Falling in love with a man and losing him, all in the same day, had been so hard. She placed her gloved hand on the top of Hank's stone, remembering the blue-eyed man in the Long Branch Saloon who had treated her like a lady so long ago. He had touched her with a gentleness she'd never known from another man.

Hank ran trembling fingers over his father's name. Didn't speak for a long while. Then he glanced at the stone next to him. Hank's brother, George. "Father was the best brother a man could have."

"To go out to kill someone is not the best way to show love, Hank. Please remember that."

"Don't worry, Mother. I know that."

HERE LIES HANK HOYT
He kept his vow
SHOT BY WYATT EARP

HERE LIES GEORGE HOYT
Beloved Brother
SHOT BY WYATT EARP

Strange. He had to've told someone about his vow to call out Earp, else why was it put on his tombstone? Probably what got him killed. But she would never know.

—*Velda Brotherton wrote for decades from her home perched on the side of a mountain against the Ozark National Forest. While known for her successful series work—the Twist of Poe romantic mysteries, as well as her signature Western Historical Romances—her publishing resume includes numerous standalone novels, including* Once There Were Sad Songs, Wolf Song, Stoneheart's Woman, Remembrance, *and her magnum opus,* Beyond the Moon. *Following the tragic passing of her longtime writing partner, legendary Western author Dusty Richards, in early 2018, she took up her pen to finish several of his outstanding works, including the standalone novel* Blue Roan Colt *and the Texas Badge Mystery Series. Sadly, Velda passed away in early 2023, leaving behind scores of up-and-coming writers she'd mentored through the years.*

The Scout by Frederic Remington

HAT CREEK

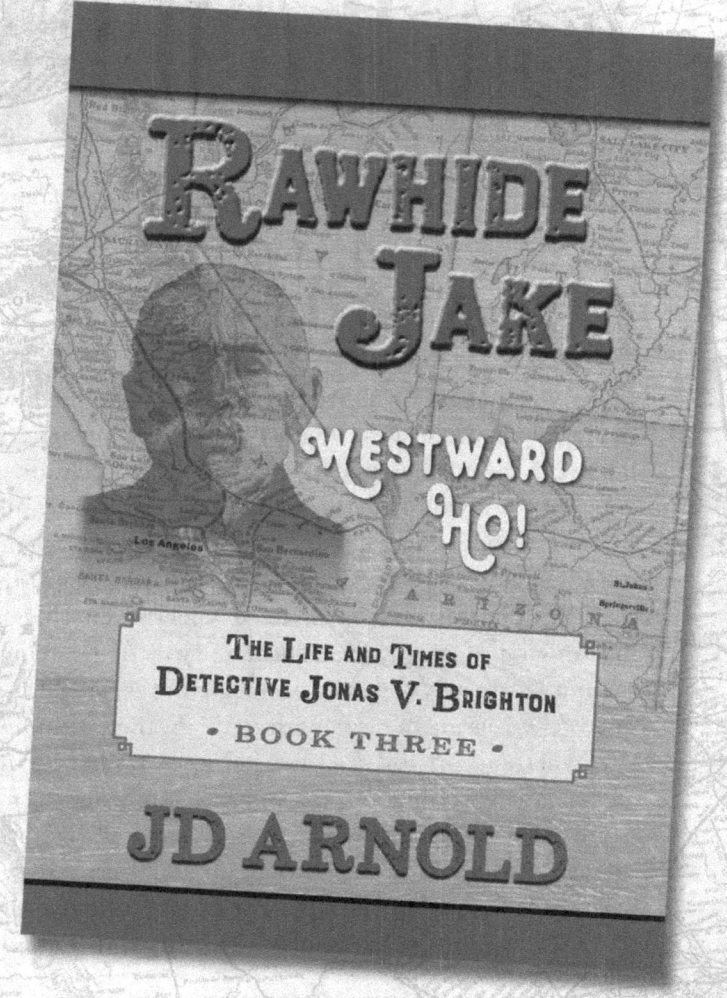

BOB GIEL

AUTHOR OF A CROW TO PLUCK

SHAWNEE

THE ADVENTURE BEGINS

NOW AVAILABLE AT ALL YOUR FAVORITE BOOKSELLERS